ALSO BY TA

~

Becoming Mrs. Smith

Stealing Mr. Smith

Breathe

A MAN CALLED SMITH

TANYA E WILLIAMS

RIPPLING EFFECTS

Printed in the United States of America

Published by Rippling Effects, Surrey, British Columbia, Canada

Visit the author's website at www.tanyaewilliams.com

FIRST EDITION

Cover design by Ana Grigoriu

ISBN: 978-1-989144-04-6

For Gem

CHAPTER 1

April 1949
Cedar Springs, South Dakota

John

I already long for the normalcy of a typical Tuesday morning. The afternoon sun filters through wisps of clouds hanging low in the April sky. The wind and early morning chill have evaporated. The same is true of the future I imagined for myself and my children, vanished like smoke through a chimney. The bright spring sun creates the deceptive appearance of a lovely day, the kind those who have been barricaded against the winter crave.

We gather around the deep rectangular hole, the freshly dug earth beside it in a small mountain of rich brown soil. The sun dips behind a cropping of dense clouds, perhaps realizing its error and apologizing for its appearance and warmth on a day such as this. I watch, my body numb, as grief dictates the crowd's movements. With a bowed head and tear-filled eyes, I scan those gathered, all of whom seem to appreciate the view of their shoes more than that of the casket in front of us.

We were married just short of three years. I shake my head in disbelief. "It wasn't enough," I whisper to nobody in particular. I might never have had enough time with her to be satisfied. But having her life cut devastatingly short, without warning, is too much for my broken heart to handle. Mere days ago, I watched in slow motion as our happiness was blown away like dust in the wind. My heart sinks further as my thoughts turn to Calla and Jarred.

Children deserve a mother. Violet is, or rather was, an exceptional mother. A rogue sob escapes my closed lips at the thought of our loss. After less than a week without their mother, Calla and Jarred moved to my parents' home at the edge of town. We made the decision out of necessity rather than emotion. My mother, well versed in raising children, took charge when the news of Violet's death reached my family. Caring for her grandchildren is a joyous privilege my mother has adored since Calla entered our world. Given the situation, I can't help but wonder if my mother's own grief spurred her into action, driving her to busy her otherwise idle hands. When I found myself with a premature infant who needed care and a two-year-old girl devastated by the disappearance of her mother from her life, my parents opened my childhood home without hesitation, embracing Calla and Jarred with warm, loving arms.

To my left, Reverend Campbell stands with his back straight and his shoulders wide, at the head of Violet's final resting place. His white robes billow gently near his feet as he opens his Bible to a marked page. I brace myself to hear his booming voice—the same voice that baptized every child in my family, prayed for me and many more during the war, and celebrated my marriage to Violet with great enthusiasm.

As his words ring out, reaching as high as heaven itself, Violet's mother startles and a few solemn shadows to my right waver. Her slight and fragile body is flanked by Violet's father on one side and my own mother on the other. Childhood friends themselves, the two mothers cling to each other for support. They both know the feeling that a mother experiences when the life of her child is snuffed out, in contradiction with the natural progression of life.

I stare at the casket, stained deep brown, and attempt to recall a time when Violet wasn't in my life. I realize after several moments of deep concentration that no such time exists. Being slightly younger than Vi, I am slapped with the reality that I have never known a world without Violet. I certainly have no desire to know one now. The tears pool at the edges of my eyes and spill freely to the ground.

The tug-of-war inside my heart is real. Part of me can't wait to escape this dreadful day. The thought of entertaining others at the reception is unimaginable. I am not certain I can resign myself to the obligation of listening to others speak of my Vi, with solemn faces and clasped hands. The desire to hide under the covers and forget this nightmare is both intoxicating and unrealistic. The other part of me doesn't want to rush this final goodbye. This is my last time to be near her, to be of this same earth with her. I stiffen my resolve and straighten my posture. I am unable to let her go just yet, and I pray for Reverend Campbell to continue speaking, to draw out the service all afternoon.

My guilt over wasted time and lost moments creeps in and stands beside me, keeping me company like a schoolyard bully. The guilt's overbearing presence is heavy, and I am compelled to swivel my head, snatching a glance to my right, ensuring that my guilt is not physically present.

Though, over time, Violet came to understand my decision to join the war effort, I regret that I was the cause of such heartache and worry for her. I wish I could take back the lost years, the pain, the fear, her worry. I know now that, once begun, a war never truly ends. The casualties of war are far too great, and they haunt both the living and the dead long after the battlefield has been abandoned.

Once overseas, it didn't take long for my preconceived illusions of war to tarnish. We felt neither gallant nor heroic as we trudged through mud, snow, and rain with the constant threat of enemy fire. The daily battle against our own fears and the necessity to fight to the end, no matter the cost to our souls, left me battle weary and with an instinct to flee at the first sign of trouble.

I was far from a violent man when I left Cedar Springs for basic training. I always chose to take the high road in potentially inflammatory situations. I had never been in a schoolyard scuffle and always practiced patience during disagreements. Any fight I might have possessed upon enlisting vanished when I learned of the kind of evil humans are capable of committing.

The war taught me that fighting disengages a man from his true self faster than anything I had witnessed. The lesson stuck, and when I laid down my weapon for the final time, I vowed to avoid battles, big and small, for the rest of my life. They simply are not worth the harm they cause.

I am abruptly wrenched from my thoughts as Reverend Campbell touches my shoulder and says my name. His compassionate brown eyes house understanding mixed with his own grief. His love for Violet is written on his face, while his concern for me creases his forehead. Those gathered are singing one of Violet's favorite hymns, swaying slightly as one, mournful and sedated in their grief-stricken states.

"John," Reverend Campbell says again. "It is time." He motions with his Bible-holding hand toward the casket that has somehow made its way into the ground. "It is time, John."

A fresh shudder of tears invades my being. Duty bound to fulfill the task, I take one step toward the lowered casket. I say a silent goodbye and release the single white rose from my grip.

After a moment, I reluctantly find my place among my family and close my eyes. A shiver runs through me at the repeated sound of a white rose being dropped onto Violet's casket. Each person in attendance steps forward in turn to say farewell to my beloved Vi.

CHAPTER 2

June 1944
Caumont, France

John

Caked in dirt, I lie molded into the uneven ground. The fighting reached deep into the early morning hours, stealing any hope of rest. I could blame the Germans at Caumont, but I know my exhaustion is days old, from the rainstorm of destruction at the beach. Sleep is the luxury of a man who has never seen war.

"It's a funny thing. War, that is," a soldier, new to our platoon since we made it past the beach, says as we crouch along the hedgerow.

Having spoken with him briefly, I only know he is a farmer's son from Idaho. I look over my shoulder in a feeble attempt to assess his sanity, all the while keeping an eye out for movement beyond the brush.

With no verbal response from me, he continues as if reciting something poetic. The breeze dances lightly across the backs of our necks, sometimes soothing the heat and other times delivering chills as cold as death itself. "I've seen so much violence in just a few short days. Feels like months though. It numbs me to know these things. The knowledge haunts me in daylight and at night. But the funny thing is . . ." He sighs. "I can see a memory in that there field, and I just don't think I know what is real anymore."

"Only real things we have to know right now are where the enemy is and whether they're fixing to shoot at us," I say dryly, hoping that holding my own emotions at bay will keep this soldier alive.

While I'm lying in the dirt, brambles tugging at every piece of cloth and skin, and searching the area with eyes that narrow and scope like binoculars, I see it. I understand what Idaho is talking about.

I am sitting beneath the large hackberry tree in Father's field. Just sitting and whittling on a small fallen branch. The wind rustles through the tall yellow crop. Like an ocean moves in waves, a field sways to its own rhythm while offering a soothing song for those fortunate enough to hear it. I must have sunk deep into my own thoughts, though I couldn't say now what they were.

A shadow catches my attention. I look up to find Violet standing a few feet in front of me, her dress swaying in the breeze, her hair aglow from the sunlight behind her. She's just standing there, smiling at me. I can almost hear her. "Didn't you hear me calling you, John?"

"John. John. Ten o'clock. Sniper in the hedge," my commanding officer hisses. I realize my elevated position and ease back down, tucking my body as low as the earth allows.

June 1949

Cedar Springs, South Dakota

John

Immersed in the dream, I burrow my face into the pillow, so deep I might suffocate. I stretch my arm across the bed, instinctively reaching for her. During these years since the war's end, she is the one person who could offer me peace and calm my mind. The coolness of the vacant spot where she used to sleep snaps me from my dreamlike state and into reality. I heave my body to a seated position, forcing my eyes not to look over my shoulder for confirmation. I place both feet on the floor to steady the dizzying sensation. Rubbing my eyes with the heels of my calloused hands, I press hard against the sockets to try to keep the tears from falling.

Two months have passed, and yet I still wake with the belief that Violet is alive and well. A shiver runs through me as my stomach turns and clenches in response to the grief that follows me like a shadow. I tug a t-shirt over my head and rise to face another day. *Another day without her.* Though reality tells me otherwise, my head refuses to accept this truth about my life.

The phone rings as I make my way into the kitchen. I reach for the receiver and glance at the clock on the wall. I slept longer than usual again. "Hello."

"John, dear." Mother has been at a loss for how to address me since Violet passed. I suspect she stops herself from saying good morning, solely because she knows there is nothing good about this or any other morning. "It is Saturday, and well, we are hoping to see you today." Her words are tentative, but her resolve pushes them out.

I squeeze my temples with one hand. By "we," she means Calla and Jarred, my children.

"Yes," I say as both an acknowledgment of my duties and a promise to fulfill them.

"I will pack a picnic." Mother's voice wavers, and I imagine her nervously twisting the phone's cord in her free hand. This loss is not mine alone. Violet was like a daughter to my parents and an older sister to my siblings. She was a well-loved woman. No matter how a person came to know her, she would capture their heart with her piercing blue eyes and warm smile. "Calla could benefit from some time out of doors."

"See you at noon, then." I hang up the phone before she can say another word. My head drops, and the anguish I've tried desperately to hold at bay escapes from the hollows of my chest. My tears hit the wood floor as I move about the kitchen, attempting to silence the agony with the distraction of daily chores. I demand that my body perform these mundane tasks. Coffee, shower, dress. These things keep me sane.

There is little food in the refrigerator, and my stomach grumbles in protest as I load my truck with boxes filled with colorful fabrics. Yesterday, I found myself in a puddle of despair on the living room floor, where Violet set up her sewing machine and supplies. Her sewing table was a happy place for her. In front of the large window that faces the front yard, she stitched together dresses for Calla and herself, along with thoughtful gifts intended for the Christmas season. She had been working on infant-sized articles in the months before Jarred arrived. A stockpile of cloth diapers made their way to Mother's when it became clear that I was in no condition to care for a newborn.

The Singer squeals across the floor as I drag the machine and the desk I built toward the front door. I wipe a trickle of sweat from my brow and survey the space. A collection of dust and a basket of half-finished sofa pillows is all that remains of the sanctuary she created. I remember her joy that first Christmas after we married. Violet's anticipation of Christmas morning had rivaled that of a three-year-old. Having been banned from the living room the afternoon prior so I could place her gift near the tree, she sat perched on the edge of the sofa, a wide smile spread across her face, eager for me to uncover her surprise.

When I lifted the bedsheet that covered the sewing machine and desk, her delight at the thoughtfulness and usefulness of the gift was apparent. All she required was the relocation of the machine to the center of the window, and every day after, Violet could be found sewing and humming along to the radio. When Calla arrived, the living room became a nap-time nursery and later a play space where the two of them would spend hours talking, singing, reading, and sewing. A fleeting smile brushes across my lips before I heave the machine and the desk into the back of my faded green truck. Its destination is Mother's home and the back bedroom my sisters share. I couldn't refuse their request to continue Violet's sewing.

Violet's scent permeates the air as I carry the basket of unfinished pillows, hugging it to my chest as I move. I open the truck's door and toss the basket onto the seat beside me. Before I even turn the key in the ignition, I know I will take the long way to my family home. I want a few more minutes with her, even if only in my imagination.

CHAPTER 3

JUNE 1949
Cedar Springs, South Dakota

John

I park the truck by the back of the house. The stench of grief permeates the air inside the stuffy cab. What only thirty minutes ago felt like an escape from reality now suffocates me with its weight. I press my finger and thumb into the pocket between my nose and eyes, determined to hold back another flood of tears. I give my head a firm shake and marvel at my body's ability to produce a never-ending supply of liquid angst.

Movement behind the screen door catches my attention. Calla is watching me with a dolly in one arm and the thumb of her other hand firmly inserted in her mouth. Her blonde curls frame her face like a halo. The screen between us prevents me from gazing into her cornflower blue eyes, but I can feel their intensity. Wise beyond her years, she offers no smile until I give her one—a habit she picked up in the last two months, since Violet vanished from her life.

I lift my hand and wave hesitantly, a smile forced upon my lips. I know she is safe. But she is also broken, and my heart lurches for her as I round the hood of the truck and close the distance between us. Before I can climb the steps and scoop her into my arms, Mother is there. She cradles Jarred in the crook of her elbow and wraps her other arm about Calla's shoulders, protecting her from the world beyond the house.

I am torn between the instinct to quell the sadness in Calla's eyes, the desire to nuzzle my newborn son, and the instinct to run far away and rid myself of the shackle of grief. Mother's eyes speak loudly. I tug on the screen door and kneel before Calla, wrapping her delicate, two-year-old frame in an embrace.

"Picnic." Her soft voice brushes against my neck.

"Yes, that's right, pumpkin. We are going on a picnic."

Calla peers over her shoulder, her arms still clinging to my neck. "Gamma come?"

"Yes. Yes of course, dear. Grandma will come." Mother smiles and nods decidedly. "I must get the pie cut and packed though. A picnic just isn't a picnic without a little pie, now is it, Calla?" Mother's warm smile washes over us as Calla shakes her head obediently.

Carrying Calla into the house, I lean across Mother's arm and kiss Jarred's forehead before taking him into the crook of my other arm. Together, the three of us make our way into the living room, Mother trailing behind us with an anxious expression.

"They need you, John." Mother's words are a touch above a whisper. "They are always welcome here. You know that. But Calla needs you to reassure her everything is going to be okay."

I sit Calla on the edge of the sofa as Mother leaves to gather the pie for our picnic. I tuck Jarred into the corner of the sofa and brace him with a cushion, and then I kneel before Calla's dangling knees. I retrieve a monogrammed handkerchief from my trouser pocket and lift Calla's foot to my eye level. She giggles as I spit into the cloth and set about polishing her Buster Browns. "I think about you all the time, pumpkin, and I miss you very much."

Calla nods, her giggle replaced with a solemn expression.

"If I promise to come visit you every Friday and Saturday, and on Sundays to take you to church and to visit Granny and Granddad . . ." I pause to add a little more spit to my cloth. "Would you be happy to stay here with Grandma, Grandpa, Edward, and the girls?"

Calla's eyes search my own as she considers my request. In a protective gesture, she reaches across the cushion and touches Jarred's cheek. Her words are soft and filled with innocence. "Go too?" The question all but stops my heart.

I pull her from the sofa and into my arms, holding her as tight as I can. My voice cracks as the emotions flow out of me. "No, sweetheart. I am not taking Jarred away. Both of you will stay with Grandma and Grandpa." I wipe my nose with the back of my hand.

Holding her at arm's length, I examine her eyes. Just as I would be unable to tear my gaze away from a slow-moving collision, I am compelled to ask, "Do you think I took Momma away?"

Calla's nodding head is the final blow my heart can take. I've been drowning in my own grief, unaware of her two-year-old understanding of her mother's absence. This, I know, is where I must begin. Mother is right. Calla and Jarred need me, and they deserve to have at least one parent present in their lives.

I smile through my tears and lift her back onto the sofa. I polish her shoes in silence, and I vow to put the needs of my children above my own.

"Picnic is ready." Mother's voice arrives in the living room ahead of her body as she peeks around the doorframe.

"Calla, are you ready for a picnic?" I force a smile into my voice.

She slides her bottom off the sofa, landing with a thud on her newly polished shoes before running to hold Mother Smith's outstretched hand.

I carry the basket Mother packed, while Calla swings my other arm, her hand grasped tightly in my own. Jarred stirs as we begin the walk to the creek's edge. Mother pats the swaddled bundle, and he settles into another round of soft, murmuring breaths.

At the water's edge, we lay out the blanket, eat sandwiches, and watch the water race toward its destination downstream. The mood, though subdued by our collective grief, is far from quiet. The creek is alive with raucous sounds as the water bounces over rocks, reined in only by the deep bank that surrounds its flow.

Mother was right again; it is good to be by the water. I feel washed clean by its presence. The occasional splash near our blanket sends Calla into a fit of giggles. This is precisely what we have been missing in our grief-infested state.

Mother lies down, snuggling with Jarred as she closes her eyes. It occurs to me that she is the one who wakes in all hours of the night to attend to his newborn needs—a task I am certain she thought was completed after the birth of Edward, her youngest child. Shame seeps in as these thoughts settle on my consciousness.

"Calla, why don't we take off our shoes and dip our toes in the creek?" My words are steady. The knowledge of how I must proceed with life sits at the forefront of my thoughts. "Would you like to do that?"

She grins at me, her eyes sparkling in the filtered sunlight. The dimples in her cheeks make my own smile grow. I slip off my shoes and socks before rolling my trousers to mid-calf. Calla waits anxiously as I unbuckle her shoes and remove her white ankle socks, placing our shoes and socks in a tidy pile at the blanket's edge.

We find a gradual slope in the creek bed, and I lower myself onto the smooth rocky surface before turning around to lift Calla. She stands beside me, mere inches from the water's flow. "Do you think it is cold today?" The hot summer weather has only begun to infiltrate daily life with its warm breezes and longer days.

Calla shrugs and inches her body behind mine, an indicator that I should be the one to test the water's temperature. "Okay then. I'll go first." I release her hand. "You stay put until I gain my balance."

She stands planted, leaning against the side of the bank, eyes wide and mouth open in awe. I step onto a large rock, smooth from years of erosion, and feel the cool water rush over my toes. I laugh out loud as the current tickles my feet. The laugh sounds foreign, as if someone else has laughed behind me. *It has been too long since I heard my own laughter*, I think as I take Calla's hand.

Together, we wade to where the water reaches just below Calla's knees. The hem of her dress graces the highest of the ripples as they sneak by. The occasional fish moves by us in the current, and I imagine Calla's squeals of delight can be heard in town. We spend several minutes admiring a frog resting on a shady section of wet ground.

In these small moments, we are able to let go of our saddened hearts and immerse ourselves in the wonder of nature. As our toes numb, we pick through the rocks, back to the shallow section of bank. I hoist Calla to higher ground, setting her bottom on the bank's edge. Her legs dangle before me, and I rub her feet to bring back the feeling.

"I know you miss, Momma," I say. "I miss her too, pumpkin. Momma had to go and live in heaven, but that doesn't mean she isn't your momma anymore." Calla's face becomes solemn, and I regret having to share these words with her. "Did you know you can talk to her anytime you want?"

She shakes her little head no as her eyes grow wide. "You can talk to Momma just like she taught you to talk to God." A puzzled expression draws across her face. "Whenever you miss her or want to tell her something important, just get down on your knees and talk to her. Just like she is right here beside you."

Her lip quivers as a single tear rolls down her face. Calla pushes her body up onto solid ground before turning her back to me. Frightened that she may be about to dash away from me, I climb the bank and reach her side in a panic. Her small hand tugs at mine as she kneels to the hard ground, pulling me with her. Her eyes close as she releases my hand, folding both of hers together in prayer, just like her momma taught her to do.

CHAPTER 4

March 7, 1964
Ferngrove, Washington

Calla

The slamming bedroom door echoes throughout the single-story brick house. Only thin walls separate my fury and her condescending glare. My fists, clenched into tight balls at my sides, want nothing more than to strike out at her. "Mother," I say to myself, my voice carrying thirteen years of heartache and disappointment. I tilt my chin upward in defiance of everything she's said. Everything she is. "She knows nothing about being a mother." No, to me, she is just Bernice.

There was a time, in the beginning, that I desperately wanted to call her my mother. At four years old and with a heart that still remembered Momma's adoration raining over me, I craved a mother's love. Things haven't quite worked out that way. Mother, as she prefers to be called, is devoid of any maternal touch. With the majority of my teen years behind me, I recognize that Mother has no compassion, kindness, or ability to hold her tongue. She spews only vengeful dialogue.

Fueled by the argument, I spin away from the closed door and survey my small room and the little I own. All my worldly possessions are in this room. I began working as soon as I was able, out of financial necessity rather than desire. I alone am responsible for the purchase of my belongings. I was given little, due to insufficient household funds and Mother's unwillingness to offer me anything more than basic necessities. I learned to secure employment at a tender age and have long paid my own way through this world. I've picked apples each season since we arrived in Washington state. I offer babysitting services to neighborhood families, while my peers enjoy the latest picture shows. Even now, with the heavy academic load of grade twelve, I juggle my high school studies with a part-time position at the hospital, and each night, I walk three miles home in darkness.

I've clung to the dream of attending college since the early years of my education, ever since my grade-one teacher, a kind and nurturing woman, told me how bright I was. For twelve years, I've held on to the belief that I would attend college, earn a degree, and walk away from this place with my head held high. At sixteen, I now realize that my dream of college, though a crucial element of my future earning potential, has more to do with escaping the hell of my daily existence in this house.

My shoulders slump as defeat creeps in, replacing the anger simmering below the surface of my skin. I shake my head, disappointed that I let my guard down. I should have known better. I misjudged the situation, and now devastation is tearing me apart. I believed Dad when he said there was a savings account just for college. My mistake was thinking he meant the funds would be available to me.

As the years went by, life with Mother became an obstacle course set precariously above bubbling molten lava. But I clung to the dream of attending college. I relished the idea of choosing a college several hours away from Ferngrove. I planned to put as much distance as possible between myself and Mother's unpredictable and unyielding wrath. I was sure that at least some of the college savings would be earmarked for my education. Mother's words, "That money is for the boys," will stay with me for the rest of my life, shaping my future. Her words guarantee that my dream of college, of escape, is no longer an option. I believe in my heart that Dad will want to stand up for me on this particular topic. I am certain he will try to reason with Mother. Sadly, I am all too familiar with Dad's inability to persuade Mother. And he has an even worse chance of convincing her in situations regarding me. With my dreams dashed, frustration builds in my head, pounding its way out through tears. I hurl words riddled with indignation. "I am the oldest in the family. Girl or not, I should be first in line for the college money."

I scan the open math textbook atop the child-sized desk. The desk's white paint is worn along the edges, evidence of hours I've spent on the hard wooden chair before it. Now it seems that time was wasted. All those nights and weekends. I gave my every spare moment to studying, and for what? I replay the argument in my head, dissecting it and trying to find a different outcome.

I was immersed in a study session, trying to wrap my head around a new math process when I decided to take a quick break. I went to the kitchen for a glass of water while the calculus equation rattled around my brain. I wasn't expecting a confrontation. Even after all these years, my mind refuses to assume a hand grenade with its pin removed is always at the ready, waiting to unleash destruction in any direction Bernice may carelessly toss it.

She stood in the kitchen in her maroon, brushed velvet housecoat. A sideways glance in my direction as she poured herself another cup of coffee was a silent directive to stay out of her way. A glimpse at the plain, round-faced clock above the sink told me the day was edging toward late morning. She returned the nearly empty coffee pot to its resting place atop the warming plate, a thoughtless act that would have me scrubbing burnt coffee from the pot's bottom this evening. Leaning against the olive-green stove, Mother crossed her arms and narrowed her eyes.

"Just getting a glass of water." I tried to sound casual, but the air indicated something more than coffee was brewing in the house.

"You've been hiding all morning." Her eyes bore into the back of my head as I reached for a glass. "If you think your chores will wait, young lady, you are sadly mistaken."

"Lots of homework this weekend." I filled the glass from the kitchen tap. "I will get to the chores just as soon as I finish the chapter questions."

"Why do you even bother?" Her sneer was a definitive sign that she wanted no answer to the question.

My eyes dropped, as if on cue, to survey the yellow, patterned linoleum floor. I knew already I could not navigate this conversation unscathed. "Bother with what?"

"With school and all that." Mother's head tipped as she emptied coffee past her pursed lips. Her red lipstick was long gone, but the lines remained.

"I plan to go to college. I've decided I'd like to be a teacher." As hard as I tried to etch it from my voice, the pride in having decided my future career slipped past.

"What makes you think you're going to college?" A snort escaped her nose as she judged my dreams. "There is no money for you to go to college."

"But—" I paused, treading carefully into a conversation full of hidden land mines. "Dad said there is a college fund. He said he's been putting away money all my life." Though I felt compelled to remind her that Dad had been saving for my college education long before she showed up, I knew nothing good ever came of mentioning Momma.

"Well, you might as well get to work on the laundry, then, because that money is for the boys' education, not yours. Wouldn't do you any good anyway. You'll only amount to being someone's lackey."

I felt my face redden. The tears gathered in my downcast eyes. I refused to give her the satisfaction of seeing me cry, so I hastily grabbed my glass of water from the counter and stormed back to my bedroom.

The final blow came as I retreated from her view. "Calla, don't forget to wash the bedding. My satin sheets are losing their shine. It's my day off for Christ's sake, and I am certainly not going to spend it doing laundry."

The argument plays on repeat across my mind, and I slump into the desk's wooden chair, pushing aside my notebook. My eyes follow the pencil as it rolls and then falls over the desk's edge, disappearing into the abyss between the bookshelf and desk. A sigh laced with frustration rushes past my lips. Fresh tears prick at the edges of my eyes. I slap my textbook closed and begin to grieve the loss of my future.

I freeze at a noise beyond my closed door—a knee-jerk reaction. Worry settles over me as I think of my hastily slammed door. I know better than to argue with Mother, and I most certainly know better than to slam doors in anger. One can never know Mother's tipping point, and I sit glued to my chair, holding my breath as I pray she is not focused on me.

The noise subsides, the threat of danger snuffed out. I take a deep breath and lower myself to the faded yellow carpet in search of my lost pencil. The carpet's rough texture rubs my bare knees as my muted plaid skirt creeps up my thighs. With my arm extended in the narrow space, my hand feels around for the pencil.

I press my shoulder and then my face against the bookshelf's thin wooden frame and stretch my arm a little farther. My fingers grapple with the smooth surface of the pencil before snatching it in my firm grip. I pull my body away from the bookshelf, a makeshift piece of furniture Dad built from scraps once he discovered Mother had spent the budget meant to furnish the whole house entirely on her bedroom suite. My eyes are drawn toward the book that hides the photograph. I place the pencil securely on the desk before retrieving my worn copy of *The Diary of a Young Girl*. I flip through the pages as Anne Frank's story washes over me. I find the photograph tucked into the book, alongside my favorite passage: "Yet I cling to them because I still believe, in spite of everything, that people are truly good at heart." I squeeze my eyes shut and clasp the book to my chest. If Anne can believe in the goodness of people, so can I.

I gently tug at the photograph with my thumb and forefinger, releasing it from its hiding place. Momma's shining eyes smile back at me. This treasured black-and-white photograph is the only proof I have that she existed at all. I must have been about seven years old when Granny Sanderson gave it to me, during an unscheduled visit to the Sanderson farm outside of town. Dad and I were running an errand in town. Instead of driving straight home, he took a detour to the countryside, unbeknownst to Mother, of course. He and I watched the fields of gold through the rolled-down windows of our family sedan.

Though he never said, I knew our time at the farm would be short. He slowed at the farm gate, his eyes surveying the house and land before he spotted movement in the field. He turned the car slowly toward the driveway of Momma's childhood home. The car bumped along the gravel drive, Dad navigating the largest of the potholes caused by frigid winters and heavy springtime rains. Grandad looked up from a fence line he was repairing, and his face spread into a wide grin.

My hand flew out the open window, waving wildly as

Grandad ducked under the fence, hollering for Granny as he half ran, half hobbled to meet us. Granny, bent over a bushel of beans in the garden, straightened her back and shielded her eyes with a gloved hand. She dropped her gathering basket to the ground and rushed to meet Grandad near the back porch, where they waited with anxious grins as Dad put the car in park. I bolted from the car to greet them, and Granny peeled the gloves from her hands just in time to wrap me in a warm embrace.

Dad remained in the driver's seat, watching the reunion from a distance. After hugs and a flurry of questions, Grandad made his way over to speak with Dad. Granny held me close and asked about Jarred and school and all the things grandparents take interest in, solely to hear their grandchildren's voices.

Our clandestine visit was brief, lasting barely long enough for Granny to retrieve the photograph from the home's interior and to smother me with more hugs before our hasty departure. Dad didn't need to tell me; I knew, even then, this was to be our little secret.

I run my thumb along the edge of the photograph and lean my back against the wooden frame of my bed. I search Momma's face peering back at me and wonder, *What would she do?*

CHAPTER 5

MARCH 1951
Cedar Springs, South Dakota

John

On Sunday, specifically during church service, is the only time I allow my guard to falter. I feel safest within the walls of this church, whether that is because of the soothing familiarity of Reverend Campbell's sermons or the vivid memory of a lifetime spent celebrating holidays, church picnics, and life's milestones here. One of the reasons I opted for a cemetery service when Violet passed two years ago was that I couldn't fathom visiting a place every Sunday that brought me so much pain. I couldn't imagine watching my children grow and thrive while the memory of their momma's funeral played on repeat in my mind.

Two years. I run my fingers through my hair and let out a long, slow breath. Life hasn't eased much since Vi passed. Oh, it has gone on. That is for certain. There is nothing quite like death to make a person realize how undeniably well the world goes on without their loved one in it. This reality is one of the crueler aspects of death. The ache in my heart still remains, weighing me down during even the most mundane tasks. Over time, I must have gotten better at hiding the pain. I decided to tuck my grief away from view. It was all but impossible at first, but Mother's words about my children stuck with me. Calla and Jarred need a father who is present for their young lives.

Each week, I fill my hours with work and household chores. I am building a small custom furniture business, and I spend weekends with Calla and Jarred. We have attempted three times to bring the children home to live with me during the week. Each attempt resulted in tearful goodbyes. Managing what comes with life and death is simply too much for me to handle. Deciding to allow the children to remain at my parents' home during the week was one of the most difficult decisions I've ever made. Stability, though, is the backbone of child's upbringing. So we spend the weekdays apart, while I work to bring a stable, happy father into their lives on weekends.

The months pass with relative ease, though far too many minutes still feel like eternities. Aside from during the nightmares that I tell myself are beyond my control, I visit Violet and the war during Sunday services. Though entirely different, the two traumatic events affected my life so similarly that it is nearly impossible to discern where one ends and the other begins. They are loops in the same circle, unable to be separated.

The swaying of the congregation transports me back in time to a ship bobbing with the choppy, frigid water beneath it. The sky was dark with angry-looking clouds, so I huddled under a slim overhang, tucking my back against the cold steel to hide from the unrelenting wind. Mail call was one of the few bright spots while I was overseas. We waited weeks and sometimes months for a word, a letter, a small bit of home to carry us through another day. In the thoughtfulness of the packages and letters, my family's love shined over me despite the thousands of miles between us. Back home, I never felt unloved in the slightest, but with the threat of injury or death as thick as an English fog, urgency to speak with frankness and affection won out over pride and embarrassment. A letter was never sent without a clear statement of one's adoration for the other.

I sliced at the twine securing the small box's sides, an added measure to ensure the contents' safe delivery. My hands dove past the letter in anticipation of the milk chocolate that was sure to be lining the bottom of the package. Never one to deny her son his favorite treat, Mother had filled the bottom of the box with an assortment of chocolate bars. With the foil paper removed, I savored the first bite. The chocolate warmed me through, despite the day's inclement temperature. Tucking the letter into my jacket pocket, I examined the remainder of the box's contents. A pair of charcoal-colored, hand-knitted mittens. Three pairs of knitted socks. A knitted cap and two jars of Mother's homemade applesauce, in addition to the quickly disappearing chocolate treat.

With three chocolate wrappers folded neatly and tucked inside my innermost pocket, I retrieved Mother's letter. As usual, Mother kept me up to date with the goings-on of Cedar Springs. She told me of Reverend Campbell's weekly prayer for those touched by war. I imagined her sitting in the pew, holding her breath until my name was mentioned. I knew hearing my name spoken aloud in church helped her feel that I was safe and well. I stifle a laugh as I recall the story she told of her youngest child. Edward had found Mother's hiding place for the treats she was gathering to send me. She found him under the bed, surrounded by a good number of empty wrappers. His back was turned to her when she entered the room, and though the carcasses of wrappers had already given him away, his chocolate-smudged face made Mother scream when he turned to face her. Father, thinking more clearly, took the boy for a walk outdoors to talk some understanding into him, while giving Mother time to regain her composure. It seems I am not the only Smith boy who has a fondness for the stuff. I make a mental note to remember Edward's love of chocolate next Christmas.

As the choir slides into a new hymn, my mind wanders back to those first months after the war. Violet held me close, letting me shed my worn-out misery. I was one of the lucky ones, after all. I survived a war that took too many young lives.

Violet would wake me from the dreams that haunted me with faces, limbs, and the putrid smell of death. She would lie awake with me for hours, pressing a cool cloth to my throbbing forehead. She never shied away from the dark stories, and she asked the questions no one else could bear to ask. She was fearless in that regard. I miss having her strength in my corner. She gave me a special confidence by allowing me to be who I truly am, even with the bruises of life visible.

I miss her presence the most—the simple knowledge that there was no worry too big and no achievement too small for her to want to hear about. Our conversations are now one-sided and take place inside my head alone. Without Vi here to listen and share it with me, my life feels less valid. Though I'll never admit it to another living soul, I am certain a piece of myself accompanied my sweet wife to her grave that April day.

The congregation shuffles and stands to join the choir, interrupting my reverie of years gone by. Calla wiggles beside me, swaying haphazardly to the music and drawing my attention back to the present. Calla is sandwiched between Violet's mother and myself, and I imagine she feels imprisoned by the adults in her life. I tweak the bow in her hair with my thumb and index finger, which garners me a brilliant smile. Her smile sends a shock of guilt through my heart. I cringe a little, knowing that I am betraying both Violet and Calla with my recent Thursday-evening activities.

I've contemplated mentioning Bernice, the woman I've been

seeing each Thursday evening for the past several weeks. I've considered testing the waters and gauging my family's response to a new woman in my life. So far, I have not been able to muster the courage. Even I myself waffle on pursuing this relationship with Bernice when I clearly have not come to terms with losing my wife.

Even as a young boy, I always knew Violet was special. She had a kind of magic that drew people in, captured their hearts, and made them want to stay wrapped in the glow of her attention. Violet's death left a hole in our family—in the lives of Calla, Jarred, and myself, but also in my parents' and siblings' lives. Violet was almost bigger than life itself, and I am under no illusion that another woman could take her place. Perhaps that is why my lips have remained sealed on the subject of Bernice. Or perhaps I am more of a coward than I realized. Vi was truly the strong one in our relationship.

As the weeks pass, I exist in two different realities. One reality is that of a widower with two small children and a childhood sweetheart I cannot let go. The other finds me in the arms of another woman, at ease and lost in the darkness, with only her to hold my attention. My time with Bernice feels like a break, a disruption from the hardness of my life since Violet passed. I recognize the unfairness of the arrangement, and yet I can't come to terms with two worlds that don't seem to fit well together. Time, perhaps, is all I can give the situation. I will let time pass and allow my two realities to breathe. Perhaps then I will see things more clearly.

As Reverend Campbell wraps up the service with a rousing and emotional plea to join him in preparations for the church's annual Easter feast, my thoughts turn to Bernice. She is young, with striking features and dark, wavy hair. She has an air of bravery and confidence, but I see who she really is—a scared little girl who, after all these years, is terrified that she is only worthy of being abandoned. I think I am drawn to the damaged part of her. If two damaged individuals come together, does that make them less damaged? I shake my head, unsure whether I have the desire or the strength to find out.

Uncertainty about continuing a relationship with Bernice has been flitting about my mind all week. The hairs on the back of my neck have raised in warning on more than one occasion, most recently during an outburst by Mrs. Perkins at the shipping office where Bernice works. I've never had much time for Mrs. Perkins, a fellow churchgoer and an avid Cedar Springs busybody, but her words of warning that Bernice was no good for me did strike with a hint of accuracy.

For reasons I cannot pin down, I am drawn to Bernice. Her coy smile conveys far more than her lips utter. The sway in her hips lets me know she wants more of me and is prepared to deliver on the suggestion. Even the stark difference between her and Violet is intoxicating. Bernice is like a long-desired sleep for a weary traveler. The thought of her makes me want nothing more than to turn off the world around me so I can bask in her presence.

My mind is no more at ease by the time the preacher sends us on our way. As I shake the exhilarating thoughts of Bernice from my mind, I try desperately to ignore the fact that the final hymn was one of Violet's favorites. She would hum the song as she worked in the garden or while sewing happily at her machine. I tuck my memories away for another week, reach for Calla's hand, and meander to the front doors, where Reverend Campbell is waiting to greet each member of his congregation.

Making our way down the steps, we gather as a large family as the sun filters through the clouds, casting rays on the dusty parking lot. The children and I will spend the afternoon at Violet's parents' farm. Shame flows through my veins as Mr. Sanderson embraces me in a bear hug and I consider how my former father-in-law would feel if he knew I was seeing someone new. In this moment, I know I am not yet ready to divulge my interactions with Bernice. It is still early in the relationship, I tell myself, too early to know if this thing has legs. Feeling bolstered by the decision, I lift Calla high in the air and spin her around. I place her on somewhat wobbly legs in front of Violet's mother, who is waiting to steady the smiling child.

Jarred, old enough now to know when he has missed out on something fun, toddles away from my mother and reaches my side. He tugs at my trouser leg and lifts his arms in the air. The game continues until the first drops of rain hit our smiling faces. We dash for cover. I set Jarred on the truck's middle seat while Calla climbs up, hiking her dress in order to reach the truck's floorboard. With the trundle of the truck's engine and the wipers swishing back and forth, it isn't long before Jarred's eyelids begin to droop. As if on cue, Calla scoots closer to her little brother and guides his body to lie across her lap. I watch from the corner of my eye as she strokes his hair before placing a gentle kiss atop his forehead. Four years old, going on twenty-three. I hold back a tear and pray that her childhood hasn't been stolen from her completely.

We make the turn toward the Sanderson farm, catching up with my parents' car at the gate. Putting the truck in park, I gaze at my children. I see my wife, their momma, in both of their angelic faces. When Calla's eyes shift toward mine, it is as if Violet has never left us at all.

CHAPTER 6

Calla

The options seem clear enough, but I feel paralyzed by them, all the same. Neither choice is ideal, nor welcome, but choosing one is my only course of action. My insides melt into a puddle of despair as Mother's words settle in the pit of my stomach. The funds I have been promised all these years, the ones certain to see me through four years of a college education, are no longer available to me.

Even if I had saved every penny I earned and hadn't been required to pay for my own clothing, school supplies, and necessities since my twelfth birthday, I would be no closer to paying my own way. The way I see it, I have two choices. I can take control of my own life and leave this house with the hope of earning enough to pursue a college education, or I can button my mouth and live as Mother believes I should. I shake my head in disbelief and wonder if other girls my age worry about matters such as these. No, I suspect other girls of almost seventeen are more worried about boys, curfews, and prom dresses, with their future education tucked away and waiting for them come September.

I weigh the choices before me. Would it be so hard to stay put, do as I'm told, and keep my head down? I've been living under this rock for so long it feels almost normal. But the fact that I've grown accustomed to this life doesn't make it normal or acceptable. I argue the options in my head. This particular homelife situation shouldn't feel anything like normal. I know from overheard, locker-leaning conversations at school that other girls experience mostly quiet, supportive, and loving relationships with their parents and siblings. Their parents attend school plays, football games, and parent-teacher nights. I'm not even certain my parents know what courses I am taking, let alone whether I have any interest in auditioning for the school's rendition of *A Midsummer Night's Dream*. If I begin an argument with Mother, I risk having a plate thrown in my direction. If I disagree, even in the slightest nonverbal manner, she humiliates me with words delivered solely to inflict deep emotional scarring. Anytime I inadvertently do anything wrong, I have to hunker down as the tornado that is Mother sweeps through the house, taking out everything in her path.

Reaching forward, I pull my turquoise piggy bank from the bookshelf. I turn it over in my hands, admiring the pastel flower design painted on each side of its bulging belly, before flipping it upside down and removing the cap located at the pig's underbelly. I shake the bank gently before adding more vigor to free its contents. Coins tumble onto my lap and spill onto the floor around me. Using my index finger, I fish out the paper bills lodged in the depths of the bank, and then I begin sorting the money at my disposal.

I am exceptionally careful with money, a skill I learned out of necessity. I have been working long hours every summer, picking apples to pay for my school supplies and wardrobe. I also have weekly babysitting obligations, and I save my hard-earned money by sewing my own school clothes. Though I am far from rich, I am pleased to count up a total of seventy-three dollars and forty-nine cents. It's not much in terms of worldly accounts, but it's enough to make a start. The Motel 6 in town, according to their frequent adverts, fits both my slim budget and my need for simple lodgings while I sort out the next phase of my life.

I fold the bills and scoop the change into the only wallet I own. The deep-purple, faux leather accessory was a splurge after learning the cost of this term's textbooks were less than I had expected. It was a prudent choice in the end, as a wallet will come in handy as I begin providing for myself.

I toss the bulging wallet onto the bed and stand before the closet, surveying its meager contents. My decision to leave wavers in the pit of my stomach as I reach for two canvas bags to hold my clothes, shoes, and personal belongings. My thoughts turn to Jarred. I feel as though I am breaking a promise never uttered aloud. Perhaps it is a promise between siblings who have known the loss of a parent. Maybe I am merely feeling the guilt of an older sister who knows the sting of abandonment. I've always wondered if Jarred felt abandoned, having missed out on the opportunity to know Momma. Not wanting to be the cause of Jarred's pain, I pause, praying for an alternate solution.

Several minutes pass as I stare at the doorless closet. The luxury of a closet door was never afforded to my bedroom. Mother's wants outweigh others' needs most of the time. I mentioned the missing doors once or twice at the family dinner table, but a harsh word from Mother about my ungrateful attitude was enough to hush me.

I sigh in defeat, unable to do both what is best for Jarred and what is best for myself. Although frustrating, this is not a new concern. I have spent the better part of the past thirteen years shielding Jarred and the other boys from Mother. My role of protector and steward wasn't immediate. It evolved over time, as Mother's unhappiness grew. I am unsure whether her misery stems from the multiple pregnancies or from her failures as a caretaker. Sometimes, when she angers me with her flippant remarks and her wayward orders, all I can think is that she is just plain mean and that mean people have no right to live in a house with children about.

I shift my attention back to the task at hand. Aware that I will be able to bring only what I can carry, I begin by placing my two pairs of shoes in the first bag. I will wear my third pair, my everyday shoes, as my traveling shoes. I retrieve the small stack of shorts and summer dresses from the back shelf of the dark closet and place them in my second bag. I fold sweaters and tunics, positioning my winter clothes at the top of each bag. I lean my head in the closet and inspect the empty space. Save for the now-vacant wire hangers and a box of childhood toys, the closet looks as desolate as my heart is beginning to feel.

Before I can entertain the notion of changing my mind, I turn my attention to the desk. I stack the school books neatly in a shoulder bag and decide I will return the textbooks on Monday when I register my formal withdrawal from classes. I am not naive enough to believe I can continue with school after leaving my family home. My need to secure employment is much more pressing. I am comforted by the knowledge that my long-standing candy striper position with the Ferngrove hospital has earned me the title of a responsible young lady. Despite my being at the hospital only one evening a week, the hospital manager has personally commended me on more than one occasion, going so far as to inquire about the possibility of my entering nursing, after earning the proper certificate, of course. I believe he may be willing to find me a suitable full-time position in the immediate future.

Placing my hand on the pile of half-used notebooks, I consider that it would be better, easier even, to walk out the door without fanfare. Heck, they might not even notice I've left. I laugh at myself for my foolish thought. Shiny satin sheets notwithstanding, they would at least notice the dirty dishes and lack of dinner. My already heavy heart sinks a little lower in my chest. It won't be easy, but writing Dad a letter will be less of a production than having to explain myself as I walk out the door. It's not like Dad and I are regulars at the heart-to-heart café. He engages in emotionally charged conversations about as often as Mother admits she may be mistaken.

Sitting in front of the desk, I tear a piece of notebook paper from its coiled prison. Pencil in hand, I consider my words carefully. How do I explain a lifetime filled with pain, fear, and disappointment? Part of me wonders if the letter is even worth my time. He hasn't taken action against my or any of his children's anguish thus far. What can I write in a letter that would make him grasp his role in my unhappiness?

"Dear Dad . . ."

The tears come easily. The words, not so much. Chewing on the end of my pencil, I think back to how it all began. I was only four years old when Mother entered our world. I don't recall spending much time with her before the abrupt change in our living arrangements. All of a sudden, she was in our lives and in our house. Jarred and I were brought back from Grandma and Grandpa Smith's home one sunny day after church. Dad tried his best to add cheer to the transition. I remember a trip to the ice-cream shop. While I was distracted by the melting vanilla cone in my hand, he told us he had married a woman and she was going to be our mother. It was an awful ordeal. I remember the sullen faces at the announcement that Jarred and I would be leaving the Smith home. Grandma and I clung to each another as if life itself were ending. Sobs and sniffles lured Jarred into the fold as he responded to our display of emotion with his own tears. I couldn't understand how someone could simply get a new mother, but I felt the eviction from the only family unit I had known and loved as I would have felt a knife splitting me in two.

A vague memory of a visit to a park smolders at the edges of my recollection. I assume we were meeting Mother, but I can't be certain. I have few details to paint a picture in my mind's eye. A feeling of uneasiness settles across me, and I wonder if the memory is true or fabricated. The mind is a funny thing, after all, sometimes protecting us from our own thoughts.

I glance down at the two words I've managed to write and decide busying myself with packing will help me formulate my thoughts before I commit them to paper.

CHAPTER 7

August 1951
Cedar Springs, South Dakota

John

The dust billows into clouds beneath the weight of my truck's tires, making an otherwise hot afternoon a little less bearable. "Ninety-three degrees," the radio man announced as I left the shop. As I make my way home, I remind myself of what is waiting for me there. I run my fingers through my hair, dispersing droplets of sweat.

Married three months now, the transition into a family has been less than smooth. If it weren't for Calla and Jarred, I might not be inclined to return to the place that was once my sanctuary. Violet always made it so, I realize now. The house wasn't a magical escape from the daily stresses of life. Violet transformed an otherwise simple house into a home, filled with the aroma of fresh-baked bread. Newly washed laundry would be strung up with precision on a clothesline. The house was always tidy, the dishes always at home in the cupboards. Her vegetable garden, though, was her pride and joy. The garden was organized in rows by height so the plants would glean the most use from the sun's rays as it crossed the sky.

She made it look easy, managing the house, the garden, Calla. She always had a smile upon her face and a childlike skip in her step. I was delusional to think I could find someone else like her. Not that I was looking. I certainly felt the loneliness of a man who had lost his way, but I hadn't been searching for another wife. Bernice caught me unaware is all, and then with the news of the impending pregnancy—well, I consider myself an honorable man. Offering anything other than marriage would have been out of the question.

I was flattered that first day she asked me to dine with her. It felt good to be seen again, to feel a woman's eyes on me—and not with a look that hollered, "What a pity. Poor John, so young and widowed, with two small children." Those looks have plagued me since Violet's death. In contrast, Bernice's attention lit a fire, and for that, I am grateful to her.

The adjustment, though, hasn't been easy. I turn the radio volume up and attempt to drown out my thoughts with a catchy new tune. Bernice seems to be struggling with our new arrangement. I've tried to give her the benefit of the doubt, given how the pregnancy is making her so tired. At least that is what she keeps telling me. She apologizes, tripping over her words until she bursts into tears and runs to the bedroom. Violet was never tired, or if she was, she certainly never lamented about it. I shake my head, desperate to stop myself from comparing the two women. There is no comparison. Other than the fact that they are both mothers to a child of mine, there is simply no resemblance.

Lazy. The word, though harsh, slips through my consciousness. It's been rattling around in my head for weeks now, likely the result of working overtime at the cabinet shop and assisting with household chores in every spare moment. Then, of course, there is the added stress of Bernice's pregnant state. The last time a wife of mine was in the family way, she died. I shake my head with a sudden jerk in an effort to rid my mind of the dreadful thought, and I admonish myself for thinking such things. I will myself to hold my tongue on the topic. I'll give Bernice as much time and space as she needs, even if it means stepping over piles of laundry until the baby arrives. It is a small price to pay, after all, for a healthy wife and newborn.

I do wonder about what Bernice anticipated in terms of keeping a house and raising children. We decided together, the day she surprised me with news of the pregnancy, that she would take care of the house and children. Instead of continuing her search for employment, after having been unceremoniously let go from her previous position, she would remain home while I made certain we had enough money. She seemed pleased with the decision at the time, but now, three months later, I wonder if she feels the same. I make a mental note to speak with her. Perhaps during dinner cleanup tonight, we can tackle both the dishes and the conversation.

The dishes have been piling up atop the counter, leaving little room for any kind of food preparation. How she manages to make a sandwich for my lunch each day, I have no idea. Then again, given the mess, if I could envision the process, I would likely never enjoy the contents of my tin lunch box again.

I admonish myself once more. Perhaps if I were to stop comparing Bernice to Violet, she would feel a sincerity that may have been lacking since we returned from our week-long honeymoon in North Dakota. It was easy to get caught up in the excitement of a trip, of time together, of unbridled and socially acceptable affection shared between husband and wife.

As wonderful as our honeymoon was, reality hit hard upon our return to Cedar Springs. Bernice moved into the home I used to share with Violet. Three days later, Calla and Jarred joined us there. Calla is wary of our new living arrangement, clinging to my side whenever I am present. Jarred is a busy little boy, always attempting to put something in his mouth. I understand Bernice's challenges, and I put energy into helping out whenever possible. I pray she will get the hang of being a wife and mother, rather than rebuking her for all the things she isn't managing well, which is currently about every part of her new role. *No wonder I am exhausted,* I think as I run my hand through my hair, feeling the hot air swirl in through rolled-down window. *I've been burning the candle at both ends, while trying to learn the ebbs and flows of our new family unit.*

But this is pushing it. I sit up straight behind the steering wheel and squint down the road to where the dusky sky meets the gravel road. I can barely make out my children, yet at the same time, I am convinced my eyes are deceiving me. I would not have even noticed their silhouettes if they weren't contrasted against the spectacular colors of the hot August sunset.

Calla appears even smaller than she is under the weight of the little red wagon she is pulling behind her. My heart finds its way to my throat, and I wonder if Calla realizes gathering water from the neighbor's pump is not a job for a four-year-old. I park the truck in the driveway. As I round the bumper, the urgency in my gait gives away my fear. My steps quicken as I imagine a similar scene in winter, with snow and ice and frozen pump handles. A shiver runs down my back, and my desire to reach her overwhelms me, turning my stride into a jog.

She must have sensed my presence on the road. She stops, switches pulling hands, and lifts her head, blonde curls bouncing as she moves. She swivels her gaze away from mine, and I hear her talk to Jarred before pointing in my direction. Jarred is sitting in the low-edged wagon, buckets of water surrounding him and keeping him from toppling out. As his face lights up with a smile, my jog turns into a full-on sprint, and I am at their side in less than a minute, huffing but relieved to find them safe.

"Daddy!" she squeals excitedly.

"Hi ya, pumpkin." I ruffle her tangle of curls. "Whatcha doing out here so close to dark?"

"Mother told us to get water," she says so innocently that I can't help but smile down at her.

Jarred lifts his arms toward me and giggles to get my attention. I reach down for him, spilling water as I extract his little body from the prison of buckets. Holding Jarred's hand in mine, I take the wagon's handle from Calla's grip, and together we begin the bumpy trek toward home.

"You gather water often, honey?" I ask, as gravel escapes the wagon's wheels in tiny bursts, causing the wagon to lurch.

"Yes." She looks at me blankly. "It's our job."

"I see. How long has it been your job?"

Calla shrugs. Having not yet entered kindergarten, time is still a relatively new concept for her. I am in little hurry to reach our front door. The words I want to hurl in Bernice's direction are pushing at the edges of my mind. I counter my anger by trying to find compassion for my new wife, who admittedly never had the guidance of a mother. She was, after all, once a young girl abandoned in an orphanage by her father. Then, later in life, she became a young woman who was cast aside and sent away for loving the wrong man. He was a married man, but the wrong one all the same. Life hasn't been fair to Bernice. But I don't imagine it has been fair to many people, including myself and my two children.

My outrage is reaching a simmer when I am struck by the thought of the water pump. "Calla, how do you reach the water pump to fill the buckets?" I ask, certain that she isn't tall enough to reach the handle.

"I jump, silly," she says, her smiling face as innocent and angelic as ever as she lifts her slight body into the air to demonstrate.

"Oh, I see. You are a very good jumper indeed." I say this

with a smile, trying to keep my words light so as not to worry the child.

Having fetched water myself since we moved into this house, I am acutely aware that pumping for water is no easy task. The pump has to be primed, which involves pumping the handle quickly and often to begin the flow of water from the spout. I close my eyes and see Calla jumping over and over to pull the water from the well. No, I decide, no matter Bernice's reasoning, this is not a task for a small child. I squeeze Calla's hand, silently letting her know that I will protect her from this.

By the time we reach the house, there is little light left to guide our way, save for the solitary light bulbs positioned near the front doors of the neighboring houses. Casting only a shadowy yellow glow, the meager light reaches no farther than their front stoops.

"There you are. What took you so long?" Bernice asks without turning to see who has opened the front door. My anger at the situation diminishes as I watch Bernice haphazardly stack dirty dishes into the sink before rummaging through the cupboard in what I interpret as a search for dinner. As misguided as her actions were, it is easy to see Bernice did not intend any harm by sending the children for water.

Violet would have had dinner on the table by now, with a fresh peach pie cooling on the counter. The children would have been washed and changed into clean clothes, faces painted with smiles from a happy day spent in the garden, playing under the watchful eye of their mother.

I clear my throat and decide to discuss the matter of gathering water with Bernice after the children are in bed. Bernice turns at the sound of my voice, smiles, and steps toward me, cheek lifted as she waits for a kiss. I kiss her cheek before retrieving the rest of the water from the wagon beside the front steps.

"Better get washed up." Bernice returns to the stove and

dumps a package of chicken legs into a casserole pan. "Dinner shouldn't be too long." She shrugs and glances at me over her shoulder. I contemplate helping her with the can opener she is cursing under her breath, but I decide better of it. I don't want to add insult to injury, since I am certain she has no idea what she is making for dinner nor how long it will actually take to cook.

She pours the can of green beans, liquid and all, over top of the chicken. My stomach lurches as she pokes the mixture with a fork before opening a can of stewed tomatoes. I catch the scrunched-up look of disgust on Calla's face as Bernice dumps the tomatoes into the casserole pan. I stifle a laugh before I realize we will have to eat this concoction tonight. I place my hands on Calla's shoulders and guide her and Jarred toward the bathroom as Bernice opens the oven door and places her creation inside. A final glance back tells me she has forgotten to preheat the oven and is now engrossed in turning dials to spur the appliance to life.

The children wash their hands and faces. I allow them to play with the soap, slippery in their fingers, to occupy additional time and stave off grumbling tummies. As their giggles wash over me, lighting my world, I consider how I will approach tonight's conversation with Bernice.

I decide to wait until dinner is over to test the waters, knowing full well that an insensitive, though warranted, comment from Calla or myself about dinner could derail Bernice's emotional state. I will myself to eat enthusiastically, though I am aware that doing so may sentence me to a life of similar meals. My objective tonight is to sort out the inappropriate demands placed upon my children. I edit my words in my mind. I will make it clear that fetching water will be my task alone, until the children reach a suitable age, not to mention height.

Though she did not display any anger toward Calla and Jarred when they returned from fetching water, I am troubled by the fact that Bernice believed it appropriate to send them for water. No matter her reasoning, I notice a cold wariness has crept into my heart. I struggle with the knowledge that Bernice has demanded Calla and Jarred perform a household task that should have been her own or, at the very least, a task for the three of them to complete together. I dry Jarred's hands with a small towel and kiss his plump cheek. I decide dressing for bed and stories are to come before the sure-to-be-tardy dinner, and I corral them toward their bedroom. *Lazy is one word for it*, I think, *but unsettling might be another.* I simmer my thoughts as Calla chooses a story from her bookshelf. I say a silent prayer that Bernice is simply unaware of what it takes to be a good parent. *That I can work with*, I think to myself as Calla and Jarred snuggle beside me on Calla's bed and I open the book to the first page.

CHAPTER 8

March 7, 1964
Ferngrove, Washington

Calla

Standing over my bed, I decide it a prudent measure to bring my pillow. I don't know what to expect at a meager establishment such as the motel, and if I am to be grown up about things, I should look out for all my needs. Thankfully there is room in the bag containing my sparse collection of clothes. I stuff the pillow inside and then fold my bed's heaviest blanket and force it into the now-overflowing bag. Tugging at the zipper's sides, I manage to close the bulging bag before dropping it near the door.

I inspect my bedside table, deciding the lamp and stack of books I've already read will stay where they are. I empty the drawer, removing a notebook, a pencil, and the palm-sized silver alarm clock I'd placed in the drawer to deaden its overeager shrill. The clock rattles its displeasure as I tuck it into my shoulder bag.

The afternoon sun, barely peeking through a cloudy sky, casts its rays through the small window situated above the desk. Specks of dust, disturbed by my movement of items around the room, dance in the sunbeam. The tiny specks, fragments, seem almost magical as they float gracefully within the shimmering sunlight.

A memory tugs at the edges of my mind. It was a sunny spring day, though the dew had yet to leave the ground. I remember feeling the concern of a four-year-old when my white Buster Browns began to collect wet blades of grass as Dad and I walked through the park. We were hand in hand, until I spotted a dandelion. I couldn't understand why, but I knew he was sad. He wore a subdued smile as he waited for me to blow the white fuzz from the dandelion's top. I watched his face through the scattered bits of dandelion fluff, a small child's attempt at assessing the situation.

The reason for Dad's sadness washes over me as the pieces of our past, not unlike specks of dust or dandelion fluff, dance into formation. I know this memory. I don't remember anything else about that day, or even that week. But through the years, this memory has often presented itself in my dreams and my nightmares. I crawl into my bed and bury myself under the remaining covers. Try as I might, the memory will not fade. Having spent most of my childhood walking a tightrope between trying to remember and trying to forget, my mind may no longer know what to do with such remembrances.

I breathe deeply, the weight of the covers cocooning me into a false sense of comfort. In the memory, Dad takes my hand again and we continue across the damp grass. The walk seems long, and that is when I notice the funny rocks sticking up in rows. Some are smaller than others. Some are as tall as Daddy and cast shadows against the sun's hearty effort. I decide I like the tall ones the least as a chill runs up my back. I am about to voice my concern about the size and tippy nature of the rocks when he stops abruptly and turns to his right.

Stepping in between the rows of rocks, Dad's hand tugs at mine, corralling me down a grassy path with oversized stones crowding us on both sides. After several paces, he stops and faces one of the stones. His face contorts as tears spill from his eyes. He kneels to the wet grass and places a small bouquet of wildflowers against the stone. I stand beside him in frightened silence. My eyes wander about the park until they find the letters cut into the stone's face. I want to reach out and trace the letters, like Grandma teaches me to do when we read the story about Dick and Jane.

Daddy washes his face with the palm of his hand before turning to me. "Calla, honey, do you know where we are?"

I shake my head no; my eyes follow his every movement. I want to tell him I don't want to know, but the words don't form in time.

"This is where Momma is." His tears flow freely with each word.

I fiddle with the hem of my blue-flowered dress. I stay as quiet as I can. Daddy doesn't always make sense when he talks about Momma. He doesn't mention her often, but I've overheard him talking to Grandma about her. They must think I am too busy playing with my dolly, not paying them any mind, but my ears perk up especially well when Momma is the topic.

I wait several minutes, watching him stare at the stone. I ought to tell him to trace the letters. Then we could both know what story the funny stone wants to share. The sun is warm on my face, and my tummy is rumbling for the picnic we left in the truck. I decide that Daddy must be confused about where Momma is, or he wouldn't be taking so long with thinking she is here.

"Momma's in heaven," I finally say, barely above a whisper.

I know this to be true, as Daddy is the one who told me, and Daddy would never lie about something as important as that. I've been talking to Momma every night when I say my prayers before bed. Grandma helps me remember the names of family members and sometimes asks me to pray for folks from church who have "fallen on hard times." But I never forget to talk to Momma. I tell her about Jarred and Daddy and what Grandma calls "Edward's funny business." I think it makes her laugh, and that makes me happy.

Edward is Uncle Edward, Daddy's littlest brother. At least that is what Daddy likes to call him. But to me, Edward is one of the big kids. At ten years old, Edward gets to set traps and go fishing. Edward told me that one day he would teach me how to fish too. I think about spending an afternoon beside the creek, just me and Edward, and I smile. I like being with Edward because he makes me laugh—especially since Momma isn't here anymore to laugh with me about silly things.

The minutes tick by without a word from Daddy. The uncertainty of where Momma really is begins to muddle my thoughts. My tummy doesn't feel good anymore. If Momma is here, then who have I been talking to all this time?

I throw the covers off my head in a burst, gasping for fresh air. I don't remember the outcome of that day. I don't recall having a picnic or driving back to town. Daddy never answered me. Instead, we walked back to the truck with nothing but the wind between us.

That was the first and last time I visited Momma's grave.

It soon became clear that speaking about Momma, even while kneeling in prayer, was unacceptable to Mother. Not long after we all settled into the little blue house together, Daddy explained that it hurt her feelings to hear me talking to Momma when she was there and ready to be my new mother. My nightly prayers stopped, and a new routine of crying myself to sleep began—and continued for too many years.

I bolt up from the bed, uncomfortable with the unresolved grief but also fueled by it. I sit forcefully on the wooden chair. Pencil grasped firmly in my hand, I write, "How could you choose her over Jarred and me? How could you choose Mother over your own children?"

CHAPTER 9

OCTOBER 1951
Cedar Springs, South Dakota

John

The crisp autumn leaves, having been gathered into heaping piles of radiant color, scent the air as neighbors burn them in household burn barrels. Besides summer, which I spend fishing, autumn is my favorite time of year. I took a hurried lunch break today so I could race home from work early for Halloween festivities.

The annual gathering at the church has provided a fun evening of bobbing for apples and costume parades since Calla's first Halloween. Tonight will be Bernice's first appearance within the church's walls. Due to the circumstance of our union, we married at a church unknown to either of us, one that could accommodate our hurried nuptials on a quiet Friday afternoon.

Bernice's lack of attendance at church each Sunday has led to several discussions and a fair amount of pestering from me. I am aware of how her unwillingness to attend church, due in part to the Cedar Springs gossip mill, may appear to the rest of the congregation, and I am not inclined to give others more reason to talk ill of Bernice. Not even the promise of Mother Smith's famous fried chicken has budged Bernice's resolve to avoid church. I've heard stories of how the Sioux Falls preacher convinced Bernice's father to leave her and her sister, Patricia, at the local orphanage. Despite my assurances that Reverend Campbell is a kind man who would never separate a child from a parent, Bernice has held firm. Instead of attending church and Sunday lunch with my family, she has used the hours to sleep late, read magazines, and regain her strength for the week ahead. At least that is what she tells me.

Tonight, though, will be a spectacular event. Without Violet here, Mother Smith and my sisters have banded together to sew Calla and Jarred costumes for the parade. Calla, I must admit, has impressed me with her ability to keep the nature of her costume a surprise. Jarred however, has let the secret of his costume slip on more than one occasion by practicing his latest favorite word: *ghost*. This past week I have been greeted at the door each evening with the swooping and swaying antics of a two-and-a-half-year-old boy pretending to be a friendly, albeit extremely active ghost, just like Casper.

Lunch pail in hand, I climb the steps toward the front door and smile at the thought of my two children, eager to join friends and family for Halloween. Calla greets me first, dressed in a baby-blue frock with a small white apron over top. Though none of us has yet seen the film, I recognize her as Alice from the newly released Walt Disney production *Alice in Wonderland*. Her blue eyes sparkle as she twirls about, making the crinolines rustle and billow. She bends her head low so I can inspect the dainty black ribbon Mother Smith has woven among her bouncing blonde curls.

"Well, hello there, Alice." I beam at Calla as she grabs my hand and tugs me into the kitchen, where Jarred, clad in a simple white sheet with two eye holes, lingers beneath the kitchen table. "Where in the world could your brother be, Calla?" I play along, knowing Jarred is taking his ghost costume seriously.

Bernice, whose growing baby belly is pressed against the counter, forms ground meat into hamburger patties. She tosses a weary smile over her shoulder at me before inclining her head toward Jarred's hiding spot. I return her smile, pleased to see she has thought to prepare an early dinner. I place my lunch box on the table with a slightly heavy hand, attempting to elicit a response from the ghost beneath. Giggles fill the air, but Jarred remains hidden. My smile is playful, given the mood in the house and the memory playing across my mind.

Watching Bernice at the counter, I can't help but move toward her, placing a gentle kiss on the soft spot between her neck and shoulder. She smiles and leans back into my chest as I wrap my arms around her shoulders. "Remember the first time we made hamburgers together?" I ask, running a finger down her forearm.

"How could I forget?" A throaty laugh erupts from deep within her. "You taught me everything you knew. One egg, salt and pepper, a sprinkle of breadcrumbs." Bernice swivels in my arms, her hands raised, elbows bent to avoid splattering me with the mixture. "Of course, we didn't eat that batch, now did we?" A knowing smile plays on her lips.

"Nope." I return her smile with a coy one of my own. I remember the two of us, caught up in a rare moment without children about, fumbling with the removal of each other's clothes in the bedroom, in a hurry to steal a moment for ourselves. "Those ones burnt right outside that door, overtop the charcoal. We were lucky, actually. Didn't burn the house down."

"We made up for it in the end." Bernice kisses my nose and leans her hip toward me in a seductive motion as she turns back to the counter. "You did have to rush off to the butcher for replacements though." A shake of her head. "Remember? Your parents were returning with the children and you had promised everyone barbecue."

I laugh out loud at the memory. "But you did master the art of hamburger-making in the end." Before I can say more, Jarred jumps out from beneath the table with a raucous noise. I feign a startled jump and grab at my heart for added emphasis, before encircling him in a bear hug. Calla laughs with delight, twirling and jumping with a wide grin spreading across her angelic face. In moments such as these, the challenges we face as a family disappear into the recesses of my mind. These are the moments I let myself believe everything will work out in the end.

I am unsure whether Bernice's choice of dinner is due to her ability to manage the task of making hamburgers or her awareness that children excited for Halloween are not likely to eat much. But I'm pleased by her selection, as hamburgers are a family favorite. The kids take little time to clean their plates before jumping back into their costumes.

Before long, we are all four piled into the cab of my truck and trundling toward the church. I notice Bernice wringing her purse straps between both hands. I slide my free arm across the back of the seat and give her shoulder a reassuring squeeze. Calla plays with the apron of her dress, smoothing it flat across her lap while Jarred works on his "boo."

Upon arrival at the church parking lot, I notice Bernice's hesitation and usher the children out my side of the truck. Calla is excited and ready to be set free. I give her a nod and say, "Be sure to hold Jarred's hand until you've climbed the stairs. I don't want him tumbling over his costume."

I walk around the truck's box, watching the children enter the oversized church doors. Opening the passenger door, I offer Bernice my hand. "You'll love it. It really is a lot of fun."

Bernice sighs lightly, forces an uncertain smile, and puts her hand in mine. "I'm not so sure about this." Her words falter a little, making her appear timid and small. "So many children and parents, all of them churchgoers. This isn't the kind of place where I fit in, John."

I give her cheek a peck. "You promised the kids. Not to mention me. They've been looking forward to tonight for weeks." I pause, my head inclining toward the church doors. "This is a good opportunity for us to be together as a family." I look at her through downcast eyes, trying to find the balance between pushing too much and not enough.

After a few more minutes of negotiation, Bernice and I enter the brightly lit interior of my Sunday sanctuary. Pews have been positioned against the walls, making room for stations of games and activities. The sound of delighted children echoes up the steep rafters before bouncing around and landing on the wood floor. Calla and Jarred sit with others their age before a puppet show put on by the church's older children, the ones too old for dress up but too little to be excluded from the festivities.

Edward is in the group of puppeteers capturing Calla and Jarred's attention. My littlest sibling has taken the role of uncle very seriously, and though he is still a child himself, he prides himself on his responsibility and care toward my children. Years of Edward tagging along behind me has grown into a stronger bond than I could have imagined.

Bernice and I edge our way into the expansive room. Mother Smith catches us in her peripheral vision, excusing herself from the baked goods table to say hello. "John, Bernice, I am so glad you could make it. The children are having a wonderful time." Mother beams at Bernice while keeping some physical distance. The two, I've noticed, do not embrace as Violet and Mother Smith used to do. They do not share moments of laughter or tenderness. *All in due time,* I think to myself.

My father extends his hand and I take it. The firm shake is a public gesture. In the comfort of our own home, we usually share hugs. "Bernice, you are looking well." Father nods in her direction. "Feeling tip-top, then?" Though the question is genuine, I can't help but feel the tension between my parents and my wife.

"Well enough, thank you." Bernice places a hand over her rounded belly and glances down. "Tired, but I am sure that is to be expected."

"Tired will be a common state, for a while anyway." Mother Smith offers a knowing tip of her head. "Edward's ten years old now, and I still can't seem to locate a fully rested version of myself." Mother Smith chuckles, her unease showing through. "It may be just the age catching up with me now. Come then, Bernice. Let me introduce you around."

Bernice follows Mother Smith, looking back at me with soft, pleading eyes. I offer her a reassuring nod and watch as Mother introduces her to Reverend Campbell and a cluster of choir ladies. Father and I make small talk as I watch Bernice's cheeks flush when Reverend Campbell's booming voice extols his delight about the arrival of another Smith child. When she glances back at me, I see Bernice is enjoying the happy attention of her pregnancy. I smile and pray we have jumped another hurdle and that things will only get easier from here.

With Bernice in the capable and kind hands of my mother, I decide to include myself in Calla and Jarred's activities. I hold back Calla's blonde curls as she bobs for apples, spearing one on her third attempt. I help Jarred with a jigsaw puzzle and am preparing to ready them for the parade of costumes when a high-pitched voice pierces the air.

Bent at the waist, tightening Calla's apron around her slight body, I swivel my head toward the commotion. Bernice's eyes narrowed in my direction alert me to danger. I straighten my back as she pivots on her heel and storms toward me.

"It is time to go." Bernice stops in front of me, almost bowling me over in her haste.

"Time to go?" I shake my head, unsure what has caused this abrupt change in demeanor. "Why? You know how much Calla has been looking forward to the costume parade."

"Well, that can't be helped now. She will just have to be disappointed." Bernice's toe is tapping in frustration, and she folds her arms defensively across her chest as fresh emotions ooze out of her. An icy glare tossed in Calla's direction heightens the unease between us.

Calla's small hand finds mine as she leans against my leg, burying her head. I imagine her trying to hold back the tears that are sure to follow after the special evening is cut short.

"But I don't understand. What happened to make you want to leave so early?" I wrap a protective arm around Calla's shoulders and try to speak in a slow, soothing voice.

"That happened." Bernice throws a look of disdain over her shoulder at a gathering of young mothers, all watching our exchange with confusion written on their faces. "I've no intention of discussing the matter here, John." Bernice lowers her voice to a seething whisper. I instantly decide that I prefer her angry, loud voice, though not necessarily in such a public venue. Bernice's steely whisper unsettles me, shooting a chill down my back, and reminds me of the *whip* of a bullet searching for flesh to pierce.

I am tempted to try to reason with her, but the frozen look on Bernice's face tells me success is not a likely outcome. I am searching for something to say, a new direction to take this conversation, when Jarred lets out a shrill scream behind me. He is lying facedown on the floor, arms and legs splayed haphazardly, having tripped on the edge of his no-longer-pristine ghost costume.

I let go of Calla's hand and scoop Jarred into my arms, peeling off his Casper costume as I position him on my hip and begin to kiss away his tears. Calla nuzzles into me, and I am aware that Bernice interprets the three of us clustered together as a personal attack, an us-against-her situation.

"Jarred is upset. I think it is best if we leave now, John." Bernice's statement is not a suggestion, and I am fully aware that arguing the case is futile.

Fighting is seldom productive, I remind myself. *Take the high road, John. Nobody wins in a war.* I repeat the words to myself before meeting Bernice's gaze. "We'll go," I utter. Defeated and exhausted, I have no desire to cause more of a scene at what was supposed to be a happy event.

I take Calla's hand, glancing at the tears staining her cheeks. The realization that I've disappointed her washes over me, and my heart is torn by my inability to provide what my daughter needs. I bend at the waist, lowering Jarred with me, and whisper in Calla's ear, "Why don't you do a quick parade over to Grandma and Grandpa, pumpkin? I'm sure they'll want to see your costume on display. Calla shakes her head no, stealing a quick tear-filled glance in Bernice's direction.

With nothing more to do, I offer Bernice a silent nod and follow her toward the doors. The room is still full of playing children, but I can't help but feel eyes on the back of my head as we shrink away from the party. I offer my parents a slight smile to ease their worried expressions, and then we escape into the crisp autumn evening.

Bernice holds Jarred across her lap as his head bobs, exhaustion settling in. I clear my throat as we drive through the center of town. I choose my words carefully. "Do you want to tell me what happened?" Bernice's head whips around to stare at me, surveying my movements. I keep my eyes on the road and do my best to convey a look of concern rather than annoyance.

"Do you know what they said?" Without waiting for my reply, she continues. "They told me how lucky I was to have found a man like you." Bernice snorts as the words fly from her deep red lips. "Like if you hadn't come along, I'd have had no hope at finding myself a husband."

There is no suitable response to this statement. What am I supposed to say? *Yes dear, you'd have done much better if I hadn't come along first.* Or perhaps, *No dear, I am the catch of the century, after all.* I shake my head, hoping it conveys what Bernice needs, while keeping me out of hot water.

"And then they gushed on and on about Calla. How sweet she is and how well-behaved she is. How her beauty just shines through with that smile of hers, and oh those eyes. Those beautiful blue eyes." Bernice's words are laced with sarcasm and a little too much disdain for my liking.

I open my mouth, planning to agree that Calla is all of those things, when Bernice bursts into tears. Calla sits beside me in silence, staring at her new shiny black Buster Browns as if none of this is happening around her.

Through gasps for air and crocodile tears, Bernice tells me the rest. "Just like Violet's."

My heart drops from my chest to my toes. I feel Bernice's pain, the sting these comments have inflicted. Yet her pain isn't large enough to draw a shadow over my own. I run my fingers through my hair and let out a whoosh of air. "I'm sure they didn't mean anything by it. Insensitive comments is all. You know how people can be. I swear they don't always think before they open their mouths." Though the words are meant to comfort her, I can't help but hope Bernice realizes what impact her words about Calla may have on the quiet four-year-old sitting between us.

Bernice's sobs fill the small cab of the truck, and I slowly inch the window down to ensure we don't suffocate. We drive the rest of the way home in silence, save for a hiccup or two from Bernice's firmly closed lips.

I tuck Jarred and then Calla into bed, telling her how much I love her and apologizing that she missed the costume parade. A solemn nod is her only response before she rolls away from my embrace and settles herself for the night. I want nothing more than to lie tucked in Calla's bed, with Violet on the opposite side, holding hands across our daughter's sprawled frame like we used to do when Calla had a fever or a bad dream. Longing for my wife has become a pastime, but Bernice needs comforting now. So I strangle my own grief, along with the grief of my children, and slide into bed beside Bernice. I wrap her in my arms and tell her all the things I assume she needs to hear.

CHAPTER 10

MARCH 7, 1964
Ferngrove, Washington

Calla

I crumple the page into a ball and mash it between both hands as
my resentment toward Mother builds. I would like to blame her
for everything. It would be easier to direct my hatred toward her,
rather than Dad. Truth be told, I know she alone is not
responsible for everything. A good portion of blame lies with
her, but not all of it. This perhaps is the most difficult piece of
information for my brain to process.

Mother is often an instigator of elaborate proportions, but
Dad continues to let her get away with her antics. That, I fear, is
the root of the angst churning within me. How can a daughter
reconcile herself to the notion that her father hasn't protected
her? Hasn't looked out for her well-being? Hasn't shown enough
gumption to stand between his own children and the woman he

married? I fear there are no answers to these questions, and soon my head feels as if I've been bouncing around the Tilt-A-Whirl ride at the county fair. I stand to look around the small bedroom again, sure of nothing except that that none of my questions will be answered by staying here.

I consider what life would have been like if we hadn't moved away from Cedar Springs. I was heartbroken when the move was announced. An image of Grandma Smith's face whispers across my memory. A strong woman in her own right, she would have surely pushed back against Mother with all her might had she known what life was like under Mother's thumb.

This fairy-tale thought is brief, as it is both true and false. In the end, there was little Grandma could do. In my heart, I believe Grandma wanted to move heaven and earth for me and Jarred. Her hands were tied, though, since Mother refused to allow her visits and dismissed all invitations to family gatherings. She went so far as to lure Dad away from the weekly church service, and before long we were completely isolated from the Smith family and Momma's family.

I remember our first Thanksgiving with Mother in our lives. I was always eager to spend time at Grandma and Grandpa's home, where Jarred and I were spoiled with attention, games, and home-cooked meals.

I remember a day of opposites, filled with confusion as I, a small child, tried to navigate our new family situation. Jarred toddled onto the porch of the Smith home, his chubby little legs straining against the height of each step. He was a mostly happy little boy, but he was happiest at Grandma's. I suppose that was true of all of us. Except Mother, of course.

Mother fiddled nervously with her hair in front of the truck's flipped-down visor mirror. She was applying another layer of bright red lipstick when Daddy bounced the truck into Grandma's gravel driveway, causing her hand to dart away from her lips. His impish smile and shrug did little to cool Mother's sharp look. I'd already started to recognize Mother's looks, and I knew to remain silent and make myself small to avoid getting caught in the crossfire.

Grandma, Grandpa, and Edward greeted us at the door, wearing vibrant smiles and stretching their arms wide. I ran to hug Grandma's legs as she scooped up Jarred and kissed his pudgy cheeks. Jarred, not one to be contained, quickly wiggled from her grasp. As soon as his feet hit the floor, he was off running. Mother and Dad stepped into the house, where they removed their coats and hung them on the hook.

Grandma and I chased after Jarred, laughing as we followed him into Grandma and Grandpa's bedroom. We watched from the threshold as he lay his head atop the bed. He closed his eyes and inhaled deeply, sighing as if all was right with the world because he was finally home. This was, after all, the only home he had known for more than two years, and the house had been filled with love and laughter. I looked up at Grandma. She was smiling, but when she bent to pull me into her arms, her face was wet. I didn't know whether she was happy or sad—that was when the opposites began.

Edward, who had been standing beside Grandma, vanished without a sound as Mother appeared behind us. She scanned the room only long enough to catch a glimpse of Jarred, deeply content, resting on Grandma's bed. She pushed past us without a word and took him into her arms. Jarred kicked something fierce, but Mother persisted, clutching him tighter while his legs flailed. "This is no place to play. We are guests here, and I won't have my children invading others' privacy." Jarred's screams echoed down the hall as Mother forced her way past us and headed for the living room.

Grandma's pursed lips looked as if they needed a kiss, so I wrapped my arms around her neck and squeezed my face to hers. "Calla, dear, this home is as much yours as it is ours." The grooves in Grandma's face were wet again. "You and Jarred are always welcome here, at home." She scrunched her nose up tight and whispered in my ear, "Do you understand?"

Though I did not understand at the time, I nodded my head and smiled at Grandma. I did not want her to be sad.

Thanksgiving dinner must have been eaten, though I don't recall sitting at the table or even saying grace. I should have remembered Grandma's famous apple pie or Edward pretending his napkin was a hat, like he always did at Sunday dinners, but the only other memory I have from that day is Mother and Grandma with fiery red faces and raised, angry voices. They woke me from my spot on the sofa. After a day filled with games and romps around the yard with Edward, I had fallen asleep with a full tummy, nestled in the familiar scents and sounds of Grandma and Grandpa's home.

I was startled awake by Mother's high-pitched voice, a warning sound. Grandma shushed Mother. "The children are sleeping, Bernice."

"My children are sleeping." Mother argued.

"Bernice, I simply cannot abide by your wishes in this instance. Violet and John's wedding photo has every right to be in this house. She was a part of our family too. Just as you are." Grandma's voice was strong and determined, as it was when she was teaching me my letters and numbers. A voice one could trust to steer you right. "Now, as I've told you before, you are welcome to bring me a photo of your and John's wedding day, and I will place it in a frame upon these walls for all who visit here to see."

"I won't do it. I won't set another foot in this house if that photograph remains." Mother's voice boomed through the walls of the old house.

Daddy's voice cut through the argument. "Bernice, what are you saying? Think about this, please. For the children. For me."

That was the end of the loud voices. We left in an awful hurry, with Mother letting the screen door slam before she climbed into the truck and waited for us to join her. Daddy stuffed my sleepy arms into my winter coat while he apologized to Grandma.

"Trouble, John. You hear me. That woman is trouble through and through."

"Mother." Daddy pleaded with Grandma as he buttoned my coat. "Not in front of the children."

After a hasty goodbye, Daddy carried Jarred and me, squished together in his arms, toward the truck. Mother sat in the cab, staring straight ahead like a statue. Even at my young age, with less than a year of experience living with Mother, I knew to hold both my tongue and my little brother as we drove home in silence.

Her disposition hasn't changed over the past thirteen years. Mother still rules the roost with an iron fist and a laser-sharp tongue. Dad usually remains quiet, offering only the occasional sigh of conformity. Grandma Smith, it seems, was no match for Mother either. Looking back, I can't help but wonder if anyone was watching out for us kids. I angle my disappointment away from Grandma, not wanting to stain the few precious childhood memories that bring a smile to my lips.

No matter how long or hard I think on my predicament, the fault for my current situation falls on those living within the walls of this house. It seems we've all arrived late to a battle, without the necessary weapons. All I know for certain is that this fledgling battle must end, at least for me. I retrieve my hand-sewing kit from the bookshelf and place it in an empty shoulder bag. "This," I say to myself, with determination in my voice. "This ends today." I sort through the remaining items on my bookshelf, selecting which items to bring and which to say goodbye to forever.

CHAPTER 11

December 1951
Cedar Springs, South Dakota

John

The wind whips the snow around me as I slam the truck's door and make a beeline for the front door of our little blue house. The sight of the cozy space we call home used to light a spark inside my chest, but today the weather matches my foul mood, engulfing me as my Mother's words and tears swirl in my mind. A few days shy of Christmas, I made a quick stop at Mother and Father's to nestle Edward's gift under the tree for Christmas morning. I made him a miniature wooden truck, an almost perfect replica of my real-life version. Given the chance, Edward will ride anywhere with me in my truck. Last May, I took him for a drive down the country roads to tell him about my upcoming wedding to Bernice. I worried his heart would break in two, given his adoration for Violet. Everyone loved Violet, but to

Edward, she was his and his alone. Until she passed, he never knew a world without her.

After selling a story, full of holes, about moving on and growing a family, I lessened Edward's tears by allowing him a turn in the driver's seat. His smile could have lit up half of Cedar Springs as the truck bounced through an empty field, his hands firmly planted on the oversized steering wheel. During the trip back to town, Edward told me he was saving his pennies for a truck just like mine. His snare was catching well, and old Mr. Richards paid a nickel for every clean hide Edward brought him. In that moment, I knew exactly what I would carve for him come Christmas: a replica 1950 Chevy truck, just like mine.

I placed Edward's gift beneath the tree. Standing, I noticed Mother wringing her hands together, a sure sign something was troubling her mind. We made small talk as her eyes danced around the living room, gracing every piece of furniture yet avoiding my eyes completely.

"Mother, what is it?" I glance at my wristwatch, cognizant of the dwindling daylight and the holiday preparations I promised Bernice I would tend to after dinner. Bernice's patience seems to be shrinking as the baby grows within her. I've no interest in being on the opposing side of a sour look this evening, so I stride toward the door in hopes of spurring our dialogue.

"I didn't want to say anything straight away, John." Mother bites her lower lip and follows me toward the door. "I was hoping to speak with Father about it first. Didn't expect to see you this afternoon. Well, I suppose you ought to know. It isn't as if I can keep it a secret. You'll find out soon enough."

"Mother, please." *Perhaps Bernice isn't the only one with patience growing thin*, I think as I soften my gaze.

"I received a telephone call this morning." Mother folds her arms across her chest, a defensive stance that signals her readiness to speak frankly. "From Bernice."

"Making plans for the holidays, then?" I am about to let out a sigh of relief. After many discussions on the matter, I had hoped I'd convinced Bernice of the importance of a family gathering to celebrate the season. Mother's agitated look says otherwise, and instead of sighing, I find myself holding my breath.

"That would be one way to put it." Mother's words are ripe with personal hurt. I've only heard her injured tone once before, on the day I announced I'd joined the army. Violet, still angered by my enlistment but kind enough to support me, sat beside me as I broke the news and quite likely my mother's heart. I've wished countless times to erase that moment from both my memory and hers.

"I don't understand." Instinctively I reach out to touch her arm.

"Bernice has informed me that we are not invited to spend the holidays with you and the children." Mother's eyes pool with tears. "Nor will you or your family be joining us. At church, at dinner, or for Christmas morning stockings."

"There must be some misunderstanding. Bernice wouldn't . . ." My words trail off, my troubling thoughts incomplete.

"No, John. There was no misunderstanding." Mother's chin juts out in defiance. "I told you she was trouble. Just look what she is doing to this family."

"Let me talk with her. I am sure it is just this pregnancy. She is overtired and not used to caring for two small children. She just needs some time is all."

"Hmph! If she is so tired, you'd think she would take us up on our offer to care for Calla and Jarred every once in a while. They are at home here, John." Mothers words ring true, but I know better than to agree with her reasoning before speaking with Bernice.

"Think of it from her perspective. She isn't used to having family around all the time. And." I pause, wishing I did not have to utter the next words. "Just think how difficult it must be, with everyone comparing her to Violet."

"John Smith!" Mother's voice rises in a scolding manner. "I have done no such thing, nor do I have any intention of comparing that woman to dear Violet, God rest her soul."

I'd like to point out the obvious, that Mother's tone when referring to Bernice as "that woman" suggests that Bernice couldn't hold a candle to Violet in a windless room. Knowing when to pick my battles and when to walk away, I kiss Mother's cheek, squeeze her arm, and promise to speak further on the matter with Bernice.

Driving home, Mother's words ring in my ears. She isn't one to exaggerate when telling tales, nor do I doubt her motivation of wanting to remain close with her grandchildren. My work is cut out for me. I'll try to convince Bernice that all the children would benefit from a grandmotherly relationship. My parents are honest folk, and I have never seen them behave poorly toward a child, no matter who the child's parents are. I assumed Bernice would understand that our child, due in a few short months, would be just as welcomed at the Smith home as Calla and Jarred. If I am honest with myself, I had hoped she would have come around and blended in with the family by now. If only Bernice recognized the benefit of having a capable and willing set of extra hands, surely she wouldn't turn down the family support.

I pull the screen door closed behind me as I enter the warmth of our small entry, tucked into the corner of our living room. A flurry of snowflakes makes their way into the house as I push the solid wood door against the wind that is attempting to sneak past me. Calla comes running toward me at the sound of the door. Jarred follows close behind as he wobbles on tiptoe, arms pumping out of rhythm with his running feet.

"Daddy, Daddy." The excited hollers of my children are music to my ears.

Jarred is chewing on a wet cloth. His cheeks are red, with raised bumps, a sure sign his molars are still trying to poke through the gums. I was hopeful that particular gift would arrive before Christmas morning, as his slowly moving teeth have caused fitful bursts of sleep for the past several nights.

The commotion coming from the kitchen indicates Bernice is attempting to put together some sort of meal. I lift Jarred into my arms and nuzzle his cheek with my nose before taking hold of Calla's swinging hand. As we enter the kitchen, Bernice turns to present her cheek to me in greeting. I lean forward and say hello with a light kiss. Jarred takes the opportunity to lunge from my arms and wrap his free arm around Bernice's neck, squeezing the three of us together in a sweet though uncomfortable and harsh embrace. Calla's hand drops from mine as she walks away, turning her attention to the doll on the floor.

As quickly as he put us in a headlock, Jarred releases us and squirms to the floor. He breaks into a haphazard run, following his sister into the living room.

"Between those damn teeth and all his energy . . ." Bernice lets the sentence hang, unfinished, before pasting on a smile and taking me into her arms for a proper embrace. Her belly between us, I feel the baby kick, and I can't help but smile at the shared moment. My family has yet to see the way Bernice can be vulnerable. I pull back from our embrace to kiss her lips.

I notice the dark circles under her eyes. A nagging worry tugs at the edges of my heart, dredging up the details of Jarred's birth and Violet's death. The gut-wrenching scene plays on repeat in my mind's eye as Bernice approaches the due date circled in red on the calendar that hangs on the kitchen wall.

I steal another glance in her direction and decide tomorrow is a good enough time to discuss Christmas and the phone call to my mother. Certain the conversation will be better received if she is rested, I direct my attention to helping her with dinner. Bernice has yet to master the art of weeknight dinners, so to save her from humiliation and the rest of us from starvation, I've taken to arriving home early most nights. Hopefully, my assistance with dinner will eventually help her improve her cooking skills. Together we create a chicken casserole from a recipe she found on the back of a soup can. I cut the carrots while she gives the potatoes a cursory scrub in the sink.

While we cook together, the things Mother taught me while I worked beside her in the kitchen come back to me. Mother was forward-thinking for her time, and she insisted that all of her children, boys included, learn the basics of cooking, cleaning, and managing a house. In the early days after Violet passed, I was exceptionally grateful for the training. Though I was far too distraught to fully care for the daily needs of my children, I was at least prepared to feed them. My ability to tend to my children's physical requirements was never a question. The pressing concern involved my need to grieve the loss of my wife without the faces of my two impressionable children peering at my every move.

I let out a silent breath and push the tainted memory aside. Bernice hands me a russet before setting her attention on the can opener and tin of soup. While she struggles with the wobbly hand crank, I rack my brain for a safe topic of conversation.

CHAPTER 12

February 1952
Cedar Springs, South Dakota

John

I pace the floor of the waiting room. This final month of the pregnancy has drained me. Bernice has assured me several times that the doctor is unworried by the baby's delay, indicating a firstborn often arrives late rather than early. Given her impatience with so many little things in life, I am impressed by her willingness to let baby come when he or she is ready. This secondhand information, though, does little to dispel the strain in my neck, pulled taut with tension, which has plagued me for weeks.

The stark white hospital walls, floors, and ceiling make my head spin. With Bernice whisked away to a delivery room several hours ago, I feel the full weight that has been sitting on my chest all these months. The memory of Jarred's birth and

Violet's subsequent death in this very corner of the three-story brick hospital rushed up to greet me when I entered, supporting Bernice's weight as she waddled to the nurse's station.

I didn't think it possible to hold one's breath for as many months as I have, but that is precisely what it feels like. A shotgun wedding, the relocation of Calla and Jarred into an unfamiliar situation with a new mother, and now the addition of two more mouths to feed has placed considerable strain on my family. I've asked far too much of my parents, my children, and myself.

Bernice hasn't fallen easily into the role of wife and mother, and my concern about her ability to do so weighs heavily on my mind. After the Christmas fiasco, I begged off sharing the holidays with my parents and siblings with the hope of waylaying Bernice's somewhat irrational worries. I decided to do what was needed, at least in the short term, to ensure the safe and joyful delivery of our baby.

Violet's and my wedding photo, the one displayed proudly in my family home, is the cause of Bernice's concern. Conversations on the topic have been unsuccessful, and Bernice refuses to enter the Smith home until the photo has been removed. In the middle, like a slice of ham between two pieces of bread, I understand both sides of the argument.

Mother Smith is unwilling to remove Violet, both in photograph and memory, from our family's history. I see her point and agree to the terms of her grief over the loss of her daughter-in-law. Bernice, on the other hand, is desperately trying to fit in as wife and mother, albeit unsuccessfully at the moment. She has never indicated, at least to me, a desire to replace Violet. Bernice only wants to be loved for who she is, and with a family and town full of people who dearly miss my dead wife, the battle must feel immense and oftentimes uphill.

I am hopeful, though, that after the baby arrives and tempers settle, life will sort itself out. I let out the air from my lungs, and the whoosh catches the attention of a soon-to-be father sitting with his head in his hands, waiting on his own happy news from the doctor.

His eyes meet mine, and he nods. "Didn't think it'd be so tough, sitting on this side of the door."

I feign a smile, not desiring the company of a stranger.

"Is this your first?" His thumbs twiddle in his interlaced fingers as he shifts positions and leans forward on the wooden chair's armrest.

"No." My voice is groggy from lack of use. "Third."

"Oh, well. You should be old hat at this, then." His light laugh does little to dissolve the tension I feel building between my eyes.

"I'm not sure this is something you ever get used to." I give a final nod in his direction before pivoting away from him and moving to pace a little farther down the hall.

With little else to do but worry, my thoughts meander through my memories. Memories are similar in nature to dreams, never taking the same route anywhere. Instead of being linear, they often crisscross and intersect with images that don't belong. I remember Calla sitting in front of her birthday cake, staring at it in apparent disbelief, before she plunged her fingers into the soft, buttery icing and squealed with delight. The sights and sounds of Calla's first birthday crashes into a memory from high school. Some of the local boys and I played a prank on the school's harshest teacher the night of Halloween. He squealed like a pig about to be caught when he opened his door and was showered with rotten eggs. To this day, I consider the whooping I got from Father to be worth the memory of the prank.

I offer a weary smile to a passing nurse and run my fingers through my hair. She smiles in return, and all I see is Violet's likeness. Her smile used to light up her entire face, while buckling my otherwise sturdy knees. Her cornflower blue eyes, gentle yet piercing, sparkled like gemstones kissed with a dash of magic. Oh, how she could draw me in. She could make me do anything with a simple glance. I was a fool for that girl. I sigh, wondering if I'll ever be able to let her go.

"Mr. Smith." My reverie is abruptly interrupted by a man's words. Barely tall enough to reach my nose, he tilts his balding head to meet my eyes.

"Yes," I stammer. "I am John Smith."

"Congratulations, then. You have a healthy baby boy." The doctor extends his hand for me to shake.

"A boy." I nod my head. "And, Mrs. Smith?" Without intending to, I brace myself, a natural reaction from the last horrific visit to this place. "How is Bernice?"

"Fine. Just fine." The doctor leans in and lowers his voice a notch. "She's a scrapper, that one, and what a vocabulary. Never seen a woman cuss quite like that before."

I feel my brows knit together as my face flushes with heat. I am left without words, unprepared and searching my mind for an appropriate response to such a comment.

"Actually," the doctor continues, clearly lost in his own thoughts, "haven't heard quite that much kafuffle since I was stationed at a military hospital in Europe during the war."

I smile as politely as I can before raising my eyebrows in question. "When can I see them?"

"Right. Right, of course. No bother, they are both doing just fine now." He motions toward the nurse's station, turning his back as he inquires with the nurse on the other side of the desk. "Just wait here for another few minutes." He gestures toward the chair closest to the desk. "We will call for you just as soon as Mrs. Smith is settled in her room."

"Thank you." I sit as instructed, relief flooding through every pore in my body.

An hour and a half later, just as I am about to drift off to sleep—the threat of danger now evaporated with the safe arrival of my little boy—a nurse nudges my arm. "Mr. Smith." She holds a clipboard tightly to her chest. "Your wife is ready for you now."

"Thank you." I scramble to my feet and follow her down the corridor. We navigate the maze of white walls in silence. A few turns later, she leaves me in front of the closed door to room number nine. I knock lightly before entering and find Bernice and our son quietly tucked into a single bed. They both have their eyes closed, and there is a gentle rhythm to their breathing. I am in love all over again. His angelic face tugs at my heart, and my eyes fill with tears. *Happy tears*, I point out to myself as I take a step closer, careful not to wake them. I didn't imagine I'd ever feel this way again, and for that, I am indebted to Bernice forever. In the simple act of becoming a mother, she has brought hope, love, and a sense of joy back into my life.

As if reading my mind, Bernice opens her eyes and smiles up at me. "He is beautiful, isn't he, John? Our Mark is beautiful." She places a kiss atop the knitted cap on his head as her eyes water with emotion.

"He certainly is, Mother." I pause and meet Bernice's misty eyes. "He certainly is."

"Mother," Bernice whispers. "Yes, I am a real mother now."

CHAPTER 13

MARCH 7, 1964
Ferngrove, Washington

Calla

A holler from the other side of the house reaches the solitude of my room. I hold my breath and wait for the skirmish to settle. In this house, one rarely knows the temperature of a situation until it is too late. I often find myself smack in the middle of a dispute I wasn't aware was happening. Thundering footsteps travel down the hall, rattling my bedroom door in its casing.

My door is a recent addition. After years of pleading for one, Father finally installed a door to give me some privacy from the rest of the family. Though the door does little to camouflage a true uprising, its presence adds a small measure of comfort, since I am the only girl, besides Mother, among the boys in this house.

Before the addition of the door, a thin fabric curtain hung in its place. The curtain was Mother's solution, after she blew through the budget for the construction of our new home. The day it became clear that several items on the to-build list were no longer an option, given her careless spending, Mother's voice rang through the unfurnished brick house. "She has a room all her own for Christ's sake, John. The boys all have to share a bedroom. Certainly Princess Calla can manage without a door for a little while."

From my room, I hear Mark's voice, deep and loud, emit a "whatever" in his smart-mouthed tone, before his own bedroom door slams shut. He is the only one of us who can get away with any sort of back talk. Regardless, I remain still as a statue, desiring zero attention from Mother while I pack.

From day one, Mark was the precious child. I've always assumed that is because he was Mother's firstborn, but I suppose Mother's favoritism toward Mark could have more to do with her disdain for me. The glad tidings Mother ushers onto Mark remind Jarred and me daily that we are on the outskirts of this family unit. Mother's past actions have never been rooted in kindness toward others, and I don't suspect her future ones will be either. I remember the day they brought Mark home. Bundled in a fleecy blue blanket, only his pink face and dark eyes were visible. I was so excited to meet our new little brother that it didn't occur to me that he would be more hers than ours.

I have no idea if I was always the mothering sort or if I developed the skill early on. Being motherless at a young age and being used to watching over Jarred, it makes sense that I was anxious to help out with the new baby. My excited welcome, however, was cut short. Mother did not take kindly to my keen interest in Mark. I was not permitted to hold him or even to stroke his cheek. If he cried, I was to step aside and out of her way as she lunged to scoop him into her arms. If he was sleeping, Jarred and I were to be as silent as mice, or else face the wrath of Mother's stern and hurtful words. After a few days, she sequestered herself in her bedroom with the door closed so she could sleep and take care of Mark. We, apparently, were no longer her concern.

The arrival of Aunt Patricia, Mother's younger sister, set us right. Aunt Patricia breezed into our lives one blustery February morning like a fairy godmother. She brought gifts for each of us, as well as a joyful personality. She laughed and smiled with ease. Whether it was to scrub the kitchen floor or to play make-believe with Jarred and me, Patricia didn't hesitate to get down on her hands and knees. She was exactly what our family had been missing.

Aunt Patricia taught me how to bake cookies, scrub carrots, and make pancakes. She never scolded and had an earnest interest in everything I had to say. She was quick to giggle at Jarred's antics and managed to make cleanup and bath time fun and lively activities. I adored Aunt Patricia and desperately hoped she would stay forever. Having her around felt like having a real mother.

Forever ended too soon though. One evening, as Daddy, Jarred, Aunt Patricia, and I were enjoying cups of hot cocoa and playing *Chutes and Ladders*, Mother appeared at the threshold of the living room. She had her hands on her hips and dark circles under her eyes, and I felt the temperature in the room chill. Daddy invited her to join us. Aunt Patricia stood quickly and offered to brew a cup of tea or fetch a bowl of broth. Mother's eyes narrowed as she declined both.

"Isn't this quite the picture? A happy little family, is it?" Mother's words weren't the slightest bit happy, and I wanted to scream at her to go away, that we didn't need her anymore. Aunt Patricia could be our mother now. I hoped with all my heart this could be true. The words never reached my lips. Instead, Aunt Patricia ushered Jarred and me to bed, leaving Mother and Daddy to argue in both hushed and raised voices beyond our bedroom door.

As she tucked me in, I begged her to stay. "Please, Aunt Patricia. Please don't go. I don't want you to go."

Aunt Patricia kissed my tears away, read me an extra story, and promised she would always carry me and Jarred in her heart.

The next morning, I woke to a heaping plate of freshly made pancakes in the center of the kitchen table, but Aunt Patricia was nowhere to be found.

I never forgot her though, and true to her word, she never forgot us. Each and every birthday and Christmas, and sometimes for no reason at all, a package would arrive from Sioux Falls. No matter what age I was turning, Aunt Patricia always managed to send me the gift my heart desired. Now, with only five days until my seventeenth birthday, there is sure to be a package wrapped in brown paper and tied with string waiting for me. I am saddened by the realization that I won't be here to receive it. I cross the room and retrieve my address book from the bookshelf, ensuring Aunt Patricia's current mailing address is written there. I toss the book into a bag and vow to send her a letter as soon as I settle myself with employment and a place to stay.

Thinking of Aunt Patricia makes me think of Momma, or at least how I imagine Momma would be. I fold two blankets in half, forming them into a shape sturdy enough to use as a pillow, and crawl into the back of my nearly empty closet. Closets and I have a long history. Despite my closet being vacant of doors, the quiet, dark cove has been a sanctuary for me when there was nowhere else to hide. I prop myself against the makeshift pillows and wrap my arms around my body, attempting to find comfort in my own embrace.

Several months after Jarred and I moved from Grandma's back into our little blue house in Cedar Springs, I stumbled upon a box in Daddy's closet. It was the same box I had heard Mother curse a few weeks before. She'd been rifling around in the back of the closet, searching for a high heel to wear to dinner with

Daddy. I was perched atop the bed, watching with wide eyes as she put on a new dress and sheer black stockings.

Grandma wasn't the sort to spend time with makeup, and as a four-year-old girl, I was rapt with attention as Mother drew in eyebrows, blushed her cheeks, and expertly applied a deep red sheen to her lips. It is one of the few happy moments between us that I can recall. Mother clearly enjoyed the attention I focused on her, and she brushed my cheeks with a hint of color before diving headfirst into the closet in search of the missing shoe.

Her relaxed and happy tone changed instantly when she placed one hand on top of a box to steady herself while she reached into the dark closet. The box, less than sturdy, collapsed beneath her, sending Mother jolting forward into the closet. She came up cursing and muttering about long-dead memories, telling no one in particular that it was a waste of space. I waited for Mother to sit back down in front of her dressing mirror to touch up her smeared lipstick, and then I quietly left the room to avoid being the one her words might attack.

Weeks after Mother's run-in with the box, I was playing hide-and-seek with Jarred while Mother was resting in the living room, reading a magazine. Since I couldn't hide in my usual spot, behind the living room sofa, I ventured into their bedroom, opened the closet door, and crouched inside. I wedged my small body behind the brown box and waited quietly for Jarred to discover me. Several minutes passed, and it seemed Jarred was taking his time finding me. I began to wonder if he had lost interest in the game and was now playing with his trucks instead. I leaned on the box to push myself up, and the top of the box collapsed, revealing a beautiful peach-colored sweater, soft as a newborn puppy. The color was pleasing, vibrant and sunny, and the scent of a familiar perfume washed over me like a misty rain. I lifted the sweater to my face and hugged it tightly.

Rummaging through the box, I found dozens of photographs of Momma, with Daddy and with me as a baby. Finally, my tiny hands found an image with all three of us. Me in front of Momma cocooned in her embrace and Daddy with his arms wrapped around Momma's pregnant tummy, a silly grin on his face. I shimmied behind the box and wrapped myself in the sweater. I placed the sleeves over my shoulders to pretend the sweater was hugging me and dropped my nose to inhale every ounce of Momma I possibly could. I held on to the photograph of the three of us and stared at it, wishing it was real.

I must have fallen asleep in the closet, as the next thing I knew, Daddy was home from work and was gently shaking my shoulders. We never spoke a word about the box or about me being in the closet. His eyes were sad as he placed the photographs back in the box, folded the sweater, and closed the lid.

CHAPTER 14

September 1952
Cedar Springs, South Dakota

John

I steer the muted gray Ford onto our normally peaceful street. A few neighborhood women mill about at the ends of their driveways, not wanting to get involved in other people's business but curious enough to gawk at the dark smoke penetrating the cloudless blue sky. I cringe at the public display and switch off the radio with an agitated swipe as I curse the slow four-door sedan. The drab, well-worn 1946 Deluxe was a necessary purchase to accommodate the addition of Mark to our family. Trading in my beloved truck for this prewar-designed boat almost sucked the life right out of me. As I drive to and from the cabinet shop each day, I covet the newer, sleeker models with colors meant to celebrate life, youth, and freedom. I crank the wheel hard and slide the car into the driveway, gravel tossed from under the tires as I slam on the brakes, horrified.

A frantic telephone call from a neighbor summoned me home. I deserted my tools, my crew, and the job that was sure to put food on the table for the coming weeks. The flames licking the air just above the edge of the burn barrel capture my attention first. *What in God's name is she trying to do? Burn down the house?* The barrel's natural home is in the far reaches of the backyard. Bernice must have dragged the barrel to this new location in the middle of our driveway, far too close to the little blue house that holds everything precious to me within its walls.

Confusion yields to panic as I step around the car door, catching the tear-stained and snotty faces of Calla and Jarred in my peripheral vision. Bernice storms out of the house, carrying a stack of dishes in her arms. I watch, stunned motionless with disbelief at the scene. Bernice, her eyes alight with the flickering flame, begins to systematically smash each scalloped-edge plate painted with the delicate flower pattern Violet favored. One after another, she snaps each plate against the edge of the burn barrel before dumping the remainder of the stack into the barrel itself. If she is aware I am standing here, she doesn't let on.

Another quick movement and she is headed back toward the house. My mind is reeling with questions as I search the faces of my children. I step toward them, edging my way around the barrel as the burning paper crackles and pops within its cavernous belly. Trying to find my voice, I bend at the waist and peer into Calla's eyes. "Are you and Jarred all right?"

There is no time for Calla to answer such a complicated question before Bernice appears again, this time juggling papers, photographs, and a peach-colored cardigan. The screen door slaps shut against its casing, knocking the wind out of me with its hollow thud as recognition hits me. I know that sweater. Bernice, eyes filled with malice, stares me down, daring me to engage her as she walks toward the barrel and drops the armful of belongings into the rising flames.

"No!" Calla screams. "That's Momma's."

Dusting her hands against each other, Bernice turns on her heels and strides back toward the house, shooting Calla a sneer as she passes. Bernice's words cut as deeply as the hate fueling them. "Well, she certainly doesn't need them anymore. Does she?"

Calla retreats, pressing her back against the splintered wood siding of the house. Instinctively, she pulls Jarred with her, arms wrapped tightly around his chest protectively, a defensive move I've begun to see more often since Mark arrived in our home several months ago. Mark's arrival should have been a happy occasion. Instead, the new baby has disrupted what little balance I had hoped we were beginning to experience.

The trouble began the day we brought Mark home from the hospital. Calla, eager to welcome her new brother into our lives, reached up on tiptoe to peek at the bundle nestled in Bernice's arms. Her little hand peeled back the baby-blue blanket with a gentle tug, only to be swatted away by Bernice's much larger and harsher hand. Until this current scene, that was the defining moment, and it was etched into my memory like a chisel attacking stone.

Fresh tears cascade down Calla's wet face as she watches the fire spit, spew, and devour the few remaining remnants of Violet. Hiccups rattle her slight body at the grief of losing her momma all over again.

The anger rising within my chest burns like acid. The familiar but imaginary smell of spent ammunition fills my nostrils. I close my eyes tight and fight against the fury that is consuming my rigid body. This is the anger of a man in battle. How dare she taunt me with my past, both that of war and of Violet. In my desperate attempt to move forward with life, I've smothered any rising anger with a steady yet firm hand. In fact, that's all I've done—put on a brave face, take the high road. But at what cost? For months now, I've hidden my guttural responses to slights against my children. I have done my damnedest to hide my longing for a life that once was mine. I have separated myself from my church and my family, my entire support system, for this woman. What more could she possibly want from me?

This is the act of a vengeful woman. If I didn't know better, I would think it the act of a scorned one. As the flames, fueled by the last remaining mementos of Violet's life, spark the air, a fresh wave of grief washes over me and tears tumble freely from my eyes. I run to the edge of the drive, where the ground is less compact, and grab handfuls of dirt, smothering the fire bit by bit with repeated trips. *I must look pitiful*, I think, with my children and my neighbors watching. My desire to flee is intense and all-consuming. To me, fleeing is safer than reacting, safer than the fight ahead that is sure to harm us.

Sweaty with grief and effort, I look to Calla and Jarred. I see past the tears to the fear behind their eyes. I cannot let this go. I cannot give Bernice the satisfaction of seeing me walk away. For once, I have to take a stand for my children. Rage moves through me like an earthquake, with peaks and valleys of tremors strong enough to tear flesh from my bones. A wave of anger rises as the thought of Bernice's actions prod my soul like a hot iron poker. How dare she torture these children with such irrevocable acts?

Bernice has clearly lost not only her temper but also her mind. I knew a storm was brewing, with the way she's been seeking attention like a desperate puppy. Her insecurities have shone even brighter since Mark was born. *What more does she want from me?* Though I ask the question, I know exactly what she wants. I've been slow to return her physical advances, her less-than-subtle attempts to lure me in with inappropriate displays at all hours of the day, regardless of who else is in the room.

At first, I was being careful, not wanting to cause her discomfort after the baby was born. Then exhaustion set in from sleepless nights, dirty diapers, and feeding schedules. Her irrational and hateful accusation that Patty and I were getting too cozy was the final wedge between us. She all but accused her younger sister of attempting to steal me away. I could list any number of viable excuses for my lack of interest in intimacy, but in my heart, I know my vanishing desire to be with this woman is due to the growing unease that now lives between us.

A hateful emotion builds in my belly. I've been here before, filled with an immense fear that transforms into anger when my back is pressed against the wall. Though I wish I could, I can't forget the first time I felt the angry beast within. I was on the beaches of Normandy. There was so much chaos and destruction in such a short amount of time. Fear, grief, and horror were all wrapped up in the massacre of war.

More recently, Violet's sudden passing had me screaming into a blackened sky, panic-stricken and cursing God for taking her away from us. I thought I hid it well, my yearning for Violet. Given the smoldering, smoky fire before me, I clearly didn't hide it as well as I thought. Bernice, full of spite and venom, knew exactly how to get my attention. But how could she hurt the children like that?

I've been kidding myself, dropping my head and averting my eyes from the traumatized faces of my children. I've known for far too long now that Bernice has a jealous side, and her envy has been pointing like a dagger directly at sweet little Calla for months. I can't understand how a fully grown woman could be jealous of a small child. I thought I was helping the situation by paying less attention to Calla, even though the child's confusion was written across her face the first time I navigated away from her, attempting to include all the family in my gaze.

Jarred sniffles, wiping his damp face with the back of his hand as his wide hazel eyes bore through me. His desperate and defeated look fuels the inferno within me as it lies in wait, ready for a little oxygen push to unleash its ugliness onto Bernice and her hateful act.

"Calla, please take Jarred and go play in the backyard." A strangled voice I don't recognize as my own croaks from deep inside me.

With the children walking hand in hand toward the backyard, my eyes narrow in on the front door. I think of the putrid blaze and taste blood from the inside of the cheek, where I've bitten down. I spit and slow my steps while I attempt to clear the vileness that consumes me. Convinced I cannot let this go, I march into the house, prepared to go to battle.

This time, I cause the heavy wooden door to slam against its casing. The windows tremble above their sills, and like a lion hunting for dinner, I search every room of the house for my prey.

Sobbing quietly in the corner of our shared bedroom, Bernice acts as if she is the one who has been deeply hurt. I am taken aback by the transformation of her venomous expression into teary, red-rimmed eyes. But the fire within me asserts itself at the sight of her playing the victim. I know this is just another one of her antics, a ploy to get what she wants. My fury boils over, and the rage I swore to never again reveal leaps up and engulfs me.

"Not this time," I roar. "You want my attention? I'll give you my attention." I storm across the bedroom floor, skirting the foot of the bed. Grabbing her by both arms, I turn her and force her to face me.

"John!" The flash in her eyes tells me she is both surprised and impressed by my anger. "You're hurting me."

My voice booms as my worry of what the neighbors might think disappears into the background of my consciousness. "I'm hurting you. You can't be serious, Bernice." A sneer of loathing crosses my face. "Do you have any idea what you've done?"

Bernice squares her shoulders, evidently not as frightened as she appeared to be. "Yes, John. Yes, I do."

I stare at her in disbelief, waiting for more. Impatience laced with dread mixes with the bile churning in my stomach. "Well?" I ask, not entirely certain I want to hear her spun version of logic.

Her hand flies to her forehead, and she swipes her thick brown curls away from her face. "I was ridding this home, our lives, of a past that consumes you."

I stalk away from her and begin pacing the floor in front of the bed that I already loathe having to share with her tonight. "What gives you the right to destroy memories that are not yours?" My voice cuts through with clarity, even as it cracks with pain. "They belonged to me. They belonged to Calla and Jarred."

Bernice places both hands on her hips in defiance. "I will not let your dead wife decide my future happiness." Bernice pushes past me, grabbing her hairbrush from the dressing table. She looks at me in the mirror's reflection as she swipes the oversized brush through her thick, brown mane, and then she turns toward me, arms raised in question. "She is everywhere. Don't you see? Violet lives and breathes within these walls. She is in your parents' home, smiling over every Sunday dinner." Bernice takes a step toward me, pointing the brush in accusation. "Christ, John, she is in every single shop I visit in town." Bernice's condescending tone mocks me. "Your oh-so-sweet Vi is haunting us, and the sooner you rid yourself of her, the better."

Silence lays between us, each of us shooting daggers at the other. Anger this intense has few places to go except out, so I consciously decide to give my anger wings. "You are wrong, Bernice." My stare is steady. My eyes pierce hers, cold, smoldering, and full of false confidence. "Violet isn't haunting us. She's haunting you."

I am not a spiteful man by nature, but the look on Bernice's face tells me my arrow has hit the target, and my harsh words create no discord in my soul. I am not ready to back down. I watch with a slight curve of my lips as Bernice stumbles, almost imperceptibly.

My eyes remain fixed on hers as she takes a moment to recover. She casually runs her hairbrush through her dark waves, attempting to appear unfazed. Bernice's voice is cold as steel, matching the ice in her eyes. "I would've never married you, John, if I'd known you were such a lost cause." She switches gears with a shrug of her shoulders. "Nobody can compete with a ghost on a pedestal. Not even me." Bernice takes a step toward me, and I take a step back. She points her broad round brush in my face. "I loved you." Another shrug ushers a chill up my spine. "Sure I did. But I wouldn't have settled on you." Bernice's arms swing wide, her gesture encompassing the modest bedroom, sarcasm tinged with disgust dripping from her lips. "I wouldn't have settled on this." Her gaze narrows like a hunter who has found a shot. "I would have held out for someone man enough to let go of the past. Someone willing to live in the present. Someone with the means to provide me with the life I deserve. I see now this is the least I deserve from a marriage."

I'm caught off guard. Her words don't add up with our current situation. My quivering voice spills out, despite my efforts to restrain it. "What do mean by you would never have married me?"

Her smirk sends a shock of disquiet through my core. I can't tell whether her confidence stems from knowing something I do not or from her sheer brashness. "I wasn't pregnant when I married you." Bernice pivots on her heel, checking her reflection in the dressing mirror. "You are a gullible one, aren't you, John Smith?"

I stumble backward, the back of my legs brushing against the edge of the mattress. I sit and try to regain my composure. "What?" My voice wavers as the knife she has inserted drains the blood from my limbs. My mind is reeling. We didn't have to get married? She's lied to me all this time? My children. Oh

God, what have I done to my children? My head finds my hands as guilt settles heavily upon me.

The bed groans as she places herself beside me. Bernice's demeanor once again changes, shifting like a chameleon as the situation between us alters. "I'm sorry, John. I didn't mean to hurt you." A soft whimper leaves her lips. "Really, I am." Bernice sobs softly, nuzzling herself into the crook of my listless arm. "I was lonely is all. I just wanted you to notice me."

There is nothing I can say. I am unnerved by this knowledge and by my desire to strike back at her. I want to hurt her as much as she has hurt me. I abhor violence, yet this ninety-eight-pound woman has managed to push me beyond my logic and morality.

I am profoundly ashamed of what I have allowed to happen, and of my own foolishness. Tricked into the lifelong sentence of marriage. A union doomed to fail. How could I be so utterly stupid? So gullible? I was so concerned with what others might think of me that I rushed into this marriage to conceal the existence of a pregnancy that didn't exist. A lie. It was all a lie.

I rub a hand over my face and vow to never tell another soul of how this marriage came to be. My head snaps up as the thought filters through my mind. "You can't tell anyone." My words sound hollow, filled with defeat. "What would people think of me?" My head swivels to face her, and I pull back just enough for my eyes to meet hers. "Promise me, Bernice, that you won't ever tell anyone how we came to be married."

She scoffs. "Now you're concerned about what sort of man you look like? A pregnancy out of wedlock is the least of your concerns." Bernice sighs before smiling in my direction. "Don't worry, John. I will keep your secret. As long as you live up to your end of the bargain."

The baby's cries propel me into action. I stand, relinquishing my body from Bernice's lazy embrace.

"It was nice though." Bernice arches her back, stretching her arms high above her head. "That you noticed me, I mean." She offers me another contrived smile. One of my hands closes into a tight fist, and the other flies to my mouth as vomit fills the empty space between my cheeks.

Before I can rescue Mark from his crib, I make a beeline for the toilet, almost missing the bowl in my haste.

Gripping the sides of the cool white porcelain, the reality of what has happened settles on me. Feeling confused and duped, I shake my head and reach for a towel to mop my face. Bernice got exactly what she wanted, and she didn't care who she hurt to get it.

The severity of my predicament hangs over me. I have no choice but to tread carefully until I can think through this. Bernice is more damaged, more dangerous than I've been willing to admit, and I alone am responsible for bringing her into my children's lives.

CHAPTER 15

MARCH 7, 1964
Ferngrove, Washington

Calla

The house is quiet when I wake. The closet, without fail, is the one place I can find peace and sleep. After Mother destroyed every tangible memory of our life with Momma, I learned to speak only when spoken to. I learned to stay out of her way. I learned to become as invisible as possible. The strategy served me well for many years. Even as a five-year-old, I learned how to survive the uncertainty of life with Mother. I run my fingers through my hair before stretching my arms above my head. After the burn barrel summoned Daddy home that day, I became more withdrawn. In response to my withdrawal or perhaps to her own unsettling behavior, Mother began to shower me with a heavy dose of sugar-coated affection. She liked to playact the part of doting mother whenever Daddy was in the room. Her sweet demeanor only lasted a few months though, as it wasn't long before she was consumed again with her role of expectant mother.

He has never said so, but I am certain Dad has always known the difference between Mother's facade and who she really is. He, too, has become quieter over the years. He began working longer hours, often leaving before we woke and returning after the sun had set. Whenever he and Mother squabbled over his long work hours, he would point to her expanding belly and cite the need to provide for his family. He avoided spending time with Mother altogether, and soon they had little to talk about.

Dad's absence was especially noticeable at mealtime. Mother's limited cooking skills never improved, and by the time I was six years old, I was making breakfast each morning. As soon as Jarred became old enough to attend school, I taught him to pack his lunch and helped him ready himself for the day. Under my guidance, Jarred became quite proficient at caring for himself when necessary, which was often while living under Mother's roof.

I stand and step out of the closet, reminding myself to pack the Betty Crocker cookbook. No one else in this house will ever use it. I don't remember whether I learned to cook because I was tired of Mother's attempts or because she told me to. I do know I learned first by examining the pictures in the Betty Crocker guide. Everything I needed to know was there, in large-picture format. As soon as I was taller than counter height and could read well enough, I made everything from homemade soup to pot roast. But my favorite meal, even now, is the pancakes Aunt Patricia taught me to make.

Soon after I'd began learning to cook, but long after Mother's fleeting attempt at a sweet demeanor had vanished, I decided to make pancakes for dinner. What could be more comforting on a winter evening than a heaping pile of pancakes?

I thought it was the perfect meal, and I was proud I could make it all by myself.

Having a plate of golden, fluffy pancakes hurled across the room at me certainly taught me that pancakes are, apparently, not a suitable dinner offering. Not understanding what I'd done wrong, I cleaned up the pancakes and the broken platter through tears.

Daddy came to my rescue when he came home that evening. Without a word, he placed his metal lunch box on the counter and helped me clean the remainder of the kitchen. Then he grabbed our jackets and took me and Jarred to the Fountain for burgers and French fries. The splurge of ice cream sundaes for dessert finally brought a smile back to my face.

With his undivided attention upon us, I remember asking what I had done wrong. How was making pancakes for dinner a bad thing?

"Nothing, pumpkin." Daddy's face was solemn. "There is nothing you could have done to deserve how Mother has treated you."

I didn't understand then, and I can't make complete sense of it now. I was only a little girl. If she had given me even the slightest chance, she would have seen how much I wanted her to like me. How helpful I could be. How much I wanted her to be a mother to me.

"Don't go blaming yourself." Daddy's calloused hands gathered mine. "You hear me, Calla? Don't you ever go blaming yourself."

I nodded obediently, though I had no clue who else I might blame. Jarred wasn't always getting yelled at by Mother, but then again Jarred was younger and maybe better at staying out of Mother's way. "Why doesn't Mother like me?" My voice was small and barely above a whisper. The words hurt to speak aloud. Mother made little secret of the fact that there was nothing I could do to win her over. Nothing at all.

Daddy hung his head, and I instantly regretted asking the question. He squeezed my hands, unable or unwilling to offer an explanation.

I don't imagine life has been easy for Dad either. I plunk down on my bed as my resolve to move out quivers in the shadows of my mind. I desperately try not to think about Jarred. Me leaving might be the closest thing to abandonment that he experiences, and I am already regretting that particular reality of my decision. Even Mark, Jamie, and Daniel deserve better than this, but at least I can reason that they technically belong to Mother, whereas Jarred and I do not.

Wishing to be anywhere else is much different than actually taking the steps to get there. Leaving means cutting off all communication with Dad. Mother, I am certain, wouldn't have it any other way. I've seen her go toe to toe with anyone who said a negative word about her John. She has embarrassed herself, Dad, and every one of us kids, cussing out anyone who didn't agree that Dad walked on water. Even he couldn't talk her down if someone got her knickers in a knot. I can't imagine a scenario that involves me leaving home without a quick and relentless response from Mother.

I am confident I will find a way to stay in contact with Jarred, but today may be the last time I see my father. I'm not entirely sure I am ready to break those ties. The frightened little girl inside me wants nothing more than for him to come to me and tell me I am worth it. I am worthy of any battle he would have to fight with Mother. I am worthy of any pain an argument or even a divorce would cause our family. I am worth so much more than his actions have shown me all these years. But I know he won't do what I need him to. I have to walk away and try my best to save myself.

CHAPTER 16

JUNE 1953
Cedar Springs, South Dakota

John

The haunting wails from the wounded echo all around me. Men with limbs blown to pieces scream in terror as the steady drum of German retaliation lashes across the length of the beach front. The dead pile up quickly as the lucky few scramble past them, up the shoreline, seeking cover first among the barricades and bodies and then among the cliffs. Outgunned and exhausted from the swim in icy waters and the dash across sand riddled with landmines, we huddled together under a small overhang, barely out of reach of the German killing machines. Every muscle in my body tenses and shivers as I scan the scene. With my back pressed deep into the cliff's rock, hundreds of soldiers lie dead or dying before me, strewn across the rugged beach in unnatural positions. The waves deliver, with consistency, more dead bodies to shore with each exhale of water meeting sand. The screams grow louder and more soul-stripping as they pierce my already deafened ears. Confusion curled around disbelief begins to set in. An air-raid siren, maybe, or—

"John!"

I shift at the sound of my name, eliciting a sharp and crippling cramp in my right calf. I scream out in pain and clutch my leg.

"John!" A pause and then again, "John! Can't you hear the baby?" Bernice is standing over me, hands on her hips, with a sour expression that indicates a misstep on my part. "I swear, John Smith, you can conveniently sleep through anything." Bernice whips the curtains back and sunlight fills the room.

I shield my eyes with one hand. The other remains in place, massaging the cramp out of my distraught calf. Bernice leaves the room in a huff, and soon James' howls begin to subside into a low whimper.

I toss the covers to the side and swing my legs with care, resting my feet on the floor. I test the cramped leg first, pressing into the floorboards with my toes before I am sure the straitjacket of tension has passed. Bernice is moving about the kitchen, her annoyance with me evident by the way the pots and pans crash onto the stove top.

A week has come and gone since Jamie was born. Jamie is the most recent result of Bernice's pestering me for attention, which eventually led to her threat about "our little secret." Working long hours at the cabinet shop with little sleep has left me exhausted enough to lure me into bed on a Sunday afternoon. The sleep was welcomed, the nightmares not so much. Walking toward the chair that holds my shirt, I catch my reflection in the dresser mirror. *A father again,* I think as I dress and prepare to face the firing squad.

The moment Bernice told me she was pregnant, guilt became my steady and constant companion. I worried a child conceived out of a loveless union might realize the oddity of such a scenario once born into this world. While I wished I could rewind time, Bernice strutted about like a proud mother goose. I hadn't thought she had taken to motherhood, yet she delighted in the attention that accompanies a married woman with a child growing inside her. I couldn't quite explain the change in her. Perhaps pregnancy suited her, but motherhood did not. *An unfortunate set of circumstances.* I button my shirt and set out to find her in the kitchen and apologize for falling asleep.

With Jamie tucked in one arm, Bernice places a pot filled with water on the largest burner. Having disliked the routine and inconvenience of breastfeeding Mark, Bernice opted to start Jamie on bottles as soon as she left the hospital. I know the drill and smile in her direction before I wrap my arms around both her and Jamie from behind and gaze into his clear eyes. "I'm sorry I fell asleep. I know you are just as or even more tired than I am." I swivel her to face me and kiss her nose. "I am sorry."

Jamie coos in her arms as Bernice's lips curve ever so slightly. She lowers her eyes in a demur fashion that I take to indicate I am forgiven.

Bernice looks over my shoulder and hollers toward the living room, "Mandy, bring that bottle from the coffee table, will you?"

"Mother, please. Why would you do that?" The tender moment of connection between us is lost. My heart sinks to the pit of my stomach as Calla enters the kitchen with the dirtied baby bottle in her little hand.

Bernice takes the bottle from Calla and shrugs as she lowers it into the boiling water for sterilizing. "I've told you before, John. It's from a book I read. I liked the name is all."

I dismiss the urge to point out that perhaps the bottle should first be washed before being sterilized, and I march forward with the matter at hand. "You cannot simply change the name of a child because you read it in a book." My voice remains low, not wanting to elicit any response from the children.

"I don't see why not." Bernice pushes around the bobbing bottle with a large spoon.

I comb through my thoughts, trying to find a more delicate way to state the obvious. In the end, I come up empty-handed and blurt out, "She wasn't yours to name."

"Wasn't mine. Wasn't mine, you say?" Bernice slams the oversized spoon on the counter. "I don't see you saying she isn't mine when it comes time to wash dishes, or laundry, or faces." Her eyes and her nostrils flare, and I back away instinctively from the hot stove and the bubbling water.

"You know what I mean." My hands find a home on my hips, taking a stance of insistence and control. "She already had a name when you met her. Her name is Calla."

Another unconcerned shrug from her brings heat to my cheeks. "I don't see what the big deal is. She answers just as well to Mandy."

I grit my teeth and try again. "Her name is Calla, and that is exactly what you will call her." I take one step toward her, my face an inch from hers. "Do you understand?"

"Whatever." Bernice turns her attention back to the boiling pot, effectively ending all discussion on the matter.

I turn to retreat to the quiet of the living room when I see Calla, still standing in the corner of the kitchen with her hands laced behind her back. Engulfed by my disdain for the interaction with Bernice, I hadn't noticed her standing there, as quiet as a shadow. So aware and watchful. Her big blue eyes follow me as I step toward her. I nudge her back with my hand, and together we leave Bernice to her own devices in the kitchen.

Afternoon turns into evening. Bernice, having retreated to the bedroom with Jamie hours before, makes no sound and gives no indication that dinner will be forthcoming. Her childish pattern of ignoring us began not long after Mark was born and became more frequent after I learned the truth about the foundation of our marriage. Her refusal to make dinner tells us that all is not right in her world and that we, her family, are to fend for ourselves.

I open the refrigerator door as Calla drags a kitchen chair to the counter. "I'll help, Daddy," she says as she climbs atop and stands ready to assist. I retrieve leftover chicken and a smattering of overcooked vegetables from last night's dinner before grabbing three potatoes from the basket in the cupboard. I place everything on the counter and then move Calla, chair and all, to a spot in front of the washbasin and hand her the three potatoes for washing. Together we place the readied ingredients into a casserole dish and preheat the oven.

We move on to creating the pastry crust that will cover our poor man's chicken pot pie. Calla delights in rolling the crust with the wooden pin, evidence of her enjoyment sprinkled across her nose and cheeks. I'm thankful my mother is an excellent cook and teacher. It takes us only another twenty minutes before we have a rolled pie crust and a counter covered with flour. With the pot pie in the oven, warming the house with its comforting aroma, Calla and I set the table, gather the boys for hand washing, and sit down to a family dinner—minus, of course, Bernice.

With stories read and dishes washed, I gather a blanket from the closet and settle myself on the sofa in the living room. I run the events of the day through my mind, trying to pinpoint the exact moment things went awry. I toss and turn on the narrow sofa, reliving every word, before succumbing to a fitful sleep. My night's rest is just as riddled with wartime images as my fraught and unhappy days. Somewhere in my sleepy, subconscious mind, I contemplate which battle zone is from a memory and which I am destined to live over and over again with each breathing moment. I tuck my body into the back of the sofa and remind myself that sleep is a luxury for the man who has never had the experience of war.

CHAPTER 17

MARCH 7, 1964
Ferngrove, Washington

Calla

The doorbell rings, pulling my attention from my melancholy mood. I glance toward the bedroom door, taking in my current level of progress. One duffel bag is packed, and my shoulder bag has space for a few smaller items. The doorbell chimes again, but there is no movement in the far reaches of the house. Mother is likely deep asleep in her favored recliner, having moved on from coffee to a good stiff drink after noon.

When the doorbell rings a third time, I am tugged back through the years to a warm, sunny day in our little blue house in Cedar Springs. It was late in the summer of 1954 and at seven years old, I was in charge of watching the younger boys while Mother rested in the bedroom. She was waiting for the third of her babies, still deep within her belly, to grace our home. The doorbell rang and I hesitated at first, unsure of whether I should trouble Mother or risk her wrath for having answered the door myself.

She was not to be disturbed. I remember the words well. I had a vivid memory from the previous day, when she had issued the same warning. I had been cleaning up the lunch dishes in the kitchen when Jarred tore into the room with a panicked expression. I could hear Mark, at two and a half years old, squealing hysterically from the living room. I was certain his high-pitched laugh would break glass if allowed to continue.

I dried my hands on the checkered dish towel and followed Jarred into the living room. The problem was apparent the moment I entered the small space. Jarred pinched his nose with his thumb and forefinger while I waved my hand wildly in front of my face. Mark, however, continued to howl with delight, clearly under the impression that Jamie pooping behind the sofa in the living room was the latest in slapstick humor.

My admonishing words did little to quiet Mark or to dissuade Jamie's antics. Jamie, having completed the task at hand, tugged up his shorts and ran to play with his favorite toy, a red fire engine. I am inclined to think that, under normal circumstances, I would have understood the desire of a child nearing the age of eighteen months to attempt potty training. Jamie's behavior, however, was far from normal. From the moment he came home from the hospital, he was a terror of a magnitude unfamiliar to me. His relatively new pooping activity is one I dislike the most. So I instructed Mark and Jarred to stay away from the pile while I went to seek Mother's help.

I knocked lightly on the bedroom door, half hoping she wouldn't hear me. I entered the room slowly after my knock elicited a groggy, "What?"

"Jamie's pooped in the living room," I said, cowering beside the dresser, not wanting to step any farther into the darkened room.

"Well clean it up, then." Mother rolled away, presenting her backside to me and the door.

"I can't." A shiver ran through me, and my stomach began to churn. "It makes me sick."

Without warning and at a speed she seldom engaged, Mother lunged out of bed and stood before me. Grabbing my arms, she shook me as she bellowed, "I'm trying to sleep." She shoved me toward the bedroom door, pushed me over the threshold, and pointed toward the living room. "Get over it. Go clean it up." The bedroom door slammed in my face as my frightened tears began to pool.

That had been the first time I cleaned up after Jamie, but it certainly wouldn't be the last.

When the doorbell rang the next day, Mother's warning echoed in my ears as the memory of the putrid smell reached my nostrils. "I am not to be disturbed," she had said. So I opened the front door.

Standing on the doorstep, looking both bashful and eager, was Granddad Sanderson. I lunged in his direction, flinging my arms around his burly shoulders, bent low to greet me, and breathed in his familiar scent mixed with the smell of horses from his farm.

"Darlin'." His eyes twinkled like a department-store Santa Claus. "It is so good to see you."

I beamed at him with adoration before I remembered where I was, or rather where Mother was. I shuffled onto the doorstep with him, squeezing past the opening, and pulled the door a hair shy of closed. Though Daddy managed to sneak me and Jarred to the Sanderson farm every few months, the visits were too short and infrequent to satisfy any of us.

"Let me get a look at you." Granddad held me by my shoulders at arm's length before drawing me into another embrace.

I looked over my shoulder, worry setting in that Mother may

appear, awakened by the doorbell. The desire to open the door wide and welcome Granddad into our home so Jarred could share a cuddle and a visit pressed against my chest. The recollection of Mother's wrath yesterday was the only thing that kept me from pushing the door aside. I briefly considered my options and wondered whether Granddad would protect us if Mother appeared. But if Daddy couldn't talk sense into Mother, then nobody could.

With the force of a tornado, the front door's knob was wrenched out of my hand. A quick glance at Mother's angry face told me I had waited too long to send Granddad on his way. She towered above me, her pregnant belly protruding in front of her, as I shrank away from her glare, willing my body to become small enough to disappear.

Mother looked up at Granddad, and her expression changed and became even less pleasant. "What are you doing here?"

"Came to see Calla and Jarred." Granddad nodded his head before he tilted his chin to meet Mother's eyes.

"I thought you understood that you are not welcome here." Mother's voice trembled a touch, and I wondered if she was afraid of Granddad.

"You can't keep them from us, Bernice." Granddad's voice didn't hold anger, nor did it waver.

"You'll need to sort that out with John. Right now, Calla is needed inside." Mother grabbed my arm and pulled me from Granddad's side.

"What are you afraid of, Bernice?" Granddad took a step closer to Mother. "You afraid they'll love us more than you?"

Mother didn't respond. She tugged at my arm again and ushered me into the living room. "Get inside and check on your brothers."

I offer a restrained wave in Granddad's direction and retreated into the cool living room as Mother closed the door behind me.

Their muffled voices echoed through the windowpane as Mother's anger unleashed, spewing, I assume, in Granddad's general direction. With Mother's voice having risen to a dangerously high pitch, I corralled the boys into the safety of a bedroom for a story.

We were halfway through the second storybook when Mother slammed the front door and stalked through the house until she found the four of us snuggled atop my bed.

"Nobody answers the door." Her piercing glare cut through the thick cardboard cover of the book in my hands and reached my burning cheeks. "Do you hear me? No one is to answer the door."

I nodded my head as Mother stomped back to the quiet of her bedroom. Her door slammed, shaking my bed, positioned against the wall. I sighed in relief before picking up with the story.

Things didn't really get any better after that, I think as I consider, only for a moment, checking the door. I listen for the doorbell, but it never returns. Whoever was there must have decided to retreat from our house. *A good choice.* I reach into the top drawer on my dresser and resume packing my bags.

CHAPTER 18

John

In the beauty of the lilies Christ was born across the sea. With a glory in His bosom that transfigures you and me. As He died to make men holy, let us live to make men free. While God is marching on. Glory! Glory! Hallelujah! The song reverberates inside me, belching me from the landing craft into the waist-deep icy water. My breath hitches in my chest as the first rain of gunfire reaches the crashing waves, the landing craft, and too many of the men still weak from vomiting over the six-foot-high swells. It is an eerie feeling when it dawns on you that someone is trying to kill you.

I struggle to reach solid ground; my sodden gear feels almost as heavy as the world we have been tasked with saving. Black smoke fills the air, ominous and suffocating. But the moon, full and round, continues to play peekaboo with the smoke and the clouds, creating a small measure of constancy in an otherwise chaotic situation. I brace myself with cotton-stuffed ears against the cacophony of machine guns. The air vibrates in defiance against the thunderous sounds of war.

"Get off the beach," echoes in my memory as the months of training off the coast of England is pulled from deep within me by my every remaining survival instinct. "Get off the beach."

I wake, bolting upright. Wiping a trickle of sweat from my forehead, I breathe deeply in an effort to slow my heart rate and warm my chills. The only way I know how to experience war is with all five senses. Without our senses to confirm the impossible, our minds simply wouldn't believe us. The body parts strewn about a battlefield. White handkerchiefs covering the faces of the fallen along the beachfront. The smell of death and decay infiltrating every pore of my body, day and night, so strong I thought it would never cease. Sometimes, still, it doesn't.

The sounds, though, haunt me the most. It is peculiar to hear the sound of a bullet hitting a man. There is a little gasp of breath when the bullet hits and the realization occurs. Then there is the percussion of the mighty machine guns, unyielding in their attack. The blast of cannons shakes the earth and anyone in the vicinity. The air-raid sirens pierce the air with haunted shrieks while the rumbling, low-flying aircraft tightens its grip on a town, a countryside, all those on the ground who never know the intent of those hovering above. The screams, though, never seem to quieten, and once I've heard the screams, I'm as good as gone.

The images spanning almost three years filter through my consciousness, often colliding with one another in haphazard formations. "It's fine. It is all going to be just fine. Only a dream," I tell myself in a low whisper as I tug at the blanket and reposition my body along the length of the sofa.

Wide awake now, I stare at the ceiling shielded by the night's darkness. Even sleep doesn't allow for rest. Sleepless nights like this one provide my mind far too much latitude for thinking.

Filling my days with busywork at the cabinet shop and my nights trying to etch out a little extra income through my furniture business has allowed me to avoid Bernice's often ill-tempered mood and my own demons. Tonight, though, the demons won't let me alone. If it isn't the war, it is Violet appearing before me like an angel transcended, right here in this very room.

How I ended up here, in a difficult marriage, doing my best to stomp down the past while being a father to five children who seem just as lost as I am, is an unsettling reality at best. One decision most certainly led to another, though it is hard to believe that a life could become so backwards in a few short years. This is where the war and my current life's allotment collide with an uncanny amount of familiarity.

A few years spent in a war alters the path for many. Lives are lost. Families are separated. Deep, irreparable wounds are left to ooze and bleed. A few years spent with a woman who loves no one but herself creates similar damage. My own life and the lives of my children have become casualties of a different kind of war. Families have been separated, and wounds continue to fester, paralyzing even the sanest of men into believing nothing can be done. Nothing can be changed. Nothing can be saved. *No, it is far too late for that now.*

Instead, I succumb to the shame and use warlike survival tactics. I keep moving forward, never staying in one place for too long, to avoid discovery by the enemy. I keep my head down and sheltered from the shells that sail overhead. I distance myself from those around me in an effort to stave off the effects of loss. Only on nights such as this do I allow myself to ask the question, *At what cost?*

When Bernice and I married, I saw in her a piece of myself. I saw the hurt she had lived, and I felt her pain like my own. I saw her vulnerability and reasoned a stable life surrounded by love could, and indeed would, fix her. I saw the lies she told, but I chose to believe they existed solely so she could persist. Knowing she'd been abandoned as a young girl, I felt her desire to be loved, to be needed by someone who didn't demand anything in return. For a while, I tried to be all of those things for her, each and every one.

The pregnancies took a toll on her, all three of them. After the birth of each child, her mood succumbed faster than a steam engine about to run off the tracks. It would be convenient to blame her poor behavior on the demands of pregnancy, but the truth of the matter is Bernice was never suited for motherhood. I'm not sure she could manage any configuration resembling a family. This fact only became clearer when she dropped the bomb regarding the ugly truth about how she manipulated me into marriage. I was only doing what I thought was right in marrying a woman who I believed was in the family way due to my actions. It was, after all, the honorable thing to do.

It is difficult to bring myself to regret my marriage to Bernice, as it has resulted in the births of three of my children. However, the marriage has also resulted in the mistreatment of those same children, in addition to the two who came before. *There is no winning at this game.* I roll over on the lumpy sofa and attempt to find a position comfortable enough to coax me into a deep-rooted sleep.

In an effort to locate a nugget of peace, I change tactics. It hasn't been all bad. I'm no saint myself. I've made my share of mistakes, spoken words I couldn't take back. I test the limits of my belief system, nudging my thoughts to respond with positive input. We've had the odd shared laugh. We've occasionally felt adoration for each other. Even a few recent conversations have reminded me of the similarities we share.

Yes, that is it. I negotiate with my weary self, hidden beneath my self-made armor. All I need to do is pay her more attention, like I used to enjoy doing. Get back on her good side. Listen to her when she talks. The actions that take so much effort when I am angry with her are precisely the steps necessary to make life better for us. Things will improve once we right ourselves again.

I decide that surprising her with a night out, away from the pressures of the children and home, is a suitable start. I'll telephone Edward tomorrow. At fifteen years old, he is both a suitable age to care for the children and always in search of a few extra pennies for the picture shows. Edward is the only member of the Smith family permitted to spend unsupervised time with the children. Bernice has made this exceptionally clear as things unraveled over the years. With Mother Smith refusing to abide by the "no Violet" rule, there was little I could do to assuage Bernice on the topic.

Edward is both the lone wolf and the go-between for me and my family. He's stuck in the middle of two worlds. His love for Calla and Jarred, though, is undeniable. Their relationship resembles that of siblings rather than an uncle and his niece and nephew. Having been part of all five children's lives since the beginning, he gets on just fine with Mark, Jamie, and Daniel too. I will call him first thing in the morning and ask him to stay with the kids this Saturday evening. Bernice and I will have ourselves a proper night out and make another go at coming to terms with the life we share.

Improving our situation will take a little more effort on my part, but isn't my family worth it? Instead of diving into a foxhole for cover, I will march up to her and show her how important this family really is to me. I am confident that I will be able to sway her by forgiving her past transgressions and showering her with attention. Bernice has always been a sucker for attention. I think that is the reason she exuded such happiness while pregnant, since a pregnant woman is certain to gain favorable attention from everyone she interacts with, including strangers. The beginnings of a smile tug at the corner of my lips as I tell myself that things will work out in the end.

With a plan of action planted firmly in my mind, I purposely toss the blanket from my body, place my feet on the floor, and decide there is no time like the present. I stride with confidence toward our shared bedroom. The door creaks a little as I gently push it open, drawing Bernice's attention. Neither one of us is sleeping, it seems, and my heart thaws a little more as I realize I am not the only one troubled by our unhappy situation.

Reaching for her, I crawl into bed and wrap her in my arms. I whisper in her ear, "We will get through all of this together." The words are as much for my own benefit as they are for hers.

Bernice clings to me as we settle into a much-needed long and restful night. *Everything will look brighter tomorrow* is the last thought I have before drifting off to a dreamless and welcomed sleep.

CHAPTER 19

MARCH 7, 1964
Ferngrove, Washington

Calla

With the top drawer of my dresser open, I begin packing socks, underwear, and pajamas. A soiled pair of socks, stained gray, catches my attention. I toss them into the garbage bin, and a memory of throwing out another pair of socks floods me with panic. Dread fills my senses, and I shiver as I remember my first visit to the basement.

By the time I was nine years old, my comprehension of life with Mother was clear. I was afraid. Not worried. Not uneasy. But truly and utterly afraid. Things didn't start out that way. I was four when Mother entered our world, and I clung to the belief that she didn't mean to hurt me. Until that time, I had never known an unkind word. I blamed myself for not understanding and quickly learned to alter my behavior in an effort to please her. If she showed me a kind gesture, I clung to it desperately, believing she was growing to love me.

I realized the true existence of my fear the day I was old enough to stack coal from the basement. In the spring of 1956, I turned nine years old with little fanfare, save for Aunt Patricia's present wrapped in brown paper. By the time November rolled around, a cold wind ushered in winter temperatures, and the coal stove situated in the living room devoured its fuel like a starving beast. To stave off the chill, the coal bucket required filling at an increasing rate as the weather turned from cold to bitter.

The basement, I remember, was part of the house but also part of the earth—a gloomy and dark part that children shouldn't be subjected to. Dad had built a set of sturdy wooden risers accessible by way of a wooden trapdoor, hidden by a rug where the kitchen and hallway met. The trapdoor, and the multicolored braided rug that hid its presence, was off-limits to us kids. It was dangerous, we were warned, if curiosity got the better of one of us. A stern word or a smack to the backside was issued with swiftness if we tried to peek under that old rug.

The chill was settling into the living room as the sun sank into the horizon, casting its shadowy veil across the afternoon sky. The coal bucket was picked empty by the time we arrived home from school that afternoon, and despite the chilling air, Mother didn't seem inclined to fetch any more. Upon removing my winter jacket and watching my cloud of breath stamp the air, I ushered Jarred, Mark, and Jamie past the darkening living room, making a beeline for the bedrooms in search of heavier sweaters.

When our sweaters were on, Jarred stayed to play with Mark and Jamie in their shared bedroom while I headed to the kitchen to scrub the vegetables for dinner.

After he woke from his afternoon nap atop a blanket on the chilled living room floor, little Daniel attempted to climb onto the sofa and into the warmth of Mother's napping embrace. His cold hands ignited a screech from Mother. I first heard the screech, then the thud of Daniel's two-year-old body tumbling to the floor, before a wail erupted. Though his wails were louder, it was the thud that had me running into the living room, a freshly scrubbed carrot in one hand.

Scooping Daniel into my arms as Mother got her bearings, I shivered as his little hands wrapped around my neck. Cooing to him and rubbing his back, I bounced up and down as I wiped his tears. Having found the source of warmth he had been seeking, Daniel cuddled into my embrace before reaching for the carrot to gnaw.

Mother staggered to her feet, looking more angry than concerned. "Why the hell is it so cold in here?" Her complaint echoed throughout the house. I felt the presence of the other three boys as they stood close enough to hear while remaining in the shadows so as not to bear the brunt of Mother's temper.

I kissed Daniel's cheek and held him even closer as Mother moved past us. Using the furniture for support, she walked toward the stove, which was barely emitting heat enough to fill a mouse's house. The darkness must have tested her vision, as she peered into the coal bucket for longer than should have been necessary to determine its state of emptiness. Snapping her head up, Mother glared in my direction. "Mandy, why is it so bloody cold in here?"

Instinctively, I took one step backward, shielding Daniel with my arms. "The bucket is out of coal." My whispered words felt overstated in the dark, silent room.

Grabbing the coal bucket, Mother took two slow steps toward us. Her footing appeared unsteady, but her pointed and accusing finger was ready to be thrust into my face. "Then go and get some!" Her slurred words hit me in the face at about the same time as the wretched and overwhelming smell of alcohol.

I had never been permitted into the basement before, and I certainly did not have any interest in going there now. I looked at her, buying time for reason to set in or for Daddy to appear and settle the matter.

Mother wrenched Daniel from my arms before shoving me with her pail-carrying hand toward the forbidden rug and the trapdoor entrance. I walked with slow, steady steps, holding my breath to control the terror that was building in my chest. I passed Jarred's room. His silhouette stared back at me from the shadows of his darkened sanctuary, the only movement a discreet shake of his head, his indication that I shouldn't go to the basement. Mother stalked behind me, nudging me forward with her alcohol-infused breath. "Hurry up, Mandy. It isn't getting any warmer in here with you dawdling."

I bent to the floor, my knees feeling the hard wood. With reluctant movements, I rolled the rug and placed it to the side of the trapdoor. Lifting the latch, I pulled the wooden door free and slid it along the floorboards to reveal the frightful basement opening. A shiver ran the length of my spine as the dank scent of earth rose up to greet me.

"Go on, then." Mother prodded my back with the coal bucket.

I glanced back over my shoulder, the cold from the basement assaulting my body. Mother's face was hidden by the bucket she held out, waiting for me to take. She gave another nudge with the bucket, and my foot touched the first step toward the bowels of our home. The dark space fueled my imagination as I thought of what was waiting below the trapdoor and what would happen should I refuse to enter the horrifying space. I considered the ramifications of not fetching coal. Would Mother yell at me? Would she strike me? Would I be sent to bed without dinner? All of these I could handle. But what if it was worse? What if she could hurt me more than I knew? As the options percolated in my mind, Mother's patience ran out.

Mother's foot, placed on the small of my back, forced me down the pitch in a rush of air and tumbling stairs. "Get down there this instant, or I'll lock you down there all night." The coal bucket collided with my entangled legs as I lay sprawled halfway down the stairs in the scariest place I'd ever ventured. Tears flowed down my cheeks as I righted myself in pitch darkness. Scrambling down the rest of the stairs, I grappled for a railing, a wall, anything to steady myself. There was none to be found.

As my eyes adjusted to the darkness, the edge of the stair tread came into formation and I realized how close I had come to falling off the top steps, unprotected from the sharp edges of the coal pile below. Using my hands to guide me down each tread, I crawled to the bottom stair, slow and steady, before attempting to stand on the uneven dirt ground that was our basement. The narrow beam of light from the kitchen cast around the stale room.

My socked foot bumped into the low-lying coal. Taking the bucket with me, I bent down to feel the coal with my hands. With tears running from my eyes and snot running from my nose, I scavenged at the coal like a hungry animal. The first few plunks of coal hitting the bottom of the bucket fanned my desire for a speedy completion of the hateful task.

I hurriedly grabbed at the black, sharp-edged morsels, eager to remove myself from this vile place. Ignoring the cold of the basement seeping through my heavy sweater and the sting of something slicing my hands, I filled the bucket to the brim before dragging it toward the light of the kitchen. Heaving the bucket up each step took more effort than I had anticipated, slowing my progress and my tears.

As I ascended out of the cave of terror, Mother met me at the opening. She loomed large and ominous over me as I cowered below her on the step. She yanked the bucket out of my hand and turned toward the living room. "Now, that wasn't that hard, was it?"

I climbed the remaining two stairs and turned to cover the trapdoor and unroll the magical rug that guarded our family from the nastiness below. As I moved the rug back in place, I noticed my hands were covered in black and striped with red. Small droplets of blood hit the wooden floor, narrowly missing the righted rug. Stumbling to the sink, I poured water from the wash bucket over my hands and cried out in pain.

Returning from the living room, Mother took one look at me and, in a voice laced with disgust, declared, "You stupid girl, why didn't you use the shovel?"

I washed my hands, removed my black-sodden socks, washed the coal and blood from the floor, and was promptly sent to bed without dinner. Mother chided me all the way to my room. "Put salve on those cuts, and don't you say a word about this to your father." Her next words made my heart sink even more. "I suppose I will have to finish the vegetables, then. Just remember this, Mandy. Just remember what I've done for you."

I pretended to be asleep that night when Daddy came in to check on me. Lying to Daddy was something I had never done before, and I was determined that Mother would not make me start.

CHAPTER 20

JUNE 1958
Cedar Springs, South Dakota

John

I wedge the sofa cushions between the kitchen table, made with my own two hands, and the bedroom dresser to keep them from rubbing against each in other in transit. I survey the contents of the little U-Haul trailer, which holds our life. A fresh start, she said, was what it would take for us to be a real family. That was a few months back, after my discovery of her daytime shenanigans at the local hotel and the infidelity that almost broke us completely. How much should one man be required to take? I asked myself that question when I discovered her, and I spoke those same words out loud after hauling her sorry, philandering butt home.

The most disturbing thought I have is how long it would have gone on, if I hadn't found her out. Bernice excels at making me look like a fool, by way of the ludicrous and embarrassing display that took place in broad daylight outside the hotel's front entrance and with the rumors that are sure to fly around Cedar Springs and make their way to my God-fearing parents. My neck warms at the notion.

Perhaps if I cared less about what others thought, I would be more inclined to stick it out here in my hometown, make Bernice the one to blame, and shatter her already fractured reputation with the news of her latest shenanigans. It was unusual for me to be near the hotel, but that afternoon I had run out to retrieve a backordered supply of hardware when I happened by the hotel's entrance. I barely glanced up as I passed. It was her laugh that caught my attention, the one I've heard less often as the years trudge by, but it was distinguishable all the same.

The laugh stopped me in my tracks, and I pivoted to see my wife, dressed in heels, a plunging V-neck sweater, and a hip-hugging pencil skirt—all red, of course, her signature color. She was hanging off the arm of man several years my junior, unknown to me. His cheek and lips displayed an array of smudged red lipstick as his gaze lingered just above the sweater's neckline.

"Bernice?" Her name uttered from my lips made me sound as weak as I felt, with my knees buckling beneath the weight of this discovery. She had little to say, surprise written across her face. The shrug of her shoulders indicated a disregard for her actions and my knowledge of them. I gathered what was left of my composure and yanked her arm away from her gentleman caller. As I dragged her down the street, she waggled her hips in the overly snug skirt, desperately trying to keep up with my hurried pace the entire way to our family sedan, parked a few blocks away.

Once within the confines of the car, I let out a whoosh of air along with a litany of heated words, none of them flattering to my wife, many of them never before uttered from my lips. The argument continued all the way home, into the living room, and for several days after. Bernice did little to ease my anger. Instead, she flung accusations. Of course, my transgressions, according to Bernice, revolved around the life I covet. The one I longed for but could not have. The one that died when Violet left this earth.

Disgust, toward Bernice or myself, colored my every decision in its ugly light as I pondered my options. Escaping the prying eyes of the small town had its appeal, and the shadows of the town reminded me what a fool I'd been.

Finally, after days of hostility and slamming doors, she came to me with a tear-stained face and an apology. The damage was done. Any love I might have had for her had vanished with her lipstick-stained kisses on another man's lips. A fresh start was what we needed, she pleaded, as she extolled the virtues and the beauty of Tacoma.

Washington State feels a million miles away. The distance is both a relief and an uncertain adventure. On the one hand, I am eager to leave behind the embarrassment and shame that dogs me in Cedar Springs, caused by my wife's perverse actions, both long ago and recent. On the other hand, leaving the only home our children have known and starting from scratch in a new town has few guarantees. For me, this is a final attempt at keeping our family together.

Though Ferngrove is not the part of Tacoma Bernice would have chosen, it has the most employment opportunities and a piece of affordable land to build a house on. Located only a few hours north of her beloved city, Ferngrove is a concession on Bernice's part, while Washington State is one on mine. After countless discussions on the topic, I refused to argue with her any further and decided Ferngrove would indeed be our new home.

If the move to Ferngrove is a success, it will have been worth uprooting the children from the familiarity and comfort of their friends and school in Cedar Springs. Should the relocation fail to right the rift and distance between Bernice and me, I've no idea what will become of us. That thought alone is enough to motivate me to act. We can't stay here, yet moving is no guarantee of a solution.

Perhaps Bernice is right. Perhaps, setting out on our own and leaving our past behind is the only way to move forward. The thought of saying goodbye to Mother, Father, the girls, and Edward only a few years ago would have shattered my heart. Today, though, the emotional distance between us is far greater than any move across the country could create. That somehow makes leaving Cedar Springs a little easier. The thought saddens me to the core, and I push it to the back of my mind where it can trouble me less.

I've thought about Violet something fierce since the idea of moving from Cedar Springs was first floated. My reluctance to leave the place that was ours wiggles into my conscious mind. The Fountain, where we used to dine together on burgers and milkshakes, always brings a smile to my face. It feels like only yesterday she was sitting across the booth, sipping sweet tea and telling me about her day. It is only a short drive from the edge of town to the fields where we used to spend Sunday afternoons, walking and talking for hours, never running out of conversation. Then there is home. Our home. The little blue house that has never felt quite right since she vanished from our lives.

Before picking up the U-Haul from town this morning, I stopped off one last time to say goodbye. The cemetery was empty, allowing me the privacy needed to explain myself to her. I told her of Calla and Jarred and how the move to Ferngrove would provide them with a fresh start. Leaving out the details of my failing marriage to Bernice, I told her how sorry I was to have let her down, how I knew I needed to do better for my children. The move, though suggested by Bernice in a desperate attempt to right her wrong, was coaxed on by the growing inconsistency of work at the cabinet shop. Cedar Springs had done its growing, and new houses with the need for cabinets was on the decline. The writing was on the wall, financially as well as emotionally. Moving towns was a good idea on many fronts.

Calla's somber face appears before me as I exit the trailer. "Hey there, pumpkin. Whatcha got for me?"

"Mother said to keep this near the back so it can be grabbed if needed." Calla hands me another ill-packed and overflowing box, a sour expression on her face.

I shake my head and smile. "Mother can't keep everything near the back. Eventually something will have to find a place at the front of the trailer." I take the box from her arms and place it on the lawn beside the other boxes, also too precious to be nestled out of reach.

Calla turns to walk away. Her displeasure with the move has remained constant since we told the children. "Hey, Calla." I catch her attention and her arm, coaxing her back to face me. "It is going to work out. I hear Ferngrove is a lush and beautiful place to call home." Her shrug tells me she isn't buying what I am selling. "We'll need to build a new house when we get there. What do you say? You want to help me with that?" Her cornflower blue eyes flicker before an almost indiscernible smile curves her lips. She nods her head one time, and I squeeze her arm to let her know I understand.

Before long, the trailer is crammed full of the contents of our little blue house. Piling into our recently acquired, pale green 1953 four-door Ford, we take one final look at Cedar Springs on our way out of town. Despite the car's bench seating being filled to capacity with the seven of us, the ride through town is silent, each of us lost in our own thoughts. I wipe a tear from my eye as we pass the Fountain, and I give it a nod in appreciation for all the memories it holds.

～

After four and half days of driving, each of us is tired, cranky, and eager to extract ourself from the confines of the car. We pull into the town of Ferngrove just after four o'clock in the afternoon. The outlying areas are lush with towering trees, and a carpet of green lines the landscape for miles on end. Cruising down Main Street with the windows down, we pass a gas station, a community hall, and a grocery store. I chuckle watching the kids in the rearview mirror as they lean over one another to gain a better view of their new hometown, craning their necks to see beyond the open windows.

Daniel, seated in the front between Bernice and myself, peers out the front window with saucer-sized eyes and an adorable, wide grin. At almost four years old, his toddler days are now behind him, replaced by a keen interest in learning about everything he can. His attention to detail and his curious questions indicate his blooming intelligence, and his sweet and gentle personality makes him a joy to be around. I pat his knee as his face grows with excitement at the scenery.

The boys in the back chatter about the apple orchards, the fields of green, and the outdoor swimming pool at the center of town. None of them can swim, but their excitement about the possibilities is contagious, bringing a smile to my lips.

We pass another row of shops. Bernice, with a poor disposition from days spent traveling, along with a poor sense of humor, thrusts her arm out the open window to point toward a shop. "Look, Calla, they have a store named just for you."

I glimpse Calla's face in the mirror as the shop's sign comes into view of the backseat window. The shop's name registers and hits her like a physical slap to the face. She shrinks back into the seat, silent, as her face glows red.

"Mother, please." I give Bernice a pleading look before returning my gaze to the rearview mirror to find Calla's face turned away from mine, tears snaking down her cheek.

"What?" Bernice whines. "It's called the Hefty Mart."

Bernice shrugs her shoulders, unaware or unconcerned how her words have hurt the child seated directly behind her.

I hold my tongue, not willing to engage her about such an uncalled-for and ridiculous assault with a car full of cranky travelers. Instead, I press on, forcing the ball of my foot a little more heavily on top of the gas pedal, suddenly eager to locate our temporary accommodations and remove myself from this car.

CHAPTER 21

MARCH 7, 1964
Ferngrove, Washington

Calla

My fingers hit a hard edge as I lift a small stack of t-shirts from a dresser drawer. I peel back the folded cotton to reveal a faded brown book with a tiny keyhole latch. I placed my diary in the drawer a few years back, after I discovered Mother reading it while sitting on my newly positioned bed. Upon arriving home from school that afternoon, I was shocked to find Mother had decided my room needed a renovation. Without asking if I wanted my furniture moved, and certainly without seeking permission to enter my room, Mother spent the day repositioning every single item in my room.

I felt beyond angry and violated when I saw her sitting there, casually flipping through my private thoughts. At fourteen years old, even I knew there was little in the way of secrets printed within those pages, but they were my pages all the same. Aunt Patricia gave me the diary for my eleventh birthday, and I had received true enjoyment from the gift that summer, after news of our impending move to Ferngrove was delivered.

I'd spent the next several days writing about my sadness of leaving Cedar Springs, my friends, and my grandparents. Despite less-than-infrequent visits, my grandparents were at least in the same town. For years they were the secret weapon I kept close to my heart. I always reassured myself that if I ever found the courage, I would run away and live with them. I thought about it plenty—dreamed about it, in all honesty—especially when Mother was being especially hurtful or unreasonable. But I never quite managed to find the courage to run away, and the possibility of my doing so would be less likely with us thousands of miles away. So I'd written and cried, and written some more. Somewhere in the process, I had found solace and resolved to make the best of the upcoming move.

I push on the latch and the mechanism clicks, unlocking the leather band. I flip open the book and smile at the childlike handwriting. The writing is certainly familiar, yet the slopes and angles appear to have come from a different version of me. I skim past the heartbroken little girl's words about moving west, and an entry dated May 15, 1958, catches my eye.

May 15, 1958

Daniel escaped again last night. This time I didn't hear him leave his room, and I felt scared for him, being out of doors all by himself in the darkness of night. It is curious to me how a three-and-a-half-year-old who can't manage to open a door in broad daylight somehow unlocks and opens the front door, while pushing past the screened one too. I can see on his face that he is a clever one, but this habit of sleepwalking makes me worry for him.

Daddy woke me in the early hours of the morning, searching under my bed, looking into my closet and behind my dresser. He apologized for waking me, but his voice was stretched thin. "Daniel is missing," he said. I leaped out of bed and began to help with the search. Besides Jarred, Daniel is my favorite, but I wouldn't tell the others that. After the entire house had been searched and all of us had been pulled from our beds, a knock came at the front door.

It was Mister Foster and he carried Daniel in his arms. Mother reached out to grab Daniel and cuddled him on the sofa the rest of the morning. I listened as Mister Foster told Daddy that he had heard a rustling at their front door as he was readying himself for the workday. He opened the door to find Daniel curled up against the door, fast asleep. Daddy thanked Mister Foster for finding Daniel and for bringing him home. Before Mister Foster left, he asked Daddy, "Has the boy done this before?" Daddy gave a sad sigh and nodded. "Not quite so far as this though." Mister Foster nodded in Daddy's direction and said, "I'll keep watch for him, then, but you might want to get the boy checked with a doctor, John. It ain't safe for a child to be wandering two blocks from home in the dead of night. Ain't safe at all."

As I read the entry of Daniel's sleepwalking, I am reminded of how many times we have found him behind the sofa, under one of our own beds, and even once in the kitchen, curled up under the table. My finger grazes the words and I smile, knowing that, besides Jarred, Daniel is still my favorite.

I return to my bed to sit on its edge as I flip through the diary, searching for more. With the warming story about Daniel, a thought flits across my mind. Perhaps I'll read enough here to find a reason to stay. I flip a little farther until I find a sentence, written in bold pencil, that I hadn't known I had been seeking.

July 3, 1958

Daddy is proud of the work I've been doing. He told me so when he showed me the plans, pointing out my bedroom with pride in his voice. "A room just for you, pumpkin." Daddy told me that as soon as the trees are cleared away, we are ready to set to work on the house we are building together. With summer just getting underway, we have been pulling whatever we can with our bare hands. They are long days, but we spend them outside and together.

Today, Mother's father and his wife, the woman Mother calls Hilda, arrived from Tacoma to help with the clearing. I imagined from the way Mother talked about her that I wouldn't like Hilda at all, but I couldn't have been more wrong. Hilda glows like a lantern, and the light travels with her, every way she moves. She is shiny and beautiful, and oh so kind. I don't know why Mother has said rude things about her, because I think she is simply divine.

Hilda brought proper gardening gloves and even an extra pair for me. Though my hands might already be stained for the rest of my life, I put on the gloves. They felt soft and lovely, and the prickles didn't scratch me nearly as much. Together, Hilda and I pulled the low brushes while Daddy and Mother's father (I'm not sure if I am supposed to call him Granddad, so for now, I don't call him anything) worked on the larger trees.

When it came time for a rest, Hilda settled us by the rear of their car with a fancy lunch. Little triangle sandwiches, real potato chips, and soda for sipping. Daddy, though, did more gulping than sipping, so he got two whole bottles of soda to himself. Even though the work is hard, I am having the best time working with Daddy and now with Hilda.

Hilda said they were going to stay on through the Fourth of July weekend and that she would convince the men to halt work early on Friday so we can all join in the Ferngrove Independence Day celebrations. There is going to be a parade and music and even a fireworks show. I am so excited I could burst.

A happy tear escapes my eye, and the corner of my mouth curls up in a smile as I remember the kindness of a virtual stranger. I am flooded with the sounds of Hilda's laughter and the weekend's festivities. That weekend, though, was the last time I saw Hilda or Mother's father. Mother did not care for Hilda spending any time, money, or attention on me, and she made her opinion very clear to anyone within earshot. I remember cringing in disbelief that Mother could speak so nastily about a woman who seemed to want only to give of herself, not only to me but to Mother as well.

A letter arrived in the mail a few months after our company had returned home to Tacoma. Mother's father had taken ill, and after a few short days of intended recuperation in the Tacoma hospital, he passed away of a heart attack. I remember my heart aching for Hilda, as I had no question about the love she held for him.

Mother seemed a great deal less fazed by the news of her father's passing, and I wondered if she had ever felt love for anyone at all. Soon after we moved into our new house in Ferngrove, Mother subscribed to the *Tacoma Times* newspaper. For months, her interest in the news outside our region baffled me. Not until she informed me that her only reason for reading the paper was to find news of Hilda did I understand the nature of her interest. Settling herself at the kitchen table, she would spread the newspaper wide in front of her. With a coffee cup to her left and cigarette to her right, she'd take a deep breath and scan the obituary columns, searching for Hilda's name.

"I'm reading it so I'll know when that woman dies. It is her fault, you know," Mother told me, cigarette pressed firmly between her lips. "It is her fault I didn't get the life I deserve. That was entirely Hilda's doing. She banished me from Tacoma without batting an eye. I was a socialite when I lived there."

Under normal circumstances, I might feel sad for Mother, but for the past thirteen years, she has done nothing to earn that kind of response from me, and so all I allow myself to feel for her is loathing.

CHAPTER 22

JULY 1958
Ferngrove, Washington

John

The sun has barely broken above the horizon as I stare at the property, now mostly free of trees and shrubs. It's a decent, flat parcel of land suitable for a modest family home and maybe even a workshop, when the funds allow, that is. I made the down payment for the land and the home from selling my remaining pieces of custom-built furniture in Cedar Springs. I suppose the years I spent avoiding evenings with Bernice by whittling away at wood in the back region of our yard paid off in the end. Though some of the intricate pieces went for far below market value, they are the reason for our head start in Ferngrove, and for that I am grateful.

The foundation was poured over a week ago, and today we begin to frame the structure. Spreading the plans on the hood of the family Ford in the dim light of the sunrise, I secure the rolled edges with my lunch pail, my thermos full of hot coffee, and a large stone I picked from the ground. I scan the drawings while creating a list of supplies needed for the week's work.

I check my watch. The crew of four, hired to help with framing the house, is due to arrive within the hour. I look back at the imprint of the slab, imagining the placement of the kitchen and the four bedrooms. Opening my thermos, I pour coffee into the lid and sip the steaming brew as the excitement of building a home for my family rises within my chest.

Early this morning, I found myself in the cramped yet economical kitchen of our temporary rental home, quietly packing my lunch and filling my thermos. I carried my boots to the door so as not to wake the rest of the family, deep in sleep. I pulled open the back door and was preparing to sit on the small square porch to lace up my work boots when Calla appeared in the room.

"I'm ready, Daddy." Her voice, filled with sleep, startled me in the quiet house as I bent to pick up my lunch pail.

"Ready for what?" I turned to take in her bed-matted head of blonde curls and her sleepy eyes. Calla was dressed in her work clothes, the same ones she'd worn for days on end as we cleared the land.

"To build the house." Though Calla rubbed sleep from her eyes and stifled a yawn, her words are filled with determination.

"Oh, pumpkin. Today is just for grownups." I walked toward her and tousled her curls. "Today, the big men do the heavy lifting. I'll need you at the ready in a couple days though." I give her a conspiratorial wink. "Why don't you visit the swimming pool with the boys this afternoon, and then tonight we can talk about you coming to the house tomorrow?"

Calla shrugged, a clear indicator that this news did not please her. Always a good girl, though, she returned to the bedroom she shared with all four boys, and I crept out of the house to be in the presence of the land I now own.

My thoughts drift back to a few weeks before, when Edmund and Hilda came to visit. Though I had heard Bernice's rendition and a fair share of stories about the illustrious Hilda and Bernice's father, it was the first time I had met them. I immediately felt at ease with both Hilda and Edmund. Two people, strangers really, were willing to drive a few hours to offer their time and services to a family member they seldom hear from. I couldn't help but wonder if Bernice had gotten it all wrong.

As Edmund and I hacked down trees, dragging them into a pile to be used later for firewood, Hilda worked alongside Calla. I heard Calla laugh and chat freely with Hilda as they tugged at the smaller, brambly growth. They were like two peas in a pod, and it quickly became evident that Hilda was fond of my daughter.

Evidence of Hilda's wealth, or "great fortune" as Bernice liked to call it, was apparent in the stately car Edmund drove and the luncheon Hilda provided midway through the workday. Their clothes, though of new fashion and good quality, were far from elaborate and were suitable for the manual labor.

I reminded myself that they owed nothing to Bernice and myself. They were family, indeed, but Bernice had done little to foster a relationship with them since her return to South Dakota. I am not even certain they knew how many grandchildren they had before meeting them. Edmund's face lighting up when the children were introduced was a sight I am sure not to forget anytime soon. His eyes twinkled with delight, just as I've seen Daniel's do when he is wrapped up in a new discovery.

The bond between Hilda and Calla warmed my heart the most. Hilda seemed to fit naturally into Calla's world. For four whole days, the two of them enjoyed each other's company. There wasn't a topic Hilda didn't know something about, and

Calla peppered her with questions of all sorts. When they stumbled upon their mutual adoration for mathematics, it was as if someone lit a fire within Calla. Their voices lifted even higher in delight as they discussed the sorts of jobs available for women in the field of mathematics. In my heart, I know Calla is capable of anything she puts her mind to. Some may call it stubbornness, but her Daddy would call it fierce determination, and he would do so with pride.

We celebrated an afternoon of festivities together during the Ferngrove Independence Day celebrations. Hilda insisted on buying the children miniature American flags to wave during the parade before ending the day with a trip to the ice cream shop in town. The first night, Bernice welcomed her father and Hilda with a stiff embrace at dinner, and she kept her distance by remaining at our rental home with the younger children while Hilda and Edmund joined Calla and me at the building site.

The fifth day was the beginning of the end. Calla and I rose early, dressed in darkness, and waited by the curb for Edmund and Hilda to fetch us for the day's work. It had been decided the evening before that Bernice would use the Ford to gather groceries and would meet us at the building site for a late afternoon picnic, since today was to be Hilda and Edmund's last day with us before they returned home to Tacoma.

The morning went as planned, with Edmund and me clearing the last of the remaining large trees before helping the girls with the final section of scrub. Though the scrub was far less heavy, as I dug at the roots and pulled at the tangles of needle-wielding branches, I gained an admiration for Hilda and Calla, who had cleared the majority of the land in a few short days.

By three o'clock in the afternoon, the four of us leaned against Edmund's deep burgundy 1955 Chrysler Imperial. We were sipping water and wiping sweat from our brows when Bernice arrived with the four boys in tow.

Our old Ford lurched onto the bare land, skidding to a stop.

All occupants of the car braced themselves as Bernice's lead foot slammed the brakes. I could tell her mood had already soured. She pursed her lips and grabbed her purse and a bag of groceries from the passenger side.

We set up a makeshift picnic table with a couple sawhorses and a sheet of plywood, and then we gathered around the table to assemble sandwiches. Hilda opened bottles of soda using the rough edge of the sheet of plywood—cola for the adults, orange for the kids—while Bernice laid out a tablecloth and paper plates.

Edmund and I took the boys on a brief and imaginary tour of our new home, showing them the two large bedrooms the four of them would share. Calla helped by adding mustard, mayonnaise, and ham to each slice of bread at the table. I could hear Hilda chatting to Bernice, the smile in her voice giving me no cause for worry. Not until I returned to retrieve a sandwich did I recognize my error in judging the situation.

"All I'm saying, Bernice, is that Calla here is a delightful young lady who is sure to change the world with her brains while she stuns them with her looks. It would be a pleasure for me to host her at our home for a few weeks, maybe even a summer if you and John see fit to let her travel to stay with us." Hilda's motherly gaze rested gently on Calla's shoulders.

"You know nothing about her." Bernice snapped as her voice leaned toward a high-pitched shriek. "You can't judge a person's future by spending three days with them. Trust me, this girl has fewer prospects than you think."

"Bernice!" Hilda placed her hands on the temporary table and leaned forward while stealing a sideways glance in Calla's direction. "How could you say such a thing? Give Calla a chance. Maybe it is you who has misread her abilities." Hilda righted herself and moved to stand beside Calla, placing a protective arm around her shoulders before meeting Bernice's eyes with a pointed look. "You were given a chance once before, after all. Or have you forgotten all that your father and I did for you?"

Bernice's eyes flared as words spewed from her lips. "Did for me?" Her voice lifted another octave. "Did for me? Have you conveniently forgotten how you banished me from Tacoma? Did you forget how you took everything from me? Did you forget that I trusted you?" Bernice shook her head. "You won't get Calla to spoil and fuss over. Building her anticipation of what life could offer before you dash her dreams to the ground and stomp on them with your Gucci shoes. No Hilda, you don't get my trust again, and you most certainly won't get Calla. Not ever."

"I see." Hilda's voice was much calmer, more reserved, and more mature. "It seems it is you, Bernice dear, who has forgotten what truly happened in Tacoma. I was being kind not to point it out at the time, but it was your own actions that initiated your departure from Tacoma, not mine. I simply responded to the situation as best as I could. I kept your secret. Your embarrassment. Your indiscretion. I hid the knowledge of your poor choices, even from your own father, the man I love with all my heart. No, Bernice, I am not the one who is not trustworthy. You are."

"I think it is time for you and Father to leave." Bernice's words were flat and cold. She grabbed her purse from the table, got in the car, and drove off without another word.

I shake my head at the messiness that seems to follow Bernice, and I watch the sky as the sun kisses it, making the blueness visible. I cringe against the tone and the disdain with which Bernice spoke of Calla, while she stood a mere foot away from her. Her words were despicable and unnecessary, surely embarrassing Calla, who was caught in the crossfire. Given the speed with which the scene unfolded and the company in our presence, I found myself at a loss of how to properly respond.

Bernice's quick exit only amplified her anger and, regrettably, my inability to speak in defense of Calla.

After Bernice left, Hilda had nothing more to say on the matter, only that should we change our mind, Calla would always be welcome at their home in Tacoma. I thanked them but decided better of apologizing for Bernice's actions. No apology would ever be great enough anyway, and it wasn't me who owed them one.

With sandwiches eaten among the discussion of much less inflammatory topics, Hilda and Edmund hugged and kissed all the kids, promising to see them again soon. As they waved goodbye through the rolled-down windows of their Imperial, I held my tongue, silently doubting we would ever see them again. I am all too familiar with Bernice's ability to hold a grudge, but it still saddens me to think our children will miss out on having relationships with two people who clearly love them, simply because they are family.

A horn honks twice behind me, and the truck carrying the crew and lumber turn into the makeshift drive to begin framing our new home.

CHAPTER 23

MARCH 7, 1964
Ferngrove, Washington

Calla

I flip through the pages of the diary, knowing my childlike scrawl should be reminiscent of happy days. The fact that it elicits no such emotions settles on me like a dense fog in which I've lost my way. Dad isn't a bad man. I know this for certain. He is well-liked within the community and is often sought for help on a variety of topics. He is generous with his time and seems to be at ease offering gentle smiles to neighborhood kids who pass our home on their way to the corner.

I've seen him rise in the middle of a dark night, summoned to help a neighbor whose cow was having trouble delivering a new calf. He's driven the boys around their paper routes when the weather was less than favorable. One of my favorite memories is the year he made sleds for us kids at Christmas and then proceeded to put on his boots and coat and take us out to the steepest hill he could find for an afternoon full of winter fun. If memory serves me right, he himself even enjoyed a ride or two down the snowy hill.

Even with Mother, he seems to be at the ready, prepared to do whatever she needs. No, Dad isn't a bad man at all. He is simply a man who prefers to busy himself with concrete actions rather than sorting through our family's emotional mess. Seldom does he talk about feelings—good, bad, or anything in between. I know when he is angered, but his anger seems fleeting, almost as if he hides it away the moment he recognizes it. I am pretty sure he loves me, but to the best of my recollection, I've never heard those words from his lips.

It is impossible for me to hate him. I love my father. Dearly, in fact. Perhaps I love him too much. I feel exhausted from the action of loving. I understand why Dad tucks his emotions away, hidden beneath the crusty edge of daily life. Emotions are difficult. They make you want to cry, smile, laugh, scream, and even lash out. Some emotions are simply not becoming, and others offer too big a glimpse of one's weakness when it is not safe for others to see it. If I've learned anything from my dad, it is how to hide my emotions. I keep them close, spreading them just beneath the surface of my skin. They are close enough for me to feel every day yet tucked away safely out of sight. Sometimes life is more about coping than living. My fingers land on a diary page, and I lower my eyes to read through the blurriness of gathering tears.

August 13, 1958

. . .

My face is red and flushed from the heat of the day. It was another long, hot day at the building site. Daddy and I were up before the roosters crowed. We lugged jugs of water and Kool-Aid and enough sandwiches to fuel us for the day ahead. It was our second day of putting the wood floors in the house, and I could tell Daddy was pleased with the progress we'd made. For two days straight, we have worked side by side, each of us holding a hammer and a pocket full of nails. Daddy cut the wood, and I placed the boards flat, neatly tucking them into one another for a sturdy fit. I was proud Daddy only had to show me once how to lay the boards properly before nailing them in.

We didn't talk much, with Daddy going back and forth to cut each board the right length, but it felt like we were the only ones in the world today, with nobody stopping by to interrupt our busy work. By the time four o'clock rolled around, my knees were bruised and my hands blistered, but we both had big silly grins stretched across our faces as we admired our handiwork. We packed up the tools, and Daddy drove us to the ice cream shop for sundaes, just the two of us. It was the best day of the whole entire summer!!!

I smile as the memory of building the house, the same house I am now sitting in, washes over me. Those were simpler times, it seems. Even though life at home was anything but easy, those days with Dad, both of us intent on the same outcome, were like magic. I worked alongside him for the entire summer until it came time for me to start school. I tried to convince him to let me stay and work on the house, but he could not be dissuaded, and come September, I was off to a new school with new teachers and new friends.

I turn the pages of the diary, and as I do, a piece of paper falls out. I unfold the paper to reveal a letter from my grandparents. The letter must have gone unnoticed by Mother the day she read my diary, sitting right here.

At first, I think the letter is from Grandma and Grandpa, but after reading a few sentences, I realize it is from Momma's parents. I return to the beginning of the letter to read with this new context.

September 16, 1958
Dearest Calla,

It was lovely to receive your letter. We are very happy to hear you and Jarred are both well and are settling in with school in Ferngrove. Granddad is sitting beside me as I write this letter, so please know that it is just as if we are writing it together. Things are busy on the farm as usual. Granddad is still training the younger horses. Some, as you know, take to the bridle easier than others. Your mother used to have such a way with the horses. Lord, how I wish she were here to give those feisty ones a calming hand.

Aunt Iris is doing well. She has moved to New York City to pursue her art, which scares me something fierce, but I haven't told her so. I want her to know how proud we are of her. A recent letter she sent indicated there is a new beau in her life. We haven't heard many details as of yet, but don't you worry, Calla dear. I plan to extract everything I can from Iris and will be sure to pass along the news to you in my next letter.

Granddad just reminded me to tell you that Susan and Mary said hello and that they miss you very much. Granddad ran into them in town one afternoon last week. They were just heading home after school. I don't imagine it has been easy making new friends at school, but I am quite confident that your beautiful personality will serve you well in that department.

I found it especially interesting that you and your dad were building your new family home together. I pray that a home built with so much love will be filled with an unending supply of it and that you and Jarred will be at peace in your new home. Granddad says he could use your help on the farm, now that you've got all those hammering skills at the ready. You didn't mention when you expect to move into your new home. We would love to know when you do. Please send us a letter once you've moved, and include your new address so we can continue to write to you.

I suppose I had better get to work on supper, as those potatoes won't be peeling themselves. We look forward to your next letter, and please do ask Jarred to write as well. I do not wish to upset you, dear, but I want you to know how much love we have for you and Jarred in our hearts. We think of you every day, just as we do our own sweet Violet. You will never be forgotten, and you will always be loved.

With love and many, many hugs,
Granny and Granddad

I hold the letter to my chest and try to remember whether I returned their letter with one of my own. When was the last time I heard from my grandparents? Did they continue to write to me? Did I write to them? There is a blank space in my memory, and I am saddened that I don't know how or where they are.

I wonder if they would still have me on their farm. Maybe I could work until I've saved enough money for a bus ticket to Cedar Springs. Surely either Granny and Granddad or Grandma and Grandpa would welcome me into their home. I consider this new option, and a small measure of relief rises to quell my anxious state. There are more options than I can see at this moment. I remind myself to hold on to that thought, and I stand

and place the letter within the pages of the diary. I stuff the diary to the bottom of a shoulder bag, where it is secure from prying eyes, and turn back toward my dresser. A renewed desire burns within me to finish my packing and vacate this house before I lose my nerve again.

CHAPTER 24

FEBRUARY 1959
Ferngrove, Washington

John

With Bernice, the usual warden of the mailbox, nestled warmly inside the house on this less-than-pleasant February eve, I trek to the end of the snow-covered driveway to retrieve today's mail. Having already informed me she is waiting for her latest edition of *Woman's Day* magazine to arrive, Bernice's voice dipped a mere octave into a whine before I grabbed my jacket and boots and headed outside. I did not wish to spend the evening listening to her complain about her missing magazine.

Bernice took over the task of checking the mail the day she discovered that letters from Cedar Springs were making their way into our home. It was one of the few times I've participated in an argument with her since arriving in Ferngrove. Bernice's antics in Cedar Springs did little to improve our already stilted relationship. Instead, any interest I had in engaging with her in any manner has all but disappeared. I am aware that, to her, my lack of interest is like a knife twisting in her back. Though this does not necessarily please me, it does not make me feel any remorse either.

The only reason I rose to the battle was for the children's sake. Bernice has done enough to inflict pain on Calla and Jarred with her thoughtless infidelities, the ones that made the move west both necessary and appealing. Surely, we owed the children the opportunity to stay in contact with their family and friends. "How," I argued with my voice raised in frustration, "is receiving letters from halfway across the country going to threaten us?" Bernice had insisted that starting fresh as a family in Ferngrove meant no contact from the "outside," which referred to anyone with a link to my past with Violet. After an evening spent bickering, I threw my hands in the air, signaling defeat, before I grabbed my jacket and boots and walked out the door.

That night, I walked the sleepy streets of Ferngrove, hands stuffed into my pockets and jacket collar turned up against the damp. The children would certainly be disappointed when they realized letters from Cedar Springs have stopped arriving. I, though, have found my own way of dealing with things.

In Cedar Springs, Violet was everywhere. She was at the Fountain, in the house, at the grocery store, in the backyard with the children. I realize now what Bernice meant the day she tried to purge Violet from our lives by burning her things. Not that Bernice's cruel and irreversible actions can ever be forgiven, but time and distance have provided me the space necessary to understand what Bernice was trying desperately to say.

She was fighting against a memory, a past she couldn't access and a future she could not own alone as my wife. The marriage is crowded, I know now, with the memory of the life I used to know. The life I still long for. I couldn't see it then because my home was familiar and comfortable for me. But during these months filled with the work of building our home, and with distance separating me from daily reminders of my past, I have found myself lost in my thoughts. Each day, I have worked in silent reverie, my mind falling into step with the vivid recollection of days spent by Violet's side. It is easy to get lost in the memories, bringing them forward as imaginary conversations. This is what Bernice was fighting against in Cedar Springs, and though the memories are now concealed, they remain just the same. One might argue they are even stronger.

In the end, Bernice won the battle of the mailbox, though I remind myself that nobody ever truly wins in a war. In response to my walking out mid-argument, Bernice issued me the silent treatment along with a reserved spot on the sofa each night for three weeks straight. If letters continued to arrive for Calla, Jarred, or myself, I am unaware. Instead, I send the occasional, though likely not frequent enough, letter home to Mother and Father, letting them know we are fine but requesting they not reply.

I open the mailbox and it responds with a squeak that penetrates the frosty night sky. I reach into the dark box and feel a thick magazine and a few smaller envelopes. I tilt my head toward the box as I pull the mail from within. The feel of the letters in my hands throws me back in time to when the arrival of a letter meant at least one more day of sanity.

I've been aboard this ship for a week now, enroute to my next post, situated along the English Channel. The quiet of men having stopped their busyness is noticeable as I brace my back against the cold exterior of the ship's steel. I slowly slide into a seated position on a rare dry spot, in an effort to get low enough to block the wind that has been whistling around us for the past few days. Winter, having long since vacated, seems to have forgotten to take its wind with it. I turn up my collar and bow my head, steadying the package in both hands.

The arrival of mail is a welcomed yet mournful time for all aboard. Sailors scatter with their packages, seeking solitude with their letters, their thoughts, and perhaps even their fears. After traveling weeks or months, A little piece of home arrives to comfort, inform, and remind us that even in this desolate, war-ravaged place, we are never truly alone. We have not been forgotten.

The time has passed at a steady rate, and though I look forward to the chocolate, I crave the words more than anything. Placing the small box on the deck beside me, I unfold the pages and, without hesitation, flip to the last page, as I always do, just to hear her say, "Stay healthy and well, John. We love you. Mother." Though months have passed, each time I read her words, I hear her voice echo around me. I see tears staining her pale cheeks as she grasps at my sleeve, her eyes still pleading with me to stay.

Exhaling slowly, I return to the first page, soaking up the news quickly before beginning again. I read more slowly each time as I take in the letter over and over. With my head tipped back toward the clouded sky, I bring the letter to life in my mind's eye. Mother is an exceptional storyteller, never failing to bring Edward's shenanigan's to life across the miles and years we are apart.

∾

A chill runs through me as I close the mailbox and shake the memory from my mind. My life in Ferngrove, though far from perfect, is at least not a battlefield. The overpowering desire to read my mother's words again, though, still burns deep within me. Edward is now eighteen years old, and I am not there to help him navigate his journey into becoming a young man. The weight of letting him down is heavy on my shoulders.

All I seem to feel these days is heavy. Heavy with exhaustion from long hours spent framing other people's houses. Heavy with the looming task of returning home to work on custom furniture, which brings only a small amount of relief to the budget stretched thin by a growing family. In addition to my sleepless nights haunted by memories, the emotional drain of life with Bernice wears me down. I exist as a shadow of the man I once was.

So far, life in Ferngrove hasn't worked out how I hoped. We moved into our new home a couple months ago, and though the house is complete enough for occupants, it is far from finished. Bernice's desire to have the latest in style and design, all discovered through her damned glossy magazines, has delayed several projects due to cost, availability, and my lack of time. I fear by the time we can afford that which she desires in her new castle, the styles will have changed and will once again be out of our price range.

I tuck the mail under my arm and meander back toward the single light bulb that glows in the carport. I cast my eyes around my workspace. A makeshift worktable stands in the center of the space, ensuring no vehicle will park under its shelter in the foreseeable future.

I decide better of getting comfortable and warm inside, as it would surely stifle my resolve to work on the table and chairs that are awaiting my attention. Instead, I open the front door and place the mail on the table. I holler to tell Bernice the mail is on the table and that I am going to work for a bit. I close the door and return to the carport.

It is easy to get lost in my thoughts as I sand and shape the wood. The rhythmic sound of the sandpaper washing over the table's leg lulls me into submission, and despite the freezing temperatures, I am at one with my surroundings.

My thoughts turn back to the letters. Letters from home hold a special place in my heart, and I am not ready to let go of them. Those letters saw me through illness, fatigue, and a tremendous amount of death during the war. As devastation surrounded me, letters from home brought some normalcy to my thoughts. I was able to retreat into my memory, coloring in details through my past experiences at home. I read the letters so often that the words, still to this day, are embedded in my mind and heart. As I run my hand over the smooth table leg to determine its level of completeness, I let the remembered letters infiltrate my present.

The letter arrived late, by almost two months, but it was welcome all the same. For a moment, I was not at the military base in England. I was home again, among the warm comforts of a roaring fire and a roast turkey spitting in the oven. I sank onto the cot I'd claimed as my own, tilted the pages toward the light of the small tent opening, and immersed myself in home.

Saturday, December 25, 1943

Dear John,

Christmas morning would not be complete without words sent to you, so I rose early this morning to put those words to paper. Edward has yet to wake, though my time may be limited, considering his excitement when he went to bed. The holidays are just not the same with a war going on. The churches seem much fuller this holiday season, so perhaps there is a silver lining. But I must admit, I would need to look with deep intent to find it.

Your letter informing us of your orders to be shipped out arrived on Friday. I can't say I am pleased to hear you are heading into the storm, but my prayers are as strong as they are constant, as is my love for you, son.

Thank you for the thoughtful gifts you sent for under the tree. Edward will be especially surprised to see one there from you. He misses you so, John, and though he doesn't yet offer much in the way of words, he clings to Violet every Sunday during the church service. Speaking of Violet, she is coming to stay for a spell the week after Christmas. We haven't seen much of her since you left, save for Sunday service. I imagine it has been difficult for her without you here, but her mother seems to think she is coming around and is ready to embrace our family once again as we wait for your return.

I hear Edward rustling about now. Must go, but I promise to finish this letter before the day is through.

I am back! Oh, what a whirlwind Christmas Day was. It is late now, and the fire is burning the final embers as I stifle a yawn. As promised, my dear boy, completing this letter to you is the least I can do. What I write next is not meant to make you long for home but instead to make you feel a part of it. John, you are with us always. My hope is that these words will help carry you through and keep you safe in all your travels, near and far.

Christmas morning began with me rising in the darkness to prepare the large bird for roasting. Father rose a short time later to stoke the fire and light the tree. Together, he and I stood, admiring the presents nestled under the decorated boughs as we waited for the rest of the family to rise. The collection of family stockings hung from the mantel and were full of sweet treats and a small toy for each little Smith. Father turned on the radio, and I went to begin this letter to you. All day long we listened to familiar holiday tunes as they played softly in the background.

The roasting bird filled the house with smells so divine that I am convinced it pulled Edward from the warmth of his covers just as the sun rose in the sky. I stood in the doorway of the living room, having heard Edward moving about, and I watched as he rubbed his sleep-filled eyes before wandering toward to the Christmas tree, strung heavily with the paper and popcorn decorations that he had made a few days before.

With everyone gathered around the tree, we held one another's hands and bowed our heads, giving thanks for the holiday, for family, and for a day to celebrate. As we gathered before the tree, we prayed for you, John. Prayers of safe travel, good health, and a speedy end to the war came from each of our lips. It was, however, Edward who prayed the most beautiful prayer of all. He said three little words filled with determination and love. As a tear rolled down his cheek, he whispered, "John, come home."

With that, I will leave you, son. If our prayers have any sway with God above, I am certain they will be heard on this glorious day.

Merry Christmas, John.
We love and miss you every day.

Much love,
Mother

My stomach rumbles at the thought of Mother Smith's roast turkey. The memory of that Christmas letter fills me up inside with a love strong enough to withstand the brutalities of war. I turn the table leg in my hands, pleased with its outcome. Even today, a letter from the past can connect me with the family I've separated myself from. *That is love*, I think again. *That is true, honest to goodness, unconditional, family love. Bernice knows nothing of the sort.*

CHAPTER 25

MARCH 7, 1964
Ferngrove, Washington

Calla

If my secondhand, well-worn dresser had a mirror attached to its brown-stained surface, it would reflect back to me my grief in having to make such a bold decision at my age. I waffle between anger, fear, and immense anguish as my thoughts and memories swirl about me. I know I need to proceed, but that doesn't mean I want to.

I tug open the third drawer down to reveal disorganized odds and ends. A movie stub from a friend's birthday party last October quickly finds its way into the trash bin. I sort through a smattering of pencils and notepaper before adding them to the belongings set to go with me. My eyes stop and hover over a photograph. My hand tentatively reaches for it, cautious at first, as if the memory is strong enough to lash out and burn my skin.

The photograph is from Christmas a few years back, a defining moment in the sibling hierarchy within which we live. Christmas of 1960 was a memorable one. Dad had sold a few extra pieces of custom furniture that autumn, and with Daniel in school, Mother had taken a position at the hospital.

Mother's employment was made possible by Miriam, a neighbor and new friend to Mother. Miriam had worked at the hospital for several years while raising her own four children. Miriam's husband, Mother said, was a no good, lying, cheating, sack of something, who couldn't hold his liquor or his tongue. Miriam and Mother became the best of friends, complaining over coffee and cigarettes about the lots they'd been handed in life. Really though, Mother did most of the complaining, while Miriam nodded her head, barely getting a word in edgewise.

Embarrassingly, to me at least, Mother told two lies about her new job. First, she told Miriam over coffee one morning that she had to work because Dad was incapable of providing for her properly. She forgot to mention that her expensive and constant demands for the latest fashions have left our family in a financial pickle on more than one occasion. Second, she told everyone she was a nurse at the hospital, but in reality, her lack of training meant her job was to be an assistant to the nurses.

Money wasn't as much of a strain that year as it had been during past Christmases, so it was with great enthusiasm and excitement that the five of us waited for the *Sears Christmas Book* to arrive in the mail. We enjoyed rare moments of happy chatter in the house while the boys and I sat together on the sofa, poring over each item. We scoured the glossy pages from cover to cover, selecting our most wished-for Christmas gifts. Even the dish sets and the men's pipe kits got our attention. No page was passed over in our quest to relish this particular year's holiday experience.

My thumb caresses the photograph of us kids seated in front of the Christmas tree, and I remember how eager I was to have a sewing machine so I could set to work sewing my own clothes. But given the expense of such an item, I kept my ask modest and settled on a small tabletop record player instead. Daniel desperately wanted the microscope set, complete with three lenses and a battery-powered light. Daniel is most certainly the smartest one of all the boys. His desire to learn more than was taught at school was evident from his first week in grade one. He begged me to read and reread the microscope's description, and then he would prattle on for hours about the slides he would create once the microscope arrived under the tree from Santa.

Jamie wished for the paratrooper action set, which had authentic fighting gear, including pretend hand grenades. I hoped Mother would recognize this as a bad idea and outfit him with a less menacing gift, but I sure wasn't going to be the one who rained on his parade. The last thing our house needed was Jamie pretending to be a one-man army, just as the catalog promised. Mark was more interested in the electric train sets, choosing the most expensive one in the catalog, not because it was the most interesting or included a coveted train-like whistle sound, but simply because it was the most expensive one.

Jarred was quieter about his selection. Though we all knew he was keen to join the local hockey team, the cost of ice skates had prevented his enrolment for the previous two years. When the *Wish Book* wasn't sequestered away by another pair of grabbing hands, I would spot Jarred tucked into a corner of the sofa as he admired the ice skates pictured on the shiny page. Given the skates he had chosen were a fraction of the cost of Mark's desired train set, I didn't see any cause for concern and felt confident his wish would be granted.

Christmas morning came, and after we wrapped ourselves in robes and placed slippers on our feet, we gathered excitedly in the kitchen, waiting for permission to discover what waited for us beneath the tree. With cups of coffee in their hands, Mother and Dad finally nodded in agreement, and we dashed off to the living room as if the kitchen were on fire. Mark pushed his way past the rest of us and was the first to arrive at the tree. Spotting his beloved train set, he squealed in delight and pulled the box away from the tree to investigate its contents.

Daniel found his microscope and quietly set about reading every inch of the box before opening it with extreme care. Jamie located his military-themed set, thankfully a more subdued version than the one he chose. My record player was smaller than I expected but included three records that I hadn't thought to request. Jarred was seated before a shiny pair of black ice hockey skates, his face lit up with a broad smile. Mother came into the living room just as he reached out to try one on his foot.

"What do you think you are doing?" she barked, her morning voice still groggy-sounding.

None of us certain whom she was addressing, so we all froze in place, stealing glances at one another in an effort to locate the culprit.

"Those aren't for you, Jarred." The words were delivered without anger, carrying a tone of satisfaction that made me uneasy. "Those skates are for Mark."

Mine wasn't the only mouth that hung open in response. Dad was quick to stand and question Mother in a hushed but firm tone, his back to us kids. "The other gift." Mother's voice was filled with exasperation. "The other unwrapped gift under the tree is for Jarred."

We all turned to face the tree and watched as Jarred pulled out a box labeled "*The Game of Life*." I looked from the game in Jarred's hands to Mother's face in disbelief. A board game? An inexpensive and not even new-to-this-decade board game? A board game that Jarred would ultimately have to share with others in order to enjoy. My stomach curdled with disappointment for Jarred. My face flushed red, with embarrassment for Jarred and anger toward Mother, as Mark reached over Jarred's shoulder, pulled the ice skates from his lap, and proceeded to try them on. Of course, they fit. They were intended for him all along.

Tears welled up in Jarred's eyes. I offered him a sympathetic look and a shrug of my shoulders, understanding the importance of supporting my brother but knowing that my getting involved would make the situation and the remainder of Christmas that much worse.

My eyes met Jamie's before his gaze dropped back to the half-opened box in his hands. Pushing the toy military set aside with a shove, Jamie glared at Mother for a full minute before he stood and left the room.

It was Daniel who didn't hesitate to intervene. At six years old, he understood the hurt that Jarred was feeling. Daniel scooted his precious microscope toward Jarred's knees and sat down beside him. He put his arm around Jarred's shoulders and said, "It's okay, Jarred, we can share mine."

Daniel's thoughtfulness helped Jarred recover from his disappointment. He wiped a tear from his eye as he bent to examine the microscope. I recognized, though, that Jarred was covering his emotions, and I am certain the memory of that horrid Christmas still haunts him today. He knew, as we all did, that to cause a scene would only make things worse for everyone.

I decide to keep the photograph with me, if only to remember the tenderness that Daniel embodies, despite the challenges he faces. I retrieve the diary from the bottom of my bag and tuck the Christmas photograph into its pages.

CHAPTER 26

MAY 1961
Ferngrove, Washington

John

I help Mother, as she prefers that I call her, slip her paper-thin, turquoise overcoat onto her shoulders. I question the purpose of such a costly jacket and shake my head at the money wasted. The jacket is certainly not sturdy enough to provide any protection from the wind or rain, not that today appears to be offering either of the two. Glancing briefly at its hem as I smooth out the coat's collar, I notice that the brightly colored shift dress underneath the coat is significantly shorter than the jacket itself, with the dress ending several inches above Mother's knees. Raising an eyebrow, I catch myself and quickly turn away from her, removing the car keys from the hook, not wanting to call attention to what I deem inappropriate attire for our weekly shopping trip.

With Bernice's latest designer purse slung over her shoulder —another extravagant purchase that could mean the inability to put meat on the table this week—we step out onto the tiny makeshift porch, the one I intended to expand several years ago. Calla is walking up the driveway, returning from a morning spent with friends at the library, as they prepare the final touches on their group history project. Her eyes sparkle and her smile is bright. I can't help but smile back at her, my instinctive response as she invokes the memory of my Vi.

Seeing Calla approach, Bernice is at the ready with her silver tongue. She strikes out at Calla with words barely hidden from my vantage point but delivered faster than I can usher Bernice toward the car. "Just what do you have all over your face?" Bernice chides, stepping in front of me and placing her hands on her hips, blocking Calla's path to the front door.

Calla, having almost reached the steps, stops mid-stride before taking a wary step back. "I am fourteen years old. I am old enough to wear lipstick now." Her voice conveys determination, but her body language deceives her. She cowers slightly, clearly uncertain of how to proceed.

"I think you look lovely." A smile touches my lips at the reincarnation of Violet's image.

"Lovely?" Bernice looks down at Calla. "If lovely is equal to looking like a tramp."

Imperceptible to most, I see Calla flinch at Bernice's mean-spirited comment. Bowing my head, I shake it lightly before I push past Bernice, descend the steps, and give Calla's arm a quick squeeze on my way to the car.

Bernice's muffled words are clear enough to reach my ears, despite her halfhearted effort to hide them. "Your father may let you get away with this kind of behavior, but as long as you live under my roof, you will march yourself right inside and wash that stuff off your face. Do you understand me?"

Bernice takes several steps toward the car before pivoting on her heel and addressing Calla once more. "The kitchen needs a good scrubbing, there is a pile of laundry waiting for you in the hallway, and oh, Jamie pooped in the bathtub again."

Bernice continues toward the passenger door that I've pushed open from the driver's seat. As if an afterthought, she looks over her shoulder once more, talking to Calla's turned back. "We'll be home by dinnertime, so be sure to get that sorted out too." Bernice folds herself into the car, slamming the door with intent before twisting in her seat to deliver me a steely look that says more than I ever wanted to know.

We drive for several minutes in silence. I've learned through the years that silence isn't always the blessed occurrence one would think. Still, it is often my preferred manner in which to navigate a day and is certainly better than being assaulted by the vile spewing from Bernice's blackened heart. So I succumb to the silence, pay attention to the road, and do my best to ignore the fuming from the passenger seat.

Our weekly outing to the grocery store has effectively replaced any other marital excursions. We seldom go out to dine with friends. In truth, we don't have much in the way of friendships. Our home is neither large enough nor kept up well enough to welcome guests for an evening of cocktails and conversation. We've lived in Ferngrove for three years now and have settled into a routine all our own. I wouldn't call it a pleasant routine, but it is a routine nonetheless.

Monday through Friday, I work with a framing company. The days begin at the crack of dawn and end just before dinner is to be placed on the table. The company hired me after a crew spent some time alongside me while we framed my very own house a few years back. Weekday nights, I eat whatever is put in front of me, more eagerly if Calla has prepared the meal. Then I head out to the carport and spend the next several hours under the light of a single bulb, crafting wooden furniture. The seasons change and the years pass by, but my existence in this life remains, though less than favorable, fairly consistent.

Saturday night is the only time the routine changes. Upon completion of our Saturday afternoon grocery shop and errands, I spend a few hours working in the carport on the custom pieces currently in progress. I finish a little earlier in the evening and shower off the sawdust before settling in for the night. Saturday is the only day of the week I indulge in a drink or two, though by the increasing need to replace the rum bottles, I suspect this is not true of Bernice. With a rum and cola in hand, we retire to our recliners, Christmas gifts to each other last holiday season, and enjoy an evening of television viewing.

The evening always begins with *Perry Mason*. Following the plot of the legal drama requires our full attention, eliminating the need to fill the otherwise dead air of the living room with chatter. The interlude between programs offers me time to refill our glasses before watching the *NBC Saturday night movie*. If the movie is dull or is of no interest to me, I allow myself to doze in my reclined position. Either way, Saturday night protocol dictates that neither Bernice nor I have the obligation to speak to each other, save for the occasional comment or request.

As we pull into the grocery store parking lot, not a word shared between us on the drive, I am eagerly anticipating our Saturday evening rituals, if only for the acceptable silence between us. I glance at Bernice's stone-cold face as she stares motionless out the front window of the car. "Have your list, Mother?"

Her head snaps back, while her eyes rake their contempt over me. "Of course I have the list. It would be a waste of a trip if I hadn't brought a list with me, now wouldn't it?"

All I can do is offer her a gentle smile. No words will fix her mood, a tact I have tried with gargantuan failure countless times before. "All set, then." I step out from the car and wait for her to join me so we can enter the store together. Bernice takes her time, leaving me to stand with a patience I've become accustomed to, before she opens her door and joins me by the trunk of the car.

By the time we return home with a trunk full of groceries, Bernice's mood has thawed, perhaps due to my lack of response as she added unnecessary items not on our list to the cart. The bags of potato chips, licorice sweets, and frozen TV dinners pushed past the upper reaches of the weekly budget. Even so, I remained quiet and conceded silently in my mind that at the very least Swanson was sure to know how to cook a turkey dinner properly.

I unload the grocery bags to the kitchen counter while Bernice, without a word, brushes past me, retreating to the only bathroom in the house. The water filling the tub can be heard through the pipes hidden within the walls. After several minutes, the water stops and the house becomes silent once again. Calla, face wiped clean, joins me in the kitchen and without being asked, begins removing the purchased goods from their brown paper bags. Her eyes widen in response to the stack of TV dinners before she shrugs and sets about making room in the freezer without a comment.

With groceries put away and brown paper bags folded neatly in the cupboard under the sink, I am about to change clothes and retreat to the carport for what is left of the afternoon when I pause to deliver my own thoughts about the lipstick. Given the privacy Bernice's afternoon bath has allowed us, I touch Calla's arm. "I want you to know that I think you are beautiful. With or without lipstick." I tilt my head to one side and search her eyes, pleading with her to believe me. "I am sorry for Mother." My words end there. There are so many things I want to explain to her, yet the knowledge of them would only make life more difficult for her. Instead I repeat, "I am sorry for Mother."

Calla's eyes rim with tears as her mouth contorts in an effort to hold her emotions at bay. She swipes at her cheek as a rogue tear escapes, before dropping her chin to her chest. I draw her into a long-overdue embrace as her tears flow freely. I am reminded once again of how I've let my children down, and though I am needed here where I stand, my desire to run as fast and as far as I can ignites within me.

CHAPTER 27

MARCH 7, 1964
Ferngrove, Washington

Calla

"Jamie Jesus, don't do that." Mother's shriek echoes down the hallway, filling my room beyond its closed door with her latest rant.

I wait for the skirmish somewhere beyond the walls of the hallway to subside. *Jamie Jesus,* I think, stifling an uprising of irritation. Not that it isn't a suitable nickname, given Jamie's heavenly status in the hierarchy of our family, where he sits at Mark's right side. But still, the nickname makes me cringe. The thought of other people, neighbors, or even Mother's friend Miriam learning of such a nickname embarrasses me further. Jamie's nickname was born out of Mother's constant repetition while scolding him, as well as her sadistic sense of humor.

"Jamie Jesus" are Mother's favorite words to start any sentence pretending to admonish her middle and, certainly in her eyes, nearly perfect son.

Jamie's devilish behavior took hold early in his life. He came home from the hospital ripe with piss and vinegar, never feeling the need to conform to other people's expectations. School brought frequent scuffles and even more frequent notes from the principal's office. If there was any sort of trouble brewing on the playground, Jamie was sure to be somewhere in the middle of it.

As a toddler, his misguided belief that he knew right from wrong made him an easy target for Mother's words. Those words often began with "Jamie, Jesus, don't do that." The words, though, were often the end of Mother's parenting. With no further action to correct Jamie's behavior, he grew up believing his daily antics and disruptions were funny and entertaining.

It is easy to think of my brothers in a gentle light when I consider the ways in which survival has molded and shaped them. Though Mother does favor her own sons, none of us in this house are unscathed by her reckless and violent nature. We each do what we must to get through the day.

Everyone, that is, except Daniel. He remains sweet, gentle, and kind despite our volatile home life. I can only imagine how out of place he feels here with us, like an angel forced to walk among the rubbles of humanity. He seldom argues. Daniel is quick to do what is asked of him. And no matter who is hurting, he gravitates toward them and offers comfort. He is one of the most forgiving people I know. I will miss him dearly.

I realize there is little I can do to protect the others. Mother has made certain that each of us stands alone when we face her. A good strategy, I suppose, as it is surely much easier for her to rule when dealing with one child at a time. She was clever, too, in pitting us against one another often enough that our jealousy festered.

Daniel seems to avoid that particular trap, which makes me wonder what turns over in his mind behind those big, inquisitive eyes. Quiet and unassuming, I suspect the others haven't yet begun to question how life actually is for him.

I've seen his distance, not glaringly obvious but present all the same. I was walking home from school a few months back when I turned the corner and saw Daniel and a gaggle of boys ahead of me. I slowed my steps so as not to interrupt who I thought were friends walking home from school.

I stopped in my tracks though, a chill running the length of my spine, when one of the boys tossed Daniel's glasses from his face. The other boy pushed his school bag from his shoulder to the wet and muddy ground. My breath caught in my chest before instinct compelled me forward.

The boys, seeing me storming toward them, took off toward whatever hovels they called home. I picked up Daniel's glasses and placed them upon the bridge of his nose. I carried his school bag in my free hand, and together we walked the remainder of the way home. Daniel refused to tell me who the boys were. Instead, he smiled and convinced me with his sincerity that it was all in the name of fun.

But I still question the truth of that situation, and I worry for his safety both at school and at home. He never did cry, never tattled, and news of kids picking on him has yet to reach our parents. His even quieter demeanor is my only cause for concern. My heart sinks as I wonder if Daniel is on the short end of the stick more often than not at school.

Is it worse to be bullied by strangers or by those who are supposed to love and care for you? Until Daniel's interaction with the boys, I hadn't thought much past my own experience. Now I wonder what, if anything, I can do to help him.

I sift through a final drawer, stuffing an extra pair of shoelaces, a recently purchased pair of nylons, and Chapstick into a bag as I consider how best to help Daniel in my absence. I could ask Jarred, being the oldest of the boys, to look out for him. I quickly dismiss the notion though, as the responsibility of asking such a thing of Jarred settles over me. Jarred and myself are not truly of this family, at least through Mother's eyes.

If Jarred were forced to fess up to knowledge of someone other than Mother bothering Daniel, Jarred would be in the line of fire. Mother, so fickle with her anger and the direction it flows, could easily blame, yell at, or threaten Jarred for both withholding and delivering such news. Eventually, I imagine, she would accuse Jarred of not protecting Daniel properly, as a good brother would do. No, I couldn't put Jarred in harm's way like that.

I sit on the edge of my bed, giving the problem a little more consideration. Mark is far too self-absorbed to be aware of anyone else's troubles, least of all quiet little Daniel. I'm not certain Mark would notice if Daniel went up in flames in front of him. No, not Mark.

Jamie is a much better candidate. He notices Daniel's existence, and I would hazard a guess that he cares deeply for him. Despite Jamie's wildness, I sense his longing to be loved and his deep love for others. I would certainly ask him to watch over Daniel, if it weren't for that temper of his—I'm not sure I could trust Jamie to refrain from pummeling a child much smaller than himself if he thought Daniel was in trouble.

I kick myself for not having considered Daniel before now. I was so busy taking care of my own plans that I allowed Daniel's needs to wither beneath my own shadow. Guilt nudges me to think of my brothers. Perhaps my best approach is to check in with Daniel on a regular basis. I could plan to meet him at school once a week before he walks home. We could sit on the swings and talk. I could be an even better big sister without the worry of Mother breathing down my neck. Yes, I think Daniel would like that, and if I am being honest, so will I.

I breathe a sigh of relief at my freshly hatched plan. I stand

and survey the room. As I turn in a circle, my eyes scan the remaining contents, to be left behind. I frown as my eyes fall upon the sewing machine waiting patiently for me in the corner of the bedroom. The reliable machine and my own creativity are responsible for the entire wardrobe crammed into my traveling bags.

Rightfully, the machine belongs to Mother. Despite her not knowing how to sew a single stitch, the machine's home isn't with me. I wouldn't be able to carry it anyhow, I reason with my disappointed self. I will just have to learn to get by and return to mending by hand if need be. A smile tugs at the corner of my mouth as I realize that Mother, too, will have to sort out a new situation for her mending and hemming. She couldn't possibly have thought I would always be here to cook, clean, and sew for her. Another pang of guilt clenches my stomach as I realize that by leaving, I've sentenced the rest of my family to meals barely suitable for farm animals.

With nothing else to tuck into my bags, I sit in front of the desk once more. I am no better prepared to write a letter now than I was a few hours ago, but I know I will have deep regrets if I leave without saying something to Dad.

March 7, 1964

Dear Dad,

I have so much to say to you, and yet the words do not come easily. A lifetime of hurt and unanswered questions lies between us.

· · ·

My mind races back to one year ago. I was about to celebrate my sixteenth birthday and was not to be granted a party. According to Mother, I was too old for parties and cake, though I do wonder if a person can really be too old for cake. Presumably I was unworthy of presents too. When Dad found out there was not a single gift waiting for me at dinner that night, his anger boiled over and landed squarely on Mother's shoulders.

A real argument consisting of two willing combatives was taking place in their shared bedroom. Though the door was closed, not a single word was lost on us kids as we sat in uncomfortable silence around the kitchen table. We poked at the chicken I had roasted and moved the peas around our plates distractedly.

Mother's abrupt departure from the house was no less uncomfortable. She pushed past the kitchen on her way out of the house, delivering daggers in my direction as she went. She was destined, I imagined, for the local pub. The slamming of the front door was her final word on the subject. It was no secret that Mother, and her only friend Miriam, had begun to spend at least one evening a week at the local watering hole.

Though this new habit of Mother's displeased Dad immensely, he'd said little about it after the first argument several weeks before had sent angry voices beyond the confines of our brick home and dishes flying about the kitchen. The dishes, I believe, were the final straw. I had been at the stove that morning, frying eggs for breakfast, when Mother stumbled into the room, still in a stupor from her drunkenness the previous evening. Dad, typically a calm and level-headed man, broached the subject firmly, telling Mother that public drunkenness was not becoming and that she had embarrassed both herself and the family.

Mother argued that he was being ridiculous. She wasn't up to anything. It was just a couple of girls letting off steam, after all. Coffee cup in hand, Dad rose from the table to pour from the pot kept warm atop the coffee maker on the counter. With his cup replenished, Dad turned to Mother and, in a steady and controlled voice, told her that if she ever found herself in that particular state again, she would have to sort out her own ride home.

The escalation was fierce and immediate. Clearly outraged by Dad's comment, Mother grabbed a plate from the stack on the table, set there in preparation for breakfast, and threw it in his direction. The plate sailed across the room toward his head, and Dad ducked out of the way. I cringed, and even though the plate was traveling the opposite direction from me, I covered my head and hunkered down. The plate shattered against the cupboard behind Dad.

His eyes blazed with intense anger, but before I could unfurl myself from my defensive position, the fury in his eyes had already subsided. Without another word raised in disagreement, he looked at me, lifted his eyebrows, and said, "I'm sorry, Calla." He grabbed his jacket, cap, and keys from the hook and walked out the door.

My first worry was one of never seeing him again. Was his "sorry" because he was leaving us? Was he sorry because of his anger or because he restrained himself from unleashing it on Mother? The questions swirled in my head. A few moments later, after the air had settled a fraction, Mother grabbed a cup from the cupboard, poured herself some coffee, and padded back to the bedroom. On her way down the hall she said, "Clean that mess up, will you?" Perhaps, that was what Dad's "sorry" had been for.

My attention was drawn back to my birthday dinner by Daniel's legs wiggling in his chair. I was not the only one, it seemed, who had been disappointed by the lack of a cake. With little eaten and nothing celebrated, I excused the boys from the table and cleaned up the dishes, packing the remaining chicken into a container. I puttered in the kitchen for as long as possible before finally retreating to my empty room.

Mother returned in the wee hours of the morning, her lack of demure a telltale sign she'd had a few drinks too many. I listened as she shuffled down the hallway and past my bedroom, and I let out a sigh of relief at the faint yet familiar sound of their bedroom door squeaking open and then closed.

A soft knock on my door came just as I was descending into what was sure to be a fitful sleep. I turned my head toward the light emanating from the hall and found Dad standing in the open doorway, his hand upon the knob.

"I didn't mean to wake you." He stepped into the room, closing the door all but an inch.

"You didn't." I rolled onto my side and propped my head up with my hand and a bent elbow. "Hard to sleep." I shrugged and I knew he understood.

"I wanted to apologize for tonight." Dad cleared his throat before continuing. "Your birthday should be special." He took a step forward and sat at the foot of my bed. "I am sorry it wasn't." Dad's eyes were sad and full of regret. "I should have made certain more attention was . . . Well, I should have made certain of a lot of things."

I shrugged again, as if none of it mattered, hiding all the places where the evening's events had cut me.

"Is there anything in particular that you wanted for your birthday? I am sorry. I should have asked you this sooner. I thought—well, I thought Mother was taking care of a gift for you. I suppose I should know better by now. I guess I just keep hoping." There was an uncomfortable silence as Dad wrestled with the disappointment laid between us. "Anyway."

I slid my body up into a seated position and rested my torso against the wall. "Yes." My resolve was strong, even though my words were shaky. "Tell me about Momma."

Dad ran his fingers through his hair before giving me a

slightly crooked smile. I leaned forward in anticipation, sensing him beginning to open up to me, and then we both heard the creak of their bedroom door. Mother's shadow cast darkness across the thin beam of light that had been penetrating my room. In an instant, Dad's smile turned to a frown. He patted my feet, tucked under the blankets, and he whispered to me as he kissed my head goodnight. "Another time, Calla. Another time."

CHAPTER 28

October 1962
Ferngrove, Washington

John

The news is grim. The stakes are high. President Kennedy has informed the nation that the USSR and America are embroiled in a battle of wills, playing hardball with nuclear missiles situated in Cuba and pointed directly at American soil. I shake my head at the television in disbelief.

"What is this world coming to?" I ask nobody in particular as I stand and switch off the offensive information radiating from the box like the odor of a startled skunk. I step over Jarred, who at thirteen years old appears to have outgrown his torso and sits tangled up on the worn carpeting, a heap of arms and legs.

"Now the rest of the country knows what it's like to be under attack in their own home." Jarred's voice is quiet but firm. His sharp gaze in Bernice's direction does not go unnoticed. Clearly, they have shared words today. I pause and linger between the living room and the kitchen. I glance at Bernice, sitting in her recliner with a cigarette in one hand and glass tumbler in the other. It's only Monday evening, but the quickly disappearing dark liquid in Bernice's glass is evidence of her now-nightly routine.

She is either choosing to ignore Jarred's words or she hasn't heard them, lost in the haze of her inebriated state. Either way, the blessing that she follows Jarred's words with none of her own allows me a bit of relief. Arguing with Bernice is a dangerous game and is one I try to avoid. The situation becomes even more difficult to navigate when she's been drinking, and I am grateful she doesn't respond to Jarred's comment, at least tonight.

I walk into the kitchen, assessing the damage. Stepping over a garbage bag fallen short of its destination, the bin outside, I place my coffee cup on the counter and roll up my sleeves. Calla is working the late shift tonight as a candy striper at the hospital, and Bernice, apparently seeing no alternative to having Calla do the dishes and cook the meals, likely hasn't lifted a finger since Calla returned home from school. Even then, I may be giving Bernice too much credit.

I clear a space on the counter by piling cups and plates together, and I wonder how Bernice can stand to live in such an unkempt home. Wiping the bare counter clean, I place what looks to be a clean dish towel atop its surface and begin to fill the sink with soapy water.

In the beginning, I allowed her the time she needed to adjust. First she was adjusting to the children, then to the pregnancy, and now to her part-time work schedule. I am kidding myself if I think any of it has affected Bernice's ability or desire to keep house.

Jarred isn't wrong. I scrub at a piece of food hardened to the plate's surface. Whether we say it aloud or not, we've all been living in a war zone with Bernice as our commander in chief. The good days are long behind me now. Everything changed, for me at least, the day Bernice let it slip that she had tricked me into marrying her. Before that day, when everything came crashing down around me as Violet's few remaining items were destroyed in the burn barrel, I had been doing my best to keep it together. As little as a pleasant moment between Bernice and myself could carry me through and convince me we could make this life together work. But now, I am not only defeated but exhausted. Any fight I had for us, for this marriage, is gone. It's wasted away as I have worked to restrain my thoughts, words, and actions in an effort to provide a loving home for my family.

The clean dishes pile up, wet and shiny. My melancholy thoughts are becoming more frequent, and they torture me, hanging around my neck more like a noose than I'd prefer to admit. If it weren't for my children, I am not certain I would see much point in continuing to live this life. My life is a lie anyway. I shield the reality from the outside world. My recent mood, though, is less about the threat of nuclear war and more about the phone message I received at work late last week.

While I was out on the job, Edward telephoned, leaving a message for me to call him immediately. I arrived home late for dinner that evening as my eyes moved between the message and the telephone, praying the news was not as dreadful as I envisioned.

Edward picked up on the second ring, and I imagined him, now twenty-one, sitting at the family table, anticipating my call. His voice was husky and masculine, and at first, I thought it was Father who had answered.

"John," he replied, letting out a whoosh of air as he spoke my name after our initial hellos. "It's Father. He has fallen ill."

"How bad is it?" My words were shaky, my voice strangled. I'd conveniently tucked thoughts of my family into a nice, tidy corner of my mind. They were all well and happy there, and this news of Father hit me hard.

"He's at the hospital. Collapsed at work. The doctor is running tests." Edward dispersed the details in a rush, barely finishing one sentence before beginning the next.

The silence on the phone line quickly became difficult to bear as Edward's sigh turned into a sob. "You need to come home, John. Father needs you to come home." The emphasis on *need* was not lost on me and only made my head spin faster. Edward's words, rich with emotion, pierced my heart, and my own tears began to fall.

The moisture returns to the corners of my eyes as I drain the sink's sudsy contents. Regret fills every vacant space in my body, its weight heavy enough to pull me under. I scrub at the kitchen counter with more force than necessary.

The weekend was a painful exercise in managing my raw emotions while dealing with Bernice's frivolous and often hysterical demands. Choosing not to disclose my conversation with Edward, I struggled through the two days, praying for a miracle and wishing Monday would come quickly and bring positive news. I debated the cost of traveling to Cedar Springs, but knowing the mere mention of the trip would elicit an argument with Bernice, I begged off disclosing the situation until Edward could provide an update on Father. I wasn't certain I would be able to maintain my composure during that argument with Bernice.

My telephone call to Cedar Springs this morning afforded me the relief of knowing that Father, after some rest and fluids, is recovering well and plans to return home to convalescence within the week. My mood, however, has not lifted as I hoped it would. Instead, my unease with the status of my life has only amplified. I dry the dishes with a towel and return them to their home within the cupboard.

Before Bernice, life in Cedar Springs revolved around

family, work, church, and fishing. It was a simple life, but that is all I ever desired. The lack of those things in my life became even more apparent with Edward's call. With my father's health in the balance, my current lack of faith glares at me. At first, I struggled to put the words together to pray. Doing so meant apologizing for my time away from God. And that meant I could not be anything but aware of where I am today and how I got here.

I worry my current situation is the result of my own cowardice—the same cowardice that keeps me from admitting to anyone that Bernice manipulated me into this marriage. I am a proud man. Bernice knows this to be true and has used it against me throughout our years together. The shame of being tricked holds me hostage in this relationship. Anytime I've found the gumption to waver outside the lines of Bernice's expectations, she has been all too willing to remind me of two things. One, she could have done much better than me. The cold and heartless insult is her way of making me feel small and unworthy, embedding my own shame even deeper into my belief system. My guilt at never managing to be fully present in this marriage only adds to my despair, keeping any ambition I might have had to leave pressed firmly under Bernice's thumb.

The second thing Bernice reminds me of, to keep me indebted to her, is my inability to let go of the past. Bernice likes to—no, that isn't right—Bernice *needs* to be reassured that my only place in life is beside her. Like a dog with a bone, she refuses to let me be with my memories. Instead, she lashes out when she feels insecure, and whenever she suspects I've been spending too much time thinking about the war or about Violet. She says I'm too much a coward to take my life by the reins and steer it. Perhaps she isn't all that wrong.

I putter around the kitchen, wiping counters and tossing outdated food items from the refrigerator into the sour-smelling garbage bag. By the time the kitchen shines, a plan is hatching in the back of my mind.

Examining my options, I filter through my failed attempts. Reasoning with Bernice is beyond futile. Appealing to her every need has been less than successful too. Making demands is ineffective and generally results in Bernice unleashing her anger on a poor, unsuspecting member of the family.

No, this time I will negotiate with her. I will offer her something she can't refuse, something she wants more than anything else in this world. Something I have been unwilling to give to her or anyone else. Anyone other than Violet, that is. Like selling my soul to the devil, I know I am the one who must be sacrificed. I have made many sacrifices thus far in our marriage, but the ultimate gift she desires is all of me, forever and without worry or question.

Bernice said it herself, that dreadful day I found her in the front yard, before the burn barrel, the damage already done. I hadn't been available to give my love or to receive the love of another woman. I've loved Violet all my life. I've carried her with me every day, even after her death. Her words, her voice, her smile, and those eyes. Oh, those piercing blue eyes. Violet never left. She remains tucked inside my heart, my mind, and my soul every moment of every day. Violet is the reason I've survived thus far. She is the silent yet steady fuel that keeps me going.

Bernice longs for the security of knowing that someone wanted her and only her. She wants to be the sole reason I get up every morning. Unrealistic as the notion is, I've kept that from her by hanging on to Violet's memory through the years, constantly strengthening Violet's presence in our marriage. Bernice knows she never could compete with Violet in life or in death, and that knowledge makes her so very angry with me and with the rest of the world.

Bernice hasn't gotten her happily ever after, and if given the chance, I am certain she would blame me. Bernice sold me a lie that day she told me she was pregnant with my child. But she sold herself a lie too. She convinced herself that I would be enough, that I would make hers a happy life. We both fell for her lies that day. The only difference is she did so knowingly.

With Violet embedded so deeply within me, there was nothing Bernice could have done. In the end, it is exactly as she told me in the beginning—she is a scared little girl, terrified of being abandoned. Only I can give her the assurance of a lifetime. Only I can promise to never leave her, no matter what happens.

CHAPTER 29

MAY 1963
Ferngrove, Washington

John

The spring weather hits my face with the freshness of new beginnings, contradicting my state of mind. Crocuses sprout along the edges of the ditch that lines our street, while the sun warms me, even against the chill of the day. I stride to the back of my recently purchased 1961 Dodge truck to retrieve the chiseling tools I left there last night. I rifle through the toolbox, moving aside items as I search for one in particular.

The warm spring air does little for my disgruntled mood. I mutter under my breath as I search in vain, cursing as my hand touches everything but the chisel I am set on. Last night's events turn over in my mind. If the truck's keys were in my pocket, I'd be tempted to get in and just drive. Away from the frustration. Away from the embarrassment. Away from Bernice. It has been just over seven months since Bernice and I came to a new understanding. An understanding that apparently meant little to her, given her unsightly display last night.

The fateful night President Kennedy announced the impending nuclear attack was the same night I decided life was too short to live this way. I went to Bernice to strike a deal and offer her all of me, my thoughts, my attention, my lifelong commitment to never leave her side. I promised her that I would never again threaten to walk away from our marriage, a habit, I must admit, that I was taking to as time went by and our arguments became increasingly heated.

I promised her that I would let my memories die. Violet would no longer be an uninvited guest within our marriage. I know myself to be an honest, honorable, and trustworthy man. My refusal to give up on our marriage, no matter its state, is a result of my upbringing. I tried to be proud of my decision to remain, though it went against every desire in my body. But in the end, I knew it to be a wise and respectable decision. In the moment that leaving Bernice for good seemed like the best course of action for both myself and our children, I promised myself to her for the rest of her life. It was a promise she couldn't refuse.

Bernice had gushed with the exuberance of a small child as we negotiated the ways in which our life together would change. I promised to spend more attention and time on her, and she promised to allow me more breathing room to enjoy some of the things my life was desperately lacking. Fishing, it turns out, was what I longed for most. I needed the quiet of the water, the connection with nature, and the solitude to examine my life and its trajectory.

I committed to being more present in our family life. In practical terms, this meant cutting back on my hours hiding out in the carport and engaging more in conversation and in disagreements. I conceded that running away from an argument was easier for me then staying to fight. I confided in her my belief that nobody ever wins in a war, gained from firsthand experience during World War II. Bernice had nodded solemnly, understanding why I might feel that way, but she had also explained that she needed me to stay and fight. She needed to know she was worth fighting for and with. In turn, Bernice agreed for me to resume regular communication with Edward, the girls, and my parents, opening a window into Cedar Springs.

We had talked late into the evening, rekindling what we had let slip away. We laughed, cried, and made love like we hadn't done since the first year we met. What started out as a negotiation turned into a connection, a fresh start for our marriage. During the days after, my footsteps felt lighter, an easy smile touched my lips, and Bernice's brown eyes began to shine again when she looked my way.

There were moments of strained tension for sure. Calla's non-birthday comes to mind, along with the issue of Bernice's weekly trips to the local pub. But the problems felt more surmountable with the awareness that we were working together on our challenges. Though I can't be certain, I suspect even the children were happier. Perhaps they were wary still, but overall the mood in our little brick house improved to include more laughter and less anger.

All this, these past several months of progress, now lie facedown in the muck, only making my frustration at the current situation that much more visceral.

Chisel in hand, I slam the toolbox closed and stalk back toward the shelter of the carport. It's shelter not only from the weather, but also from the storms of my fractured life. A question keeps popping up in my mind: *Why?* Why did Bernice go and embarrass herself, embarrass me and the family? I remember the look of horror on ten-year-old Jamie's face as he watched his mother from the living room window. Bernice, in a drunken stupor, narrowly missed the ditch beside the driveway as she skidded her green 1949 Austin into a parked position. Abby, as she calls the car, crashed only last week into two of our garbage bins, crumpling them like tinfoil. Bernice claimed that Calla had been behind the wheel for a driving lesson, but holes appeared in that particular story at the sight of Bernice's condition.

Her public drunkenness was enough to ignite a fury deep within me. It is, however, the sight of her companions exiting the car in a similar inebriated state that gnaws at my soul this morning, like a fresh battle wound festering in the breeze. Miriam, Bernice's only friend and partner in crime, stumbled from the car, tossing a delighted wave in my direction before staggering home. If Miriam had been the only accomplice in Bernice's game, I could have moved past it. Miriam, after all, is a good and kind individual, given the raw end of the stick with a drunk for a husband. After Miriam supported his habits financially for far too many years, all while raising his four kids, he simply vanished from her life and, as far as I can tell, from this town.

In hindsight, perhaps I should have made sure Miriam arrived home safely. She is, after all, the one who assisted Calla when she was sick with tonsillitis, home alone and on the verge of passing out. Miriam is also the angel who recommended Bernice for the job at the hospital. During the winter months when framing was lean work, the extra funds from Bernice's part-time job made the difference between a happy Christmas and a nonexistent one.

After Miriam's wobbly departure from our driveway, my mind was sent reeling when a man several years younger than I stepped out from the car, looking as dazed as he was drunk. Unaware of Jamie's presence at the window and of mine in the darkened driveway, he proceeded to locate my wife, scooping her into an elaborate though clumsy embrace. He smothered her with kisses like some high school teenager until, woken from my shock at the display, I spoke.

My words were far from strong, and I was mortified at appearing to be the weaker male in the scenario. "Bernice?" The question, her name, broke whatever drunken spell had come over the two of them as they groped each other in front of our family home.

Like deer caught in headlights, they swayed, unsure of which way to run. I stepped toward them, intent on dragging my wife inside before showing the man the bottom of my boot. I grabbed Bernice's arm and wrenched her toward me. "Get inside." I shoved her toward the front steps. "Before you cause even more of a scene." I spit the words, fueled by embarrassment.

I lay a steady hand near the edge of the chisel and gently guide it down the side of the cabinet, smoothing the detail with several passes before taking sandpaper to its curve. Things with Bernice had been going better than I anticipated, save for a few hiccups along the way.

I had thought the agreement between us was working. I was attentive to her needs, and I gave her my attention, both in dialogue and in physical affection. In exchange for my promise to never leave her or our marriage, Bernice agreed to loosen the reins and cease controlling everything under our roof.

Though she didn't encourage one, she did permit a short fishing trip with Jarred, Jamie, and Daniel at the end of the summer. Mark, though invited, wrinkled his nose at the offer and declined. I scratch my chin with the back of my hand and examine the cabinet. Calla has been the biggest stumbling block on my way to making peace with my life, at least until last night. No matter how I position the suggestion, Bernice refuses to let go of her jealousy toward Calla. The years, along with Bernice's illogical jealousy, have etched ruts that Bernice, and perhaps Calla too, cannot veer around.

My face flushes hot as I consider the distasteful irony

between Bernice's jealousy of Calla and her own recent actions. I've known Bernice was jealous of Calla from the beginning. Bernice's reaction the first time they met was cool and watchful. It didn't make much sense to me then, not that I understand Bernice's behavior any better today. As a small child, Calla tried to be what Bernice wanted. As time wore on, it became apparent to anyone with eyes that Calla could never measure up to Bernice's expectations—which, I have guessed over the years, are that Calla not be a reminder of Violet. My sigh is heavy and loaded with the guilt of my failure to protect my only daughter.

The door to the house opens with a groan. A sideways glance toward the small porch tells me Bernice, still clad in the clothes she wore out last evening, has finally risen from her hungover state. I exhale a long, slow breath, measuring my anger against my disappointment and finding neither to be comfortable.

"John?" She says it as a question, clearly expecting me to fill in the blanks with what she means to say.

I ignore her presence as best I can and rotate around the cabinet so my back is to her. I am aware of the uncomfortable silence between us, but I decide better of trying to fill it with conversation. Her rebellious and immature actions elicit more embarrassment than loss of loyalty from me. Even though I promised to remain in the marriage completely, with all of me invested, my heart must have been waiting for a reason to disengage. The wiser part of me must have known it was only a matter of time before Bernice burned yet another bridge.

"John?" She calls again. "I'm sorry. I wasn't thinking is all. You know what happens when I feel lonely." She pauses, leaning against the screen door, which mimics her voice as it whines. "I was feeling a little lonely, John."

I turn with an abruptness that startles both of us. "No!" Words build forcefully in my mind, shuffling into place to be unleashed one after another, like a machine gun seeking a warm piece of flesh to pierce. "You don't get to feel sorry for yourself.

Not this time." I shake my fist at her, clenching the chisel. "Do you even know what you've done? Who you've hurt?"

Bernice's silence and downcast eyes do little to encourage empathy from me. She shrugs, but instead of conveying a demureness, the action screams her lack of concern for her actions.

I let the words fall. "Jamie was watching." Bernice's head snaps up, her eyes wild with distrust. She doesn't believe me, doesn't remember the details as clearly as they are emblazoned in my mind. "It's true. He was standing in the window, watching you." I let the realization sink in. "Watching all of it. He was mesmerized and horrified." I search Bernice's face for a crack in her armor. I see her expression falter, and then I pounce. "Imagine what he thinks of his mother now."

I turn back to the cabinet, raising my voice only enough for the words to reach her ears. "I kept your secrets last time. I won't do it again."

CHAPTER 30

MARCH 7, 1964
Ferngrove, Washington

Calla

I've waited for more years than should have been necessary to learn about Momma. I have visions and dreams of her, but I worry that I have confused the desire of a little girl who desperately wanted her momma with the real person she would have been. She couldn't possibly have been as perfect as I've imagined. With Dad offering few details, I've been left to my own fairy-tale version of the momma I lost.

I glance out the window and notice the light moving toward a late afternoon sky. Determined to vacate this house before dark, I plunk myself back in the hard wooden chair and finish the letter to Dad. Teardrops stain the paper a damp, transparent gray as the words tumble out, under the steady weight of the pencil grasped firmly in my hand.

The words are as real as the pain I feel in having to write them. I never had the courage to tell him to his face. I feared he would crumble into pieces if he heard the truth from my lips. In the end, under the weight of it all, we are both broken. No, we are all broken, every single one of us. Even Mother. Though no amount of brokenness makes Mother's words or actions acceptable. Being broken does not have to coincide with being full of hate. I refuse to let her off the hook she has put herself on. With my imminent departure, I am far less concerned about understanding Mother's ways than with removing myself from her line of fire.

I shake my head as I fold the letter in half and stuff it into the waiting envelope. I stand and take one more look around the room. Terror claws at my neck, insisting I remain precisely where I stand. I am wary of what waits for me on the other side of the bedroom door. The hairs on the back of my neck stand at attention. A trickle of sweat snakes down the length of my spine and I shiver. My anger from this morning a distant memory, I fumble with the letter in my hand, turning it over in my damp palm.

I've talked myself out of leaving a hundred times before. A nervous laugh sneaks past my lips. When I was little, I would pack a bag that held only my dolly, a favorite book, and a container of snack crackers. I would drag Jarred by the hand and, through a tear-stained expression, I would tell Mother we were running away. She always scoffed and waved a hand of dismissal in our direction. Together, Jarred and I would leave through the front door. Typical of a small child who knew to stay within the confines of the yard, I don't recall ever getting any farther than the front steps. I smile at the memory of my juvenile efforts. With any luck, today's departure will be met with the same scoff and dismissal. If only it were that easy.

I take a deep breath and wipe my damp hands on my skirt, before taking a step toward my readied bags. "I've come this far," I tell myself in a firm whisper. "The only thing to do now is go forward." I hook two bags over my right shoulder and slowly open the bedroom door.

The house feels oddly quiet. I sense the eeriness over the nondescript quiet and I tread carefully. I grab a duffle bag in each hand, Dad's letter creasing under the weight of the bag's handle. I shuffle past the bedroom door, only glancing back for a moment. The floor of the hallway is lined with piles of laundry. A satisfied smile creeps across my lips as I realize the piles of dirty clothes and bedding are waiting for me to launder them. *Not today,* I think as I take careful steps toward the kitchen.

Daniel spots me first, sitting on the living room floor, reading one of his favored science magazines. His eyes meet mine and widen beneath his dark-rimmed glasses, giving me away. I hear Mother's voice as she hisses at him. "What are you gawking at?"

Daniel remains silent, dropping his gaze from mine. A single tear spills to his lap. His nine-year-old head nods one time in understanding. I offer a weak smile and return his nod with one of my own. "I love you," I mouth in silence. The glimmer in his eyes tells me he accepts my decision and my love.

"Jesus! What is the matter with you?" The squeak of the recliner righting itself follows the callous words as Mother stands and steadies herself. She takes a few steps closer to Daniel's spot on the floor and follows his gaze into the kitchen. Her hate-filled smirk transitions from annoyance to anger as she takes in the view of my many bags. "Just where the hell do you think you are going?"

Liquor sloshes in her glass tumbler as she gestures toward me. From the unsteadiness in her step, I assume this isn't her first drink of the day. Still garbed in her morning housecoat, with her brunette, cropped curls sticking up in all directions, Mother looks anything but the dictator she is. I am surprised at what I see now. Knowing I never have to step foot in this house again has cleared my vision. All I see is a sad, defeated, mean-spirited, pathetic, drunk of a woman who can't harm me any further.

"I've decided to move out." I jut my chin forward in defiance, not willing to show any sign of weakness.

Mother steps toward me, bracing herself against the threshold between the kitchen and living room. "What makes you think you can just walk out of this house?"

"I am old enough to start my own life." I search for words that will not inflame the situation, while battling the desire to spew obscenities at her. The weight caused by years of abuse lifts from me as I watch her stagger closer. I stare her down. Holding my ground is the only measure she might respect.

Jarred enters the room from the hallway behind me. "What's going on?" His words are wary and tentative, to keep from drawing Mother's attention.

I swivel to face Jarred, my face contorting with the grief of knowing I am leaving him. "I'm moving out." My shoulders slump. The words and the bags feel heavier as I tell him my decision. "I can't do this anymore." A tear trickles down my cheek and follows the curve of my face, descending down my jawline. "I'll come for you. Just as soon as I am able." My eyes plead with him as I whisper my promise.

Jarred snatches a glance over my shoulder at Mother. "You best be going, then." He pauses, taking another quick look. "Before it gets out of control."

By "it" I assume he means Mother, and I smile at the private joke between us. I heave up my bags and prepare to walk past Mother, to the door that is calling my name.

"Not so fast, Mandy. You're not going anywhere." I catch Mother's velvety, maroon arm in my peripheral vision as she raises it, throwing the now-empty tumbler in my direction.

The tumbler sails through the air. A quick duck of my head and a sidestep to the right removes me from danger as the glass implodes against the wall behind me. The sound of shattering glass pierces the air, and my shoulders retreat upwards toward my ears, an all too familiar defensive move.

The glass seems to shatter in slow motion, piece by piece, each fragment its own shimmering star.

The front door closes firmly with a thud, tearing my attention from the wall and the shattering glass. "What is going on?" Dad's voice cuts through the chaos as the last shards of glass tinkle onto the linoleum floor like the final notes of a symphony.

CHAPTER 31

MARCH 7, 1964
Ferngrove, Washington

John

The kitchen holds a familiar silence after the final shards of glass find a resting spot atop the wide, yellow pattern of the linoleum floor. The silence is one of contempt. One of anger. The air reeks of disdain and self-righteousness. Having lived with Bernice for the past thirteen years, I've learned that silence does indeed have a voice. It also has a message. The warning beacons from a hollow place, notifying those in the vicinity of trouble.

I look from Bernice to Calla, assessing the damage that has already occurred. Neither one gives anything away, save for icy stares. I examine the surroundings, looking for clues. Daniel is in the living room, tucked into a corner, hidden partially by the long drapes. Jarred is to Calla's right, hiding behind his sister. Long ago, Calla instilled in Jarred the familiar placement as she endeavored to protect him. If the situation before me weren't so intense, I might manage a small smile. I'm proud of their sibling love and of Calla's instinct to protect Jarred from harm. Though neither of my children should have had to know danger, their bond has served them well.

Calla's torso slumps as one of her bags loses its place atop her shoulder and cascades down to her full hands with a thwack. My eyes search her blue ones, alight with indignation. "Calla, what is going on?" I nod to the bags in her arms. "Where are you going?"

With a shake of her head and a sniff of her nose, she stiffens her posture. "I have decided to move out."

"Move out?" I step toward her. "Calla, you don't have to move out." My head is spinning with this news. "You're still in school. I thought you liked school." I plead with her as I take another careful step forward, trying not to spook the wild beast raging within her slight frame. "Surely, we can talk about this." I reach out my hand to take a bag from her, an offering of sorts. "Why don't we sit down and talk. No need to make a hasty decision, Calla." My voice is soft and soothing, falling effortlessly into the fashion of coaxing a horse into a bridle for the first time.

Calla sniffs and looks sharply over my shoulder at Bernice, and then I understand. Bernice is at the root of this situation. I glance back pointedly at Bernice, my voice hardening with the knowledge that Calla has once again been assaulted by this woman and that the result, building for years now, is her decision to leave our family home. "Maybe you should take the boys and go to town," I tell Bernice. "Pick up a pizza for dinner or something." It's more a directive than a request, and I assume it will be met with acceptance.

"I'm not going anywhere." Bernice pouts and pulls out a kitchen chair, lazily scraping it across the floor. She sits with directed force and folds her arms across her chest in defiance.

"Besides, I've had three drinks, and I know you don't like it when I drive after indulging a little." Bernice's smugness is difficult to miss as a smile plays at the edges of her lips. I marvel at her words. It is barely four o'clock and she is already into her third glass of nightly distraction.

I search Calla's eyes again, trying to find a way in so I can impress upon her how badly I want her to stay. What I see startles me. Calla, now a fully grown young lady, has a fierceness I've never noticed. A sharp edge to her otherwise sweet disposition radiates from within her. Where did this come from? What has Bernice done? Where is my little girl? The one who gave me butterfly kisses and issued soft giggles at the drop of a hat.

My mind reels backward in time, searching for the moment everything disappeared. How could this happen? *More importantly*, I ask myself, *how could I let this happen?* Calla's arms are limp within my hands. There is a distance between us that human touch seems unable to traverse. A minute passes as a lifetime of memories filter through my mind. "Calla, please. Let's talk about this."

Clearing her throat, she shakes her head once, a sure and intended movement. "Talking isn't going to change anything. We've had years to talk. You chose not to."

My head drops to my chest as her words pierce my heart. The truth in them does not lessen the blow. I've been too careful all these years. Tiptoeing around Bernice consumed so much of my energy that little was left for my children. In hindsight, I imagine that was how Bernice wanted it. I've spent Calla's lifetime trying to locate a steady path for this family. Often though, I resorted to disappointing one or all of my children to hold Bernice and her fiery temper at bay.

Calla clears her throat again and, with a fierce expression, tilts her chin toward Bernice. I stand at the ready, bracing myself. Calla looks as if she is about to explain. I steal a glance in

Bernice's direction, imagining that Calla's explanation will most certainly lay bare another of Bernice's transgressions. I am under no illusion that I have not been privy to all of Bernice's misguided interactions. Some Bernice has hidden from me herself, which is no surprise, as she is always looking out for her own self. Others, though, my own children have hidden, I assume as a protective mechanism, an effort to stem the bleeding for themselves and each other.

Calla appears to be finding some enjoyment in outing Bernice. Her words are crisp and laced with a disdain she has likely wished to shower over Bernice on more than one occasion. "Mother has informed me that my time with school is wasted. No need for me to continue when there won't be any college funds available for my education. The boys, it seems, get it all." Calla's eyebrows raise against her forehead. "What was it you said, Mother? Ah, yes. I'll only amount to being someone's lackey." Calla's head nods in a quick up-and-down motion. "Stick with what I'm good at. Right, Mother? That was what you said?"

I hear Jarred's voice behind Calla, a soft but assured whisper. "I'd give mine up for you, Calla. I will if you want it."

Calla shakes her head no. "I can't," she whispers over her shoulder.

Jarred nods, and I realize how wrong I've been to remain silent against Bernice's never-ending list of demands. The more she demanded, the more I retreated. I side-stepped each battle in the hopes of winning the war. I was certain I was acting in the best interest of everyone involved. Bernice was jealous of Calla, so I paid less attention to my daughter. Only, all it got me was a nonexistent relationship with Calla and an unwelcome one with my wife. I see now that I've lost both the battle and the war. *What is that saying?* I think to myself. *The road to hell is paved with good intentions.* From this vantage point, it seems I've had a lifetime of good intentions.

Bernice's words pierce the air. Even with a slight slur, her volume and disdain make the hair on the back of my neck stand up. "See, Mandy, I told you. You aren't going anywhere." Bernice lights a cigarette, blowing the smoke toward the ceiling with an arrogant and insolent look in her eye. "Nowhere at all."

I watch Calla's body visibly deflate at Bernice's words. Out of an instinct to protect, to do what little is left for me to do, I holler back at her. "Her name is Calla!" My hands, clenched into fists, shake with intensity. "That is what you will call her. Do you understand?" Bernice is silent, sucking on her cigarette and avoiding answering my question. She stands, bypassing the ashtray already filled to the brim with discarded, lip-stained nicotine, and crushes the cigarette into a rogue dish on the table. Then she makes her way to the cupboard, where the quickly dwindling number of glass tumblers live.

I pivot toward Bernice and slam the flat of my hand on the kitchen table, the sound spinning her to face me. "Her name is Calla and that is what you will call her." I fix my gaze into Bernice's dark eyes and bore into them with all my might. "Do you understand?"

"John, seriously. I know her name," Bernice whines as she tries to wiggle free of my angry gaze.

"Do you understand?" My hand slams against the table again, hard enough to garner her attention once more.

"Yes," Bernice spits at me with a new level of anger, rising to meet my own.

"'Yes' what?" I am determined to make my point to both Bernice and Calla. I want to show Calla that I am here for her. I am standing up for her. I am prepared to go to battle for her. I can no longer live in my fabricated world. I must be present. I must do what is right for my children before it is too late.

"Yes. I understand, John. Her name is Calla and that is what I will call her." Bernice's mocking tone fosters no belief in the truth of her words, but the words were what I came for and I delivered.

I straighten myself, removing my hand, red and stinging, from the table's wooden surface, and I watch as Bernice retrieves a new tumbler and an entire bottle of whiskey from the cupboard. Taking both with her, she retreats to the living room to lick her wounds.

Tears cascade down Calla's face. Her voice is barely above a whisper. "Do you know why she calls me that?" Calla wipes at her cheek with the back of her hand. "Why she calls me Mandy?"

"Something about it being in a book she read. She said she liked the name so much she wanted to give it to you." My voice sounds haggard, older than my years.

Calla shakes her head. "No. That's not it."

My face must display a puzzled look. I lift my shoulders again, not knowing what Calla is trying to say.

"Mandy is the name of the girl in a book, yes." Calla sobs, a whir of air escaping her lips. "Mandy is the slave."

The breath whooshes out of me, leaving me wobbly. *All those times Bernice was calling my daughter, my beautiful, sweet Calla . . .* I am unable to complete the thought. I gasp for air and my lungs burn, just as my heart burns with a knowledge I will never be free of. My knees buckle and I hit the ground with a thud. Calla's sobs match my own, and together we sit on the floor in a puddle of tears, surrounded by fragments of broken glass, clutching each other in a desperate embrace. Jarred steps from the shadows of the hallway and kneels between us. Together, we grieve for all we've lost and all that will never come to be.

CHAPTER 32

MARCH 7, 1964
Ferngrove, Washington

John

Several minutes pass as the three of us hold on to each other. Each of us is a wayward soldier tossed into the icy chop of the frigid water, desperately clinging to one another like life rafts drifting in a sea of uncertainty. Bernice's mutterings from the other room finally break through, capturing our attention like a warden armed with a billy club. It is not lost on me how, once again, Bernice's ability to cut through our bond is what pulls us apart, forcing each of us to do what we must to survive.

We stand, holding on to one another's hands. I am unwilling to let this moment pass. Calla's bags lay scattered at her feet. Jarred is the first to move. Grabbing the broom from the closet, he sweeps at the shards of glass, averting his red-rimmed eyes and concentrating on the broom's movement. As the glass scratches against the floor, I search Calla's face for any sign that she has decided to stay.

Calla's face, though contorted with far less anger, remains set with determination. I study her eyes and realize I have lost my opportunity. *Too little, too late.* Too much water has flowed under that bridge, and it has swept my daughter from this house. I filter through the depths of my mind, hoping to find a solution to this situation. Surely, there must be a way to convince her to stay.

Before I can find an answer, Calla's voice, quiet yet assured, jolts me from my thoughts. "I should be going." Her four little words crush my heart to pieces. A gasp escapes my lips, and I cannot hide my pained expression or the grief bubbling up inside of me. None of it, though, alters her course of action.

Calla slings two bags onto her left shoulder. Picking up an envelope from the floor, she examines it closely, turning it over in her hands. In a hasty motion, she thrusts the slim envelope into my palm and squeezes her hand closed over mine.

I look at the envelope in my hand as Calla turns with one swift movement, picking up her duffle bags and striding toward the door.

"Hey," Jarred's constricted voice squeaks out. "Be seeing you."

Calla's lips turn upward a fraction, a movement so slight the *Mona Lisa* would be envious. "Be seeing you."

The closing door followed by the thud of the screen door falling against its casing spurs me into action. By the time I step onto the porch, Calla is halfway across the driveway. The sun has lost its warmth as it turns the sky into an inky painting, a sailor's sky of blue, pink, and orange. *Sailor's delight.* I scoff at the notion.

"Calla. Wait. Please don't go. We'll find the money. I want

you to go to college." I jog after her, reaching her side in a few quick strides. "I do." I plead with her. "I want you to go to college. That money was for you, for all of you. Mother doesn't have the right to say otherwise." I catch my breath and search her eyes. "I'll figure it out. Just come back inside. Please."

She smiles, but sadness lingers on her upturned lips. "I have to go, Dad." Calla examines her shoes, the gravel, and finally the horizon before she continues. "Don't you see? It's too late for me. I can't stay here any longer." Her eyes remain set on the road ahead. "I can't live like this anymore. She'll have it out for me even more now." Calla nods her head toward the large picture window of the living room, where Bernice stands, arms folded across her chest, fiery eyes glued on us. Silence hangs in the air between us as I try to find the words that will make her stay.

"I shouldn't have had to live this way, Dad." A small, defeated sigh escapes Calla's lips. "None of us should have." She stiffens her back, adjusting the bags in her hands, as well as her resolve. "I'm going." She sniffs, tears brimming in her eyes again. "It's sorted now."

Thwack! The screen door slams against its casing, demanding both my and Calla's attention. Daniel, wearing only his striped t-shirt, stained with this morning's juice, and a well-worn pair of jeans an inch too short for his steadily growing legs, leaps off the stoop and runs full speed toward us. He brushes past me, pushing his dark-rimmed glasses farther up his nose and heads straight into Calla's middle.

Calla's bags drop to the gravel as Daniel's arms circle her waist. His sobs eliciting a pained expression on her previously determined face. "Don't go, Calla. Please don't go."

Calla strokes Daniel's head with one hand as the other one wraps around his shoulders, squeezing him tight to her body. "I don't want to, Danny Boy, but I have to go." Calla sighs, her resolve to leave, I pray, wavering with Daniel's embrace and her special nickname for him.

Daniel's shoulders heave within Calla's arms as she kisses the top of his head, whispering comforts to him. I watch through glassy eyes, convincing myself that, if anyone can make her stay, it will be sweet, young Daniel.

Calla and Daniel remain locked together as the minutes tick by, Daniel desperate to hold on to his sister, to make her stay, and Calla determined to comfort her sad brother. A shiver runs through me and I see Daniel's unprotected skin prickle with goosebumps.

Calla rubs Daniel's arms to warm him, before reluctantly breaking their connection. Calla bends at the waist, her eyes meeting his. "You'll be all right. Remember what I told you. Look for me after school, okay? I'll be there. I promise."

Daniel nods, wiping his eyes and nose in one messy smear.

I put my hand on her arm, with Daniel sandwiched between us. "There must be something we can do. Please. This—" My hands open wide, gesturing to the space between us. "This can't be the only solution."

Calla's sideways glance is that of a young girl wishing to be mindful of her words to her father while also needing to speak her mind. "Just try to protect the others now." Her voice softens as she inclines her head toward Daniel. "Do that for me. Do that for him."

With nothing more to say, Calla repositions her bags and strides to the end of the driveway, where the road begins.

"Calla." I call out to her one final time, a last-ditch effort to make her stay. She turns right and walks swiftly, with a speed that contradicts the weight of her possessions

My voice does not reach her. Though I speak loud enough for her to hear, it's far too late in her life for my words to penetrate her mind or her heart. My shoulders slouch, succumbing under the weight of my many mistakes. I know Calla is right. There is no longer a place for her within our walls. Though I wish with every ounce of my being that weren't true, I know her life holds more promise away from this family. I hold my head in my hands and allow the tears to flow freely.

Daniel folds himself into my body as it shakes with grief and then anger. I am angry with myself for letting this happen and angry with Bernice for her cruel and unnecessary jabs toward Calla. I've spent far too long standing on the sidelines of my life —of my children's lives.

I wrap an arm around Daniel as I look back over my shoulder and see Bernice, still standing in the window. I watch her with eagle eyes as a small smile creeps over her lips. She turns her back to me and moves away from my line of sight. I wonder what she has to be smug about. But Bernice never truly seems to lose at anything. Having given it plenty of thought over the years, I've noticed that she doesn't really win either. She simply changes her point of view to suit her current situation.

Bernice's smug smile dashes across my mind. "What in the world do you have to be pleased about?" I holler at the now-vacant window, my worry about eavesdropping neighbors far from my immediate concern. "You've driven a child from our home. Who does that?" My question hangs in the air, with nobody there to hear it.

With Daniel at my side, I reluctantly meander toward the house.

Home should be a safe place, I think, *a place of warmth and laughter. Who am I kidding?* A laugh laced with pain and irony sneaks past my lips. I'm not sure Bernice is even capable of living in such a haven, much less fostering one. I pause, removing my arm from Daniel's shoulder. My head finds my hands again, and I press my fingers forcefully into my scalp in an attempt to stop the spinning.

"Dad?" Daniel's tear-filled voice pierces my silent angst. "Did she go because of Mother?"

I squeeze Daniel's shoulder, hugging him tighter to my side.

"Yes, son. She left because of Mother." There is no sugarcoating the reality. Not this time.

Daniel nods, and I am saddened by the awareness that, at nine years old, Daniel has more experience with hostility than I could have imagined at his age. At nine, my biggest worry was whether I would have time to go fishing after my chores were done. I shake my head, a fresh wave of shame rising in my belly.

"Say, Daniel." I pause to look him in the eye. "What would you say about going fishing with me next weekend?" A thought percolates in the corner of my mind. Perhaps I can offer the boys a reprieve from the warzone that is our home life. Perhaps I can show Daniel what it is supposed to mean to be nine years old.

Daniel smiles and nods. What would have normally been an enthusiastic response is muted by the loss of Calla. Still, he agrees to the outing.

Stepping closer to the door, I tell him I have some work to do in the carport, in light of our new weekend plans. "Why don't you find Jarred. Ask him if he, Jamie, and Mark would like to join us this weekend?"

Daniel climbs the steps, before he turns once more to me. "Calla didn't leave because she doesn't love us. She left because she loves us so much. That's what she told me. I just thought you should know." Daniel pulls on the screen door and pushes himself into the house with the clatter and the innocence of a little boy.

Seeking refuge in a lawn chair at the back of the carport, I collapse into the sun-faded-red, woven plastic. I'm exhausted, as if my legs have journeyed far distances, instead of the length of the driveway. Daniel's words pierce my heart, causing an ache that comforts me before stealing any joy that remained out from under me. Only once before have I experienced the ability of words to offer comfort while delivering immense grief. The day Violet left this world, she told me through a smile and tears,

"I've always loved you, John Smith. You were my dream that came true, after all."

Fresh tears brim in my eyes as I consider the similarities between Violet and Calla—both gentle as a summer breeze but strong and fierce when they need to be. I hate to admit it, but I understand Calla's reasoning, even though my heart stubbornly resists accepting her departure.

I wonder if Bernice has considered the details of daily life in a home without Calla as a maid and cook. I presume that was why Bernice was determined to make her to stay, to have "Mandy" at her disposal. I cringe at the knowledge of the meaning behind Bernice's nickname for Calla. I never deemed the name acceptable, but now that I understand its origin, the desire to wretch is overwhelming.

The scene plays over and over in my mind, repeating every detail, every word, every tear. I admonish myself for not asking Calla more important questions. I was so fixated on wanting her to stay, I forgot to ask where she was going or whether she had enough money. How will I get in touch with her now? Is she staying with friends? Will she remain in Ferngrove? The questions pour a thick sense of dread over me. The reality of Calla's disappearance from my life may be more than I can handle.

I reach for the envelope, the one Calla inserted into my hand. The same one I shoved into my jacket pocket before chasing after her down the driveway. I gently tear at the sealed flap, trying not to damage the thin paper.

Tugging the page from the envelope with my thumb and forefinger, I unfold the paper and hold it in both of my shaking hands, as if it were a precious piece of heirloom china. I read the first line and melt into a puddle of despair, uncertain of whether I can withstand reading her words. I wipe my face with the palm of my hand and look into the distance.

Calla's final words echo in the darkening sky. "Protect the

others." Her parting directive told me with heartbreaking honesty that it is too late for us, but that I can take action now. I stuff the letter into my jacket pocket, wipe the tears from my eyes, and walk toward the house, ignited to do what I've never before had the courage to do. "Protect the others."

CHAPTER 33

JULY 1965
Ferngrove, Washington

John

Calla's words are emblazoned across my mind like a scratched record. My thoughts refuse to move forward beyond the scratch, and her instruction plays on repeat, drilling the message into my subconscious with each skip of the needle. "Protect the others."

I stand in the doorway of the bedroom that used to belong to Calla. The space has become more of a dumping ground than I would prefer, but at least the piles of laundry have been relocated from the hallway floor. We can at least close the door to Calla's old room should Miriam pop over.

Scanning the room, even in its haphazard state, I can pick out memories of Calla. I see her little Blue Willow tea set, a Christmas gift from Violet's parents. The two of us used to gather around the living room table for Saturday afternoon tea.

Sitting on the floor cross-legged, she served me tiny cups full of warmed milk, one after another, until the pot was empty and teatime was complete. I smile at the thought of four-year-old Calla, her sweet face delighted by my appreciation of and interest in her tea service.

I am comforted by the knowledge that Calla has remained in Ferngrove. She's close enough to our home five days a week, but she's far enough emotionally to remain out of my reach. Working the nightshift at the hospital as part of the cleaning crew, she is managing to afford for herself, without risking an inadvertent meeting with Bernice during her dayshift hours.

Calla has remained in touch with both Jarred and Daniel since her departure from the family home. More recently she has begun to accept my occasional invitations for a cup of coffee. I try not to press Daniel, but he is always eager to share news about Calla's visits. Once a week, as the dismissal bell rings at the end of Daniel's school day, Calla checks in with her brother. Their time together is short, and the day of her visit changes weekly. I am uncertain whether she changes the day to align with her work schedule or as a safety measure to guard herself from any uninvited family contact. With school out for the summer, I wonder if Calla will continue to seek out Daniel, and if so, where and when?

My desire to see my daughter has never waned, not even for a minute. Today, though, with firm decisions made, the urge to speak with her is stronger. I need to tell her that I am protecting Jarred, just as she asked me to do. Tomorrow I will put my eldest son on a bus back to Cedar Springs. It breaks my heart to know that two of my children, Violet's children, have been forced from their own home because my wife wouldn't accept them as part of her family.

At sixteen years old, Jarred is plenty capable of making the journey and a life on his own. The realization that he shouldn't have to is a tough pill for me to swallow. The fight had been building for the past several months, gaining steam with every family meal, every chore demanded of him. Jarred, gaining in height and confidence, began to challenge Bernice and her constant requirements for him. I kept my head level and told her how boys will test boundaries, how those who push against the family rules grow into strong men. I tried to show her the similarities to her own two eldest boys, the ones who have been pushing limits since they were old enough to talk.

No words of reason could guide her down a path of productive conversation. She's taken to fuming less and firing more hostile insults. She has little patience for others' opinions, especially Jarred's. Instead, she twists every incident into a battle for my attention, insisting that I take her side in arguments with Jarred.

The final straw landed two nights ago. Jarred was obstinate and vocal about the fact that he would not clear and wash the supper dishes for the fifth night in a row while his younger brothers frittered around watching television and playing card games. Since Calla's departure over a year ago, dinner has become much less anticipated and is basically a chore of consumption. This has only added to the growing tension around the table each evening.

Mark and Jamie, eager to vacate the kitchen and the less-than-desirable food in it, are seldom asked to clean up. Jarred, apparently fed up with the status quo, decided enough was enough. He proved that he'd chosen the hill he wanted to die on when he went toe to toe with Bernice that night.

The irony of the situation would have been almost funny if it weren't so dire. From the threshold between the kitchen and living room, Mark and Jamie watched the iconic battle unfold. A few far-from-kind words leapt from Bernice's lips, and I jumped in with a demure, "Mother, you don't need to talk like that." This, however, only fueled the fire within her. She shot me a pointed look before returning her attention to Jarred and his refusal to complete the chores.

Jarred made me proud that night. He kept his argument emotionless and heaped full of sound reasoning. His refusal to accept Bernice's half-baked ideas of what was and wasn't fair infuriated her the most. Thirty minutes of raised voices and Bernice's hurled insults ended abruptly. Jamie, clearly sensing Jarred's frustration and that the situation was not likely to end well, ventured into the kitchen. Jamie put himself in the line of Mother's fire by reaching for a dirty dish on the table.

"Put that down," Bernice demanded, her voice filled with intense anger.

Jamie, avoiding eye contact with his mother, shrugged and turned to place the dish on the counter near the sink. Jamie glanced in Jarred's direction, offering him a knowing and somewhat cocky smile. I held my breath as the room went icily quiet. "If you know what is good for you, boy, you will leave those dishes right where they are." Bernice's words were harsh and threatening. Jamie, however, already used to Mother's threats, must have felt little worry about her barked order. He was on the receiving end of her threats daily, and she never actually acted on them. Follow-through is her biggest downfall when it comes to parenting her own three boys.

Jamie plugged the sink with the stopper, added a squeeze of liquid soap, looked back over his shoulder at Bernice, and turned on the water. All eyes were on Jamie's back as he placed the dish into the sudsy water. All eyes except Bernice's. A faint smile crept onto Jarred's face as Jamie, in a show of brotherly unity, defied his mother's orders. But Jarred's smile contorted into a look of terror as a flash of silver whipped by him.

The small but sharp knife flew through the air toward Jarred, sticking with a thud into the wall behind him, narrowly missing his left ear. Jarred's face flushed red. His fists, balled at his sides, shook as he glared at Bernice. Satisfied with her attention-grabbing stunt, Bernice rose from her seat at the table, shrugged in mock defeat, and said, "Oops, missed." Then she walked from the room, leaving the rest of us with our mouths hanging open, staring at her back as she retreated to the bedroom.

A defining moment was before me. I went to Jarred and spoke in a hurried whisper. "I won't let this happen again. You can't stay here any longer. Do you understand?" A nod was his only response. "I am calling home. I will take care of this. You will be on a bus to Cedar Springs in a matter of days." Jarred gave another nod.

Concerned he might be in shock, I placed my hands on his biceps. "Jarred, do you understand?"

"Yeah, I get it. Keep my head down and my mouth shut until you can ship me off." Jarred's words were fringed with fear as well as hurt.

"It is all I know to do. I won't let her hurt you anymore." I implored him to understand his physical safety was at stake.

"Maybe you should have thought about shipping her off so the rest of us could live in peace." Jarred pushed away from my hands clutching his arms and retreated to the bedroom he shares with Jamie, slamming the door for good measure.

"Sorry, Dad." Jamie's voice was subdued and sincere. "I didn't mean to make it worse."

"I know, son. I know. You were standing up for your brother, and I appreciate the effort." I carried the dirty dishes from the table, and together Jamie and I cleaned up the kitchen.

With the dishes washed and everyone tucked into the quiet, if not safety, of their own rooms, I pulled the telephone cord as far as it would stretch. I positioned myself on the front porch and closed the front door as much as was possible. It's been a long time since I spoke with my family in Cedar Springs. I'd given them nothing but worry and grief, and I had no right to ask a favor of them. My mind flashed back to the knife so close to cutting Jarred's ear, and without hesitation, I dialed the number to my childhood home.

I close the door to Calla's bedroom and sigh as the memories mix with my present dilemma. Mother and Father, of course, had no issue about welcoming Jarred home. Their home was Jarred's home and always had been. I wonder why I didn't think to send Calla first. I was selfish, I suppose. I wanted her close so I would know she was all right. I should have purchased two bus tickets that day and sent them together to a safer, happier life. It's too late now, I know. Calla has moved on in life. Just last month, I met her at the coffee shop before her shift at the hospital. Before we said goodbye, she shyly told me of the young man she was seeing. She smiled, picture-perfect like Violet, when she said Peter's name, and that made me smile too.

Jarred's anger toward me has begun to thaw, a sign that somewhere inside he recognizes my solution as a saving grace. Bernice has holed up in our shared bedroom for the past couple days. If I didn't know she was still in the house, I might think we were a normal family. Except for my choosing to sleep on the sofa each night, life eases a little. The boys and I prepare meals together, do chores, play card games, and enjoy television shows without argument or fuss.

Tonight, the five of us have ventured out for a farewell dinner. I've not spoken with Bernice for two days, and I don't expect the streak to end anytime soon. I have no idea if she is aware that Jarred is moving back to South Dakota. Given her lack of concern for him, I don't consider it important information for her to know. Instead, I watch as my four boys talk, laugh, and share fries and memories as their final night together comes to a close.

I am protecting the others, I remind myself once more as a tear sneaks past my defenses, making its way to my cheek before I can swipe it away. I breathe a sigh of relief, knowing that at least of one my boys will be safe and well.

CHAPTER 34

June 1966
Ferngrove, Washington

Calla

Thank heavens the sun decided to shine, I think as we step out from the arched doorway of the small church. Peter squeezes my hand and smiles, a reassurance of our immense love for each other and a reminder of the promises we made to love, honor, and respect each other in sickness and in health. I am far from familiar with living in a happy, healthy, love-filled home. This, however, is something Peter is determined to show me. We have no secrets between us. He believes in me in every way possible, and that is enough to make me believe in myself. He's wearing a simple, pale-blue tux, complete with a contrasting dark bow tie, and it is impossible not to smile back at him. My life and my future are before me. Happy tears rim my eyes, and I squeeze his hand.

The church bells chime, our cue to descend the steps to the crowd of happy wedding guests. It was a short ceremony, and the guest list is modest, consisting mostly of a few mutual friends and Peter's large family. We duck our heads as rice and well wishes cascade around us. We dash to the waiting 1958 Ford Fairlane convertible, on loan from Peter's oldest brother in celebration of our nuptials.

The car lurches forward and the tin cans tied to its bumper begin to clatter, announcing our wedded bliss all the way through the center of Ferngrove. Our destination is the photography studio across town, and then the reception at the community hall. Our laughter fills the air as we wave to people who are out for their Saturday errands, my short white veil blowing gently in the breeze.

～

John

We waved goodbye from the bottom of the church steps. My little girl is all grown up and married. I swipe a tear from my eye as relief fills my chest. Pure bliss radiated from her smile. Calla is happy. That smile alone gives me hope that, if she hasn't already, she will soon recover from the unsatisfactory life she has lived at Bernice's hands. Perhaps I will sleep a little easier now, knowing Calla is safe.

A neighbor catches my attention and pulls me from my thoughts, as he waves me over to chat with Peter's mother and siblings. I scan the crowd for Bernice and the boys. Not seeing them, I venture over and join the conversation, offering my congratulations to Peter's mother, Evelyn. She is a petite and friendly woman, who raised seven children by herself after her husband perished in an automobile accident. I admire her strength, as I know all too well what it means to live without the one you love.

Today, though, the conversation is light and rich with hope for the happiness of two we hold dear. I notice how Evelyn's daughters and younger son remain at her side, not hovering but holding a presence. I scan the crowd again and wonder where my own family has disappeared to. Strain edges into my consciousness as I think of where Bernice might be. On one hand, she is out of sight and not creating a spectacle on Calla's happy day. On the other hand, I worry Bernice's silence may indicate mischief brewing.

Evelyn is asking me a question. I beg her pardon, lean in, and ask her to repeat herself. We exchange polite conversation about the ceremony, the upcoming reception, and the plans of the two newlyweds. I wonder how much she knows. Has Calla confided in her about our family life? Is this sweet woman aware of Bernice's fiery temper and disdainful actions, past and present? What does she think of me? As a father? As a provider? As a man?

I am considering these questions when I spot Bernice in the distance. She is shamelessly flirting with a young friend of Peter's and has clearly nipped in somewhere for a drink. I feel a flash of disappointment, knowing I will have to cut short my participation in Calla's special day. I excuse myself from the conversation with Evelyn and stride purposefully toward Bernice. I refuse to let her ruin this happy occasion for Calla. Instead, I thank God that Calla asked me to walk her down the aisle. I beg off attending the reception, collect Bernice and the boys, and head home, forsaking any further celebrations with my only daughter.

CHAPTER 35

John

"Jamie Jesus, don't do that."

I cringe. Who gives their child a nickname like Jamie Jesus? I shake my head at the absurdity of the endearment, instinctively glancing toward the neighboring driveways as Bernice's hollers echo like an air-raid siren. The cat wails, disturbed from its place on the stoop by the hastily opened door. I turn my head in time to see the cat sail a few feet from the porch, before landing on all fours. Clearly perturbed by the unwanted attention, he scowls and gives a mean meow to the shadow looming behind him. Then he scurries off to seek refuge in the garden shed.

Jamie narrows the gap between the front porch and the driveway, anger fueling his fast-clipped cadence. The thwack of the slamming door reverberates in the crisp, dark air, rattling the glass in the front windows while giving rise to a shiver from deep within me.

Jamie is moving at full speed, like a freight train with no more track before it. Forcing the tailgate closed with a creak, I step into his path and attempt to slow him. Jamie pushes past me, in a hurry to disappear. "Jamie, what is it?" I ask, already knowing I will not receive a reasonable response.

"What does it matter?" he says in a strangled tone. "Nothing you will do about it anyway."

Jamie stalks down the road, white clouds of breath charging ahead of his every step. His tall frame, cloaked solely in a light jean jacket, disappears before I can suggest otherwise.

The barrage of cupboards colliding with their inner shelves reaches my ears before my foot lands on the first step. *Another delightful dinner,* I think as I tentatively ease myself onto the tiny, square porch.

The doorknob clicks as I open the door. The kitchen, visible from the entrance, is in its usual state of disarray. Surveying the mess, I take stock of the papers scattered on the floor. An open tin is spilling thick tomato soup onto the stove top. I watch with disgust as a dollop of red paste drips down the gap between the counter and the stove. Every cupboard door, either fully open or not quite closed, has recently served as a punching bag.

Bernice, retrieving her favorite scotch glass, slams another cupboard shut, demanding my attention. I hesitate and then hang my cap on the hook near the door before stepping farther into the kitchen, lunch box in hand.

Pouring herself a good helping of burning brown liquid, Bernice announces that dinner is whatever I can find and claim from the refrigerator. Brushing past me, she casts an exasperated look and dryly announces, "We should have just had cats."

I watch her settle in her living room recliner. Daniel takes the silent but directed cue and gathers his books, retreating to the safety of the back bedroom he shares with Mark. He gifts me with a shy smile as he snakes past me, toward the hallway.

Another delightful evening at the Smith house, I think as I survey the counter, looking for a clean spot to place my lunch box. Finding none, I decide better of remaining here, under the fog of Bernice's resentment of her unhappy life. With lunch box in hand, I replace my favorite cap atop my head and quietly exit the house. I don't have to venture far to find a little piece of solitude. The carport, though far from temperate, is the closest thing I have to a safe haven.

I tuck myself into the back of the space, secluded behind a stack of storage boxes, ensuring privacy for a quiet dinner alone. I unfold a worn lawn chair and turn a piece of plywood and two sawhorses into a makeshift table, where I place my half-eaten sandwich and apple, leftover from lunch.

The October sky sends a chill up my back, and I button my faded brown work jacket. Thankful I thought to fill my thermos with the remaining coffee from the pot in the office before it was tossed out for the day, I pour the stale but steaming brew into the lid of my thermos. Settling in to the lawn chair, I unwrap the wax paper and gulp the half sandwich in a few bites.

I think back to the letter concealed in my jacket pocket. Jarred sent the letter to my office address in an effort to avoid interception by Bernice. When I inquired about receiving the occasional personal letter at the company address, Grace, the office secretary, had asked few questions and had instead offered an understanding nod and a kind expression.

More than a year has passed since Jarred left for Cedar Springs. Once the initial sadness of having sent my eldest son to live several states away finally vacated my every thought, I expected to see a shift in life at home. I assumed removing a stressor from the situation would improve daily life, but that assumption has been anything but a reality.

Bernice's temper has yet to wane. Her disgruntled attention

has merely shifted to our other three boys. No one who remains is safe from her tirades. All these years, I have been under the misguided impression that the presence of Calla and Jarred, Violet's children, was at the root of Bernice's attacks. But during recent months, as the dust of Jarred's departure settled, I have been more than a little surprised to discover the volatile nature of our home life unchanged.

I bite into the apple and wipe its juice from my chin as I sneak a look through the sliver of a view from my hideaway. I look past my truck, to the road beyond it. Worry creeps into the edges of my mind as I think of thirteen-year-old Jamie walking in the darkness, fueled by anger. He's too young to be left to his own devices yet too old to be forced to sit there and take whatever Bernice is dishing out. My concern over the trouble he might find or the friends capable of leading him astray runs through my mind.

Mark, due to his year of seniority over Jamie or perhaps his careful navigation of his mother's moods, somehow avoids receiving Bernice's spirit-crushing directives. Seldom do I know where Mark is or what he's up to, while Jamie seems to live under a microscope. I decide that no matter how much the winter weather chills me, or how late the hour becomes, I will sit right here and wait for Jamie to return home. That is the very least I can offer my wayward son.

I pass the time by rereading Jarred's letter. Happy tears prick my eyes as I imagine him fishing this spring with the new pole I've planned for his Christmas gift. He is set on visiting the same river that brought me so much comfort as a young boy. In preparation for the upcoming holidays, I have managed to sneak a small stipend from the family finances over the past few months, sending it to Father for the purchase of a coveted fishing pole for Jarred to open on Christmas morning. Jarred has settled in at the high school and has taken a part-time job at the local hardware supply store in an effort to ease the expenses for my parents. He is an almost grown young man, after all, with a continuously hungry, growing body.

Tucking the letter back into the safety of my pocket, I breathe a sigh of relief. Jarred is doing well. He is safe and happy in Cedar Springs. With things less than settled here at home, it is time to focus my attention on Jamie. Sending him away will be difficult to sell Bernice, I know. Part of me believes she enjoys having a capable sparring partner in Jamie. He is certainly able to engage her in her favored sport of insult tossing. She isn't likely to give up her baby. Despite him being the middle child, Jamie is the one with the longest leash, though I am certain Jamie himself does not feel this is the case.

The hours pass and I nod off, huddled in the lawn chair with my arms wrapped tightly about my torso. The gravel crunching underfoot stirs me from my light slumber. I take another peek through the narrow opening between boxes, and Jamie's shadow appears. I wait in silence as he crosses the drive and climbs the porch steps two at a time. The screen door groans when he tugs on the handle, and within seconds, he is within the comfort—if not safety—of home.

I bide my time, waiting for kitchen lights to go out, not wanting to startle him but determined to ensure a full night of sleep for myself on the sofa with the knowledge that all members of my household are well and accounted for. I slip quietly through the door and settle myself on the sofa with a pillow and blanket. Morning will come soon enough. I yawn and roll onto my side. Perhaps tomorrow will be a better day.

CHAPTER 36

NOVEMBER 1966
Ferngrove, Washington

John

With a long weekend ahead of us, my four-man crew leaves the job site earlier than usual. We return to the construction company's office and warehouse to organize the necessary supplies for Monday's project in an effort to get a head start after the short workweek.

I am not impressed by an extra day away from the job. With shorter, colder days on the horizon, I'd prefer to work straight through so moving on to another project is a possibility. We could use another few paychecks before winter shuts down production. My sullenness is noticeable, even to myself, and I can't help but acknowledge the Veterans Day holiday is partly to blame.

I keep to myself as we pile lumber to the side of the loading shelter, not wishing to dampen the mood of the other men as they chatter about their weekend plans.

November the eleventh is bittersweet for me. Each year, it brings unresolved feelings about those we've lost. Guilt of having survived invades my every pore. The distasteful reality covers me and feels thick enough to be washed off in a hot shower. But no shower is ever enough. The guilt oozes out of me the minute I step out of the cleansing water. It is the cost of having survived, heavier each day as November eleventh draws nearer.

My mind shifts to a memory of Idaho, a young farm boy nicknamed for the state of his origin. He soon became my left-hand man, after we were tossed together in a reorganized platoon consisting of those men who had made it past the beach. He was always the guy to my left, until one day, he wasn't. My head bows instinctively, and I habitually tip my cap in his memory. We navigated through France, listening to Idaho telling stories in the quiet moments. He was tough as nails and funnier than any comedian I've heard since. He had a view of the world that was part make-believe and part reality, with a handful of pure farm boy bullshit thrown in. Anyone listening had to question the truth and reasoning of his stories. A poet in his own right, Idaho was gifted as all get-out when it came to weaving a tale.

The screaming siren pulls me from my memory with a jolt. I look out the large opening of the loading bay just in time to see the lights of the sheriff's car rocket past. Moments later, another police car with lights and sirens ablaze whips past, followed by an ambulance. We all lean toward the open air, trying to see which way the car is headed.

With the excitement over, we recount the stack of lumber and double-check the list of supplies for any missed items. The boys and I are shooting the breeze, talking about the timeline for pushing through and finishing our current project before moving on to a last-minute work order. A local lawyer, or rather his wife, wants an addition built on to their home to accommodate a growing list of guests for their New Year's party. The timeline is tight, but the money is good. The lawyer is willing to pay a higher rate to ensure his wife is happy.

"John!" Grace, the office secretary and keeper of all incoming correspondence from Jarred, stands in the doorway between the loading bay and the office. "Something's happened, John." A distraught expression registers across Grace's young face as she struggles to hold her emotions in check. Her voice is shaking, stammering, drawing me closer to hear her words.

"Grace. What is it?" I touch her elbow in an offer of support as her body sways with the weight of her intended message.

"I'm so sorry." Tears erupt from her eyes like a garden hose full of holes. "Oh, John. I am so sorry."

"Slow down, Grace. Deep breaths. What is it you are sorry about?" I speak in as soothing a voice as I can muster, and I search her eyes for further details. The members of my crew gather behind me, silenced by Grace's presence.

"It's Daniel." Grace blurts my youngest son's name with a burst of forced breath, washing me with the scent of peppermint from a recently consumed mint.

My blood turns cold, and dread infiltrates my body. "What about Daniel?" The words leave my mouth before I can think to hold them back.

"The sirens." Grace points with a shaky hand to the open air beyond the loading bay. "They are for Daniel."

The words settle upon me for what feels like an eternity, moving in slow motion until they suddenly snap into place with a force that knocks the wind from me. I am spurred to action, pushing past a distraught Grace and into the office building. I reach for the phone, positioned in the right-hand corner of Grace's desk, its handpiece off the cradle, waiting to deliver me dreadful news.

Placing it to my ear, I hear a commotion from the other end. "Hello." My voice is filled with the gravel of uncertainty.

No answer is forthcoming. I listen intently, picking out Bernice's high-pitched sob and the sheriff's commanding voice issuing instructions to, I imagine, other police officers. "Hello!" I yell into the phone.

The phone crackles and the deep and assured voice of the sheriff comes on the line. "John? John, is that you?"

"Yes, it's me. What is going on? Where is Daniel?"

"John. Listen to me, John. I think you better come home right away." The sheriff pauses as Bernice's sob turns into a hysterical wail, one I've never heard before. "John," the sheriff says loudly, his voice penetrating the office beyond the phone's handpiece. "Can somebody drive you home?"

"Yes, yes," I stutter and hang up the phone.

I turn to find the office behind me crowded. Jacob, a tall, lean man who, true to his biblical name, climbs ladders like an acrobat, steps forward. "I'll take you, John. My truck is out front."

I nod, holding my cap in both my hands, and scan the faces of the men I've come to know as reliable, trustworthy, and competent. Though I cannot put into words why, I know my relationship with these men will never be the same.

I nod silently to the men before me as I pass, making my way to the front door. They pat my back, grip my arm with quick squeezes, and part to allow me passage. My steps feel heavy and slow, and I will my feet to move with speed.

The ten-minute drive home is a blur. Jacob stops in the middle of our street, unable to pull into the driveway full of police cars and an ambulance, all their lights whirling. The sheriff meets me where the driveway intersects the road, a dour look upon his face. "John." He offers his hand to shake. "I am sorry to tell you, John. Daniel has passed away."

My legs buckle beneath me and I fall to the cold ground, my

hand still clutching the sheriff's. I shake my head in disbelief. "How? Why? What happened?" The questions spill forth, racing my tears to my lips.

The sheriff bends low, meeting my face with his. "We can't say for sure right now, John, but it looks as if Daniel may have taken his own life."

This new blow knocks me back so hard and so fast that I find myself sitting atop the gravel and dirt of our unpaved driveway.

"We'll have to do an autopsy to be sure, John." The sheriff sighs, the unpleasantness of this part of his job written across his lined face. The sheriff's words are slow and steady as he delivers the details. "The coroner is with him now. Jamie is the one who called us. He already identified Daniel, but since he is a minor . . ." The sheriff pauses. "John, we are going to need you to identify the body."

The horror must show across my face instantly, as the sheriff reaches out his large hand and steadies my shoulder. "Jamie?" My questions seem too unsurmountable to voice, and yet I need to know the answers. "Jamie found him?"

The sheriff nods his head, before averting his eyes toward the front of the house. "We've got them separated for now. Your wife and the boys, that is. She is pretty distraught, talking nonsense and such. The medic has given Bernice a sedative. She is resting in the bedroom. Jamie is in the living room with Mark and one of my men."

My head bobs. "Where is Daniel, then?" Daniel, my sweet, sweet boy. Fresh tears erupt as I think of Daniel, with his kind heart and shy smile. I was so preoccupied with protecting Jamie that I didn't recognize that Daniel was in need of protection too. My next question sends a chill down my spine as it formulates on my lips. "Why? Why did you have to separate Bernice from Mark and Jamie?"

The sheriff helps me to my feet, and we stumble in the direction of the carport, his firm grasp around my shoulders.

"Daniel is in the garden shed." The sheriff appears to evaluate my face upon delivering this news. "There was rope, John."

My head drops to my chest as I prepare myself to see my little boy, knowing the memory of this moment will never fade. We cross the damp grass, taller than it should be this time of year, our pant legs grabbing hold of the moisture as we walk.

Stopping before the half-open shed door, the sheriff turns to me. "The coroner has moved his body already, but still, don't touch anything until my boys can finish up in here. Do you understand, John?"

I nod as the sheriff gives a swift knock to the shed door. The door creaks open, and my mind races back through the years, trying to latch on to a memory. Perhaps the garden shed was a playground for the boys or a clubhouse or— My thoughts are interrupted as the door opens fully and Daniel's lifeless body comes into view.

The sheriff's hand on my back nudges me forward, over the threshold and into the dark shed. "John, this here is . . ."

I hear no further words. My eyes are fixated on Daniel's angelic twelve-year-old face. His jaw is slack, as if he is merely sleeping. The freckles that dot his nose look the same as they did this morning when I tousled his sleepy head and ducked out the door into the early morning darkness. With Calla and Jarred gone, Daniel has been the only one in the house to wake early enough to see me off each morning. We settled into a nice routine of coffee for me and hot cocoa for him. I suspected on more than one occasion that he rose solely for the cocoa, but I was unwilling to tell myself the honest truth on the topic.

I am desperate to reach out and touch his hair when I notice his glasses are missing. "Where are his glasses?"

"Here." The man in the white coat with the clipboard points to an upturned bucket. "They were like that when I arrived."

"He took his glasses off?" I ask nobody but myself as I take note of the other items in the shed. A rope, thick enough to moor a small boat, is tied into a perfect sailor knot on one end. My stomach coils as I remember an afternoon of fishing. The fish had vacated the lake, so to pass the time, I taught Jamie and Daniel to tie a solid knot, like I learned in the army. It was one of my prouder moments, passing down useful information to my boys without resurrecting past anguish. Now, I am overcome with regret.

I bolt from the shed, swinging the door open. Clutching my stomach, I sequester myself in the tall grass behind the shed and heave until nothing but bile remains in my gut.

The sheriff waits patiently as I retch, handing me his own handkerchief when I come up for air. I wipe my mouth with the back of my hand and face him, staggering from grief and the type of exhaustion only made possible by death. I muster up all my strength to say the words he needs to hear. "That's Daniel. That is my little boy." My words waver as grief roars out of me, splitting me in half like I've been struck by lightning, my life forever altered.

CHAPTER 37

November 1966
Ferngrove, Washington

John

Days pass at a snail's pace. There is nowhere to go from the loss of a child. The grief is all-consuming, punctuated only by the ringing doorbell when neighbors bring casseroles and condolences. Our fridge has never looked so appealing, and yet not one of us has an appetite.

Bernice spends her days and nights hidden away in the bedroom, medicated by a prescription issued by our family physician. I dreaded calling home. Summoning Jarred from Cedar Springs for his brother's funeral was as heartbreaking as the call I placed to Calla and Peter's home, informing her of Daniel's passing.

The autopsy report was issued five days after Daniel was discovered, and the report confirmed the cause of death to be suicide. The coroner released Daniel's body, and a funeral date was set. Such details are immense and overwhelming. Part of me will be grateful to have it behind us so we can grieve in peace as a family, providing there is any semblance of a family left intact.

The sheriff never answered my question about why he separated Bernice from the boys on that dreadful day. I imagine he was hoping we would have forgotten in our flurry of grief. The details, however, emerged two days later, as we trudged through sleepless nights and tear-fraught days. Mark brought it to my attention. Rarely the one to speak up about topics not directly pertaining to himself, Mark broke protocol and confided in me. He told me what he witnessed upon arriving home the afternoon Jamie found Daniel's lifeless body hanging from the rafter of the garden shed.

Mark, having visited town after school for a soda with his buddies, arrived home later than usual. He could see the flashing lights from the top of the hill, and when he realized they were in front of our home, he raced down the hill and learned Jamie had found Daniel in the shed.

Mark's eyes were full of tears as he replayed the scene for my benefit. "The police and ambulance were already here when I arrived. Jamie had called them." Mark twisted his hands within one another, nervousness exuding from every inch of him. "Jamie didn't know what to do, so he told the police officer Mother worked at the hospital. I guess someone went there and picked her up, telling her the news along the way." Mark's body rocked back and forth, distress written over every muscle, reminding me that each of us will wear battle wounds from this experience. "When I arrived, Mother was distraught. She was yelling at Jamie." Mark's eyes darted up to meet mine. "You know how she can be. She was out of her mind. She was cussing and crying and carrying on like a wild animal."

Mark paused to catch his breath, or perhaps to consider his next words. "She blamed Jamie, Dad. She hollered loud enough

for anyone within a two-mile radius to hear. She got right up in
Jamie's face. Pointing a finger at him, like she does." Tears slid
down Mark's cheeks and he batted them away. "She said, 'You
call yourself my son. If you had been here, then Daniel would
still be alive. Why weren't you here? Why weren't you here to
stop him, Jamie?' That was when the sheriff came in and took
Mother to another room. Jamie just collapsed to the floor. I
wasn't able to catch him in time. I tried, Dad. I really tried. I'm
worried about him. She had no right to cast blame. She had no
right."

Mark's words stung like a slap across the face, and my head
reeled at the thought of Jamie feeling at fault for his brother's
demise. "It's not Jamie's fault," I say aloud to bear witness to the
truth.

"I know, Dad." Mark's eyes shift between the wall behind me
and the floor. "I'm just not sure Jamie knows that."

Until this moment, I didn't believe my heart could shatter
into any more pieces, but there it goes, crumbling all over again.
And there is little I can do to stop it.

The day of the funeral, we gather as a family. And yet each of us
is a solitary piece of a mismatched jigsaw puzzle, none of us
fitting within the same design. Bernice emerges from the
bedroom, and a sigh of relief leaves my lips. She is, at the very
least, dressed in a charcoal gray dress. Though a tad clingy and
shorter than I'd like to see, the color is suitable for her son's
funeral.

Jarred arrived home yesterday, stashing his small overnight
bag in Jamie's room, a suggestion from me in an attempt to coax
Jamie into a dialogue. Calla has agreed to meet us here at home
this morning so we can travel as a family to the graveside. This
will be the first time Calla has been home since she left over two

and half years ago. If only for the sake of appearances, our family will look put together, save for the empty hole in each of our hearts caused by Daniel's death.

My suit jacket feels tight, almost suffocating, as I step outside to meet the driver from the funeral home. The long sleek car reversed into our driveway ten minutes ago, and the engine is running while the driver waits patiently as we collect ourselves.

Calla parked her car at the top of the driveway, and she steps out as the front door closes behind me. I bypass the funeral home driver and make a beeline to Calla. I don't ask permission, nor do I plan to ask forgiveness. I wrap my arms around her and hold her tightly as she weeps. Dressed in a plain black dress, with a winter overcoat to block the chill, Calla wipes the tears from her eyes before telling me how sorry she is. "I stayed in touch." A small smile escapes her sad expression. "I don't know if you knew. But I made a point of seeing Daniel every week, even after the wedding."

"I did know, and I appreciate you making time to be with him. He missed you so, when you left." I didn't mean it to be an accusation, but Calla's expression indicates she has taken it as one.

The door to the house opens and Jarred, Mark, and Jamie, draped in grief, stumble down the porch steps. Few words are said, but hugs of comfort are forthcoming as the siblings embrace one another. Their loss is different from that of a parent. For the first time, I consider what this might be like for them. Had they known Daniel was unhappy? Did they even talk about such things? I steal glances at my four remaining children and wonder how much they know but do not say.

Bernice exits the house, slamming the door behind her in her haste. I doubt she intended to garner our attention. She would likely prefer to slink away unnoticed. She walks with a false display of assuredness toward the waiting car. "Calla, thank you for coming." Those are the only words she manages before opening the car door and climbing inside to hide behind its darkened windows.

Calla catches my eye with a sideways glance. I am certain she is thinking the same thing I am. Of course she would be here —Daniel was her brother. I temper my frustration with a nod of acknowledgement. At least Bernice did not choose this moment to spew anything more damaging.

I signal the boys to climb into the car, and I position myself between Bernice and the others in an attempt to keep the peace on this already difficult day. In silence, we drive from the house to the funeral home, for a small service. At the end of the aisle, Daniel's casket is dressed with flowers and open for viewing.

We squeeze into the front row, having managed the trek from the wide double doors to the front of the room with hardly a glance at the surroundings. My peripheral vision took in the guests in attendance, overfilling the small space with their grief. In the row immediately behind ours, Peter squeezes Calla's hand as she slides into her seat, and I am thankful for his presence in her life. I offer a nod in Peter's direction, before biting down on the inside of my cheek in a futile effort to remain in the moment. I will myself not to travel back in time, knowing it would only lead to tears.

The service is short, and I am grateful for the reprieve. We are directed to follow Daniel's casket as it rolls down the aisle, flanked by Jarred, Mark, Jamie, Peter, myself, and a neighbor friend from down the road. Daniel is loaded into the back of the very car that transported us here, and I am struck by the notion of our final drive together as a family.

At the graveside, Bernice wipes silent tears from her cheeks as I stand straight as a rod beside her, just as the army taught me. Her arm tucked into my elbow for support is the only physical contact we have shared in weeks, partly due to my choosing the sofa over our shared bed and partly because of her anger over something that is now forgotten.

A preacher I met only a few days ago does his best to help us understand death. He talks about heaven and how all God's children are welcome there, and I pray that he is right, especially in Daniel's case. I think about Violet, about her funeral, and I wonder if she would be waiting for Daniel in heaven. From what I know about my Vi, I am comforted by the knowledge that no matter whose child Daniel is, she will take him under her wing and love him like her own.

The preacher's words, though filled with passion, cannot answer my only two questions. Why did Daniel choose to take his own life, and what could I have done to prevent it? The graveside service passes like the service before it, in a blur of words and tears that barely register in my consciousness. The crowd disperses. I wonder how many weeks, months, or years will pass before time resumes its natural state in our lives.

CHAPTER 38

November 1966
Ferngrove, Washington

John

The procession of cars follows us on the return trip to our home. I step out of the car, offering a hand to Bernice. The boys and Calla follow Bernice up the porch steps and through the front door. I peer over my shoulder at the cars lining our driveway, the roadway, and beyond, and I realize we will have little reprieve within the walls of our home before the throng of funeral-goers let themselves in to offer condolences.

Miriam, Bernice's only friend, and an angel in physical form this week, is blitzing around our kitchen as I walk through the door. I offer her a weak smile as she bustles past, carrying trays of food to be placed atop any space available in the living room. Other than the emergency responders and family members,

Miriam was the first person to arrive at the chaotic scene that day. At the hospital, she took the keys from Bernice's purse and followed behind the police cruiser, driving Bernice's green Austin to where the police, the ambulance, and Daniel's lifeless body were waiting.

Since that day, Miriam has fulfilled a lifetime of chores in a matter of hours. The house sparkles anew under Miriam's spell and elbow grease. Only yesterday, she set about organizing the fridge full of casseroles into appropriate containers before sorting them into tidy stacks in the freezer. Once the fridge had been emptied and cleaned, she moved on to the oven. As the oven cleaner fumed under the heat and chemical spray, Miriam popped into Bernice's car and shopped for groceries suitable for today's company.

Today, Miriam again arrived early, coaxing Bernice to dress and ready herself for the funeral before setting to work on the platters she is now distributing about the house. The furniture has been pushed against the walls to create more standing room, and the television cabinet now sits at an odd angle, with its screen facing a vacant wall and a platter of vegetables instead of bunny ears atop its surface. Either Miriam has the gift of flight or she was the first to leave the graveside, arriving home before the procession to ensure everything was in place.

The doorbell rings and, without intending to, I inhale sharply, bracing myself for what is to come. Miriam answers the door with a pleasant but downturned smile before ushering us into a line with our backs against the living room picture window. I am at the front of the line, with Bernice wavering beside me. Mark is next, followed by Jamie, Jarred, and finally Calla. Whether by design or comfort, Mark and Jarred surround Jamie with a physical and emotional wall of support. Calla, always most comfortable when Jarred is near, stands close to her brother and supports her unsteady body against a recliner located to her right.

Once the first guests arrive, there is a steady stream of people for what feels like hours. I spoke to Daniel's teachers and the school principal. The librarian appreciated Daniel's keen interest in books so much that she spoke for several minutes about what a bright young boy Daniel was. Most of them are strangers to us, but they all admired Daniel and enjoyed his company. After an hour and a half in the receiving line, I've heard many similar stories and perceptions of Daniel, and frustration begins to gnaw at the edges of my mind. If he was such a well-liked, well adjusted, curious, and deeply intelligent individual, then why would he end his own life?

Convinced there are no answers here in this room sucked free of Daniel's joy, I squint my eyes and try to focus on the neighbor before me. As the neighbor steps to the right, offering his condolences to Bernice, a stream of sunshine fills the space between us. *Daniel's sunbeam,* I think. The one he used to lie in, scooching his body as the rays moved across the faded green shag carpeting while he read from one of his many science books.

I smile at the memory, and a glimmer of truth appears in the corner of my mind. There are few children here Daniel's age. I swivel my head around the room, taking in the guests. The absence could be due to a funeral not being suitable for a younger crowd, but I consider the possibility that Daniel, though well-liked by adults, perhaps did not fit in with his peers.

My chin drops to my chest as the gravity of this new awareness settles uncomfortably within me. This was something I could have helped him with. *Why didn't he come to me with his problems? Isn't that what dads are for?*

I am thinking about my own dad and how much I learned from him when my memory opens up and swallows me whole. Daniel did come to me. He came to me every morning before work for cocoa and conversation. The shame I feel for not having noticed my son was seeking my help consumes me, and fresh tears spring forward, out of control.

My head turns toward Calla, who is clinging desperately to her mother-in-law, Evelyn. Calla weeps freely in Evelyn's arms, and I wonder if Calla knew about Daniel. I wonder if she was looking out for him from afar by keeping in touch and meeting him after school. The pain is intense, and I pray for the ground to open up and take me, grief and all, right here in this bloody receiving line as I reach out to shake the hand of yet another stranger.

Bernice fidgets beside me, drawing my attention. I grasp her hand in mine and give it a squeeze. Her red-rimmed eyes meet mine, and I swear I can see the little girl she once was, abandoned and afraid. *Another hurdle to overcome,* I think. I am utterly exhausted, and I am not certain this marriage can handle much more strain. But with my emotions flopping freely about the floor, all I know for sure is that I simply do not have the energy, nor the strength, to walk away.

Someone hands me a cup of tea. The cup sitting atop the saucer rattles in my shaky hand. I decide better of taking a sip and instead place it behind me on the window sill. I am turning away from the window when I notice Bernice's eyes on someone in the crowd. I follow her gaze and see a familiar fellow. Though I can't place him immediately, I am certain we have met before, but I'm too tired to waste precious energy locating him in my memories. Anyway, I do not even recognize a good third of the people currently chatting quietly in my house. I reason that he is probably one of Daniel's teachers, and I greet the next person before me.

With the final person received, we disperse from the line to mingle with the remaining guests. Calla, I notice, makes a beeline for Evelyn and her two daughters. She sits beside them on the sofa, Evelyn's hand placed gently in Calla's. I can't help but bristle at the image. Wanting desperately to be in Calla's life and seeing her find comfort in the company of others is a bitter pill to swallow. I hope to someday remedy that situation.

Jarred, Jamie, and Mark head to the kitchen, taking handfuls of sandwiches and then grabbing their jackets as they leave through the front door. I don't blame them for wanting to escape. Hell, I would leave in an instant if it were acceptable. I peruse the room's options before strolling over and inserting myself into a gathering of men from the framing company. At home and fairly at ease with my crew, I listen in silence as they talk about the weather forecast and a difficult client who has them pulling their hair out. Apparently, the lawyer's wife didn't know exactly what she wanted. Several changes later, the project is delayed, with cooler temperatures arriving fast on our heels.

The afternoon passes slowly, like molasses in wintertime, but I am thankful for my crew. They keep me distracted, if not entertained, with the retelling of stories from the week and a half I've been away from the team. The distraction alone is a good enough reason to return to work next Monday. However, the lack of a paycheck is the other, more pressing reason. The bills don't care that I just buried my youngest son in the hard, cold earth, and I have informed my boss to expect me first thing Monday morning. As it is, I will be paying off the cost of Daniel's funeral long after Christmas has passed. The only silver lining is that my family surely will not miss a celebration this holiday season. Instead of buying gifts, we will set aside money to replace the funds that have been diverted to pay for Daniel's casket and flowers.

The sky beyond the window begins to darken as guests bid their farewells, each goodbye tucked inside another round of condolences. As the house clears out, I poke my head around the room, searching for Bernice. Not finding her, I assume she has retreated to the quiet of the bedroom, too tired to hold herself together any longer. I spot Miriam, who is taking dirty dishes to the kitchen. Calla excuses herself from a conversation and assists Miriam by clearing trays. As she walks by with the remnants of a meat and cheese platter, my stomach grumbles. I reach out to snag a piece of sausage, but Calla dips the tray out of my reach.

"No, Dad. This has been sitting out far too long." She offers me a weak smile. "I'll make you a sandwich, okay?"

"Okay." I run a hand through my hair as my cheeks flush with color. *Calla is making me a sandwich,* I think. *My Calla is going to make me a sandwich.* I feel almost giddy until I turn my head and see the room still askew from the mourners, and I remember. Daniel is gone.

I remove my suit jacket, drape it across the arm of an empty recliner, and roll up my sleeves. All who remain are folks we've known since we moved to Ferngrove. This small group of people are sure to still be in our lives ten years from now. My comfort level increases as I stride to the kitchen in search of glasses and a good stiff drink.

Once aware of my plan, Miriam offers me a tray for the glasses. I pick out two bottles of bourbon that I've stashed in the rear of the cabinet. I was hoping to hide them from Bernice and save them for the holiday season. I carry the bottles to the center of the living room, placing them on the offset coffee table. Miriam follows behind me, carrying the tray of glasses.

I pour a good amount into each tumbler before I realize we should include Bernice. I ask Miriam to fetch her as I continue to pour, speaking with an emotionally fractured voice to all who remain. "Let us drink to Daniel. A boy who deserved to live a long and happy life."

Miriam returns to the living room as I am distributing the glasses. A single shake of her head and I know Bernice will not be making an appearance. I hand Miriam a glass and raise my own. "To Daniel."

"To Daniel." Voices ignite the room in unison as teary eyes and bourbon mix in a futile attempt to ease our pain.

With the toast complete, our last remaining guests leave us be. Goodbyes accompany promises of stopping by next week as they filter through the front door, leaving the house with an even more uncomfortable quiet.

Calla places a ham sandwich before me at the kitchen table before sitting at the table with a cup of hot tea. The boys, having come in from the cold an hour ago, are all crammed into Jamie's bedroom, listening to the radio.

Miriam enters the kitchen and sits down, the bourbon and two glasses in her hand. "John, I didn't want to say anything with everyone here, but . . ."

I pause with my mouth open, primed to take the first bite of food I've had all day. "What is it, Miriam?"

A heavy sigh leaves Miriam's lips, and Calla's eyes fall to the teacup. She is acutely aware of how to disappear and remain in plain sight at the same time. "Bernice wasn't in the bedroom."

"What?" I place the sandwich on the plate. "Where is she, then?"

"I don't know. I'm sorry, John, I didn't see her leave. There were so many people mingling about. She must have slipped out unnoticed." Miriam's shoulders sag. She pours two tumblers, each half full of bourbon, and places one before me.

The day feels as if it will never end. My head hangs over the bourbon and the uneaten sandwich as conversations repeat in my mind, looping without ever resolving themselves.

With the announcement of Bernice's disappearance, all the pieces of the puzzle snap into place like a Bayko building set. I remember where I met the man I recognized but couldn't place earlier in the day. I first laid surprised and widened eyes on him over three years ago, at the edge of my very own property. He was the drunken piece of riffraff groping my wife as Jamie watched from the living room window, while I stood four feet in front of them in the driveway. Bernice, having been out on the town, carousing at the local bar, had brought him home, though I've no idea why.

He was younger then, baby-faced and clean-shaven. He

appeared to be several years my junior at the time. The moustache he wore today would be enough to make me question whether he is indeed the same man. The only confirming fact is the way Bernice's eyes followed him around the room this afternoon, like a lioness watching her mate.

My stomach roils at the notion that I've shared my wife with another man for the past several years. I don't imagine a lifetime of showers will remove the stench of Bernice's adultery from my skin.

Calla excuses herself from the table and stays only long enough to visit with Jarred, warning him about the night's potential threat, I presume, though she never said as much. Miriam leaves about nine o'clock, heading home to care for her own family. She squeezes my forearm as we stand on the porch. Her hand is warm, her smile sympathetic. I tell her how lucky her family is to have her, and I thank her again for taking such good care of mine during this difficult time.

I sit in the kitchen alone until the clock above the sink reads just after midnight. Bernice has yet to return, or telephone. My worry subsided hours ago and was replaced by disappointment before finally collapsing into complete loathing of the entire situation. I empty the tumbler of its dark brown contents. The bottle lays empty on its side as I roll it backward and forward across the kitchen table. A defeated sigh escapes my lips, and one final push sends the bottle over the edge of the wooden table, crashing to the ground in a thunderous display of shattering glass.

My hands are holding my throbbing head when I hear the creak of a bedroom door. "Everything is fine, Jamie. I just dropped a bottle is all. Go on back to sleep. There is no need to worry."

The bedroom door closes without a comment, the latch catching and clicking in place. I retrieve the dustpan and broom from the closet and proceed to clean up the glass. I take purposeful, wide sweeps of the entire linoleum surface, ensuring the floor is safe to welcome barefoot boys in the morning.

By one thirty, I settle on the sofa with a blanket and pillow. I turn out the lamp, and assisted by an over-consumption of bourbon, sleep descends over me with little effort and a great deal of speed.

CHAPTER 39

John

Though it's cloudy, the brightness of day is magnified by the living room's picture window. Having forgotten to draw the curtains last night, I am woken by a late and unremarkable sunrise. Thankful for the undisturbed sleep, I wipe the corners of my eyes and stretch my arms over my head before the memory of the past few days slaps me in the face. I am reminded of Daniel, the funeral, and the hole that now resides deep within me.

Wiping fresh tears from my eyes, I stand and make my way to the kitchen. The boys will be up soon, and somewhere, sometime, life will resume. Though it may be much more difficult to navigate. I grab the carton of eggs and the leftover ham in the Tupperware container. I suspect that Daniel's death, like all of the other tragic and unpleasant memories of my life, will be with me forever. Like a heavy cloak that, even in the heat of summer, I cannot shed, I will wear this grief like I have worn the rest, close enough to my heart so it will suffocate all other joy from my life.

With coffee brewing, I heat the cast-iron pan, cracking the eggs one by one onto its sizzling surface. The smell of ham cooking is enough to raise even the most begrudging of young men, and I am soon joined in the kitchen by Mark, Jamie, and Jarred.

"Mark, grab the plates and let's get the table set." My voice is soft, but the request is fulfilled without argument or comment.

"Jarred, there should still be some juice in the fridge."

Jarred locates the juice jug, as well as four glasses, and places them on the table in our usual spots. Nobody dares set a place setting where Daniel sat.

Without my mention, Jamie finds the cutlery and, alongside his brothers, prepares the table for breakfast.

I try to focus on the sizzling pops and cracks as the ham and eggs cook through. But I wonder, if it had just been me and the kids, would we have lived a more stable, less jarring life? Would I have known more about Daniel's struggles and worries? We will never know, and it is too late to change anything. Nothing will bring Daniel back. Nothing at all.

We eat quietly. No one fights over serving sizes or how many eggs someone else has consumed. The house is quiet enough that when the front doorknob turns, all eyes look to one another in a silent but wary exchange.

Bernice enters the kitchen, still in her dress from yesterday. I do my best to strangle the thought, but I am certain she took it off at some point during the night. Her brown, curled hair stands up at odd angles, and the bags under her eyes tell of a less-than-restful night's sleep.

"You are all up early." Bernice drops her purse on the small table beside the door with a light thud.

Jarred is the first to take his plate to the sink, rinsing the bits with a shot of water before retreating to the safety of the bedroom.

Jamie and Mark follow suit, nobody wishing to be in the line of fire. I surprise even myself. Instead of slinging the obscenities and accusations that haunted me late into the night, I rise, pour a cup of coffee, and place it in front of the chair Bernice usually sits in.

"Thank you." Bernice pulls the chair back from the table and sits, cradling the warm cup in her hands.

"There is more ham if you want." I stab the last remaining piece of egg with my fork before pushing the plate to the center of the table.

Bernice nods toward her cup. "Coffee is fine. Thank you."

I glance in her direction as she sips from the steaming mug. Two thank-yous in a matter of minutes. Perhaps this is the way it will be from now on. Cordial, polite, and detached.

"John, I should have called. I'm sorry if you worried. I just needed—"

I stand abruptly and refill my cup from the pot on the counter. "I wasn't worried. But yes, you should have called."

Bernice frowns and nods once. "It won't happen again."

I shrug as if I couldn't care less what she does or doesn't do. Or rather, who she sees or doesn't see. Somehow the air between us is different. Sometime during the night, the words became true. I no longer worry about her. I truly don't care what she does or who she sees. She can no longer hurt me with her lies and philandering. All I have to show for my life is a disengaged daughter, a son I've sent away, and another I can never hold in my arms again. No, nothing Bernice does can hurt me anymore. The damage is already done.

"Jarred's bus leaves at three. I will take the boys with me to say their farewells." I clear my plate and the empty platter. Gulping the remainder of my coffee, I retreat to our previously shared bedroom for a change of clothes before I beg a hot shower to wash my grief away, if only for a few minutes.

CHAPTER 40

MAY 1967
Ferngrove, Washington

John

The winter was difficult. Work slowed at the framing company, leaving me with a few spare days a week. I found myself underfoot in a house not used to my continual presence. All of us felt the weight of Daniel's absence, making each day as gut-wrenching as the one before. We couldn't find the momentum needed to spur us back into life. Jamie was moodier than ever, and Mark was more distant.

I am stacking lumber and supplies for tomorrow's job site. My mind is consumed by a sea of numbers, a reprieve from the ugly thoughts of what I've lost, when Grace calls my name. She calls twice before I look up, fighting the memory of the last phone call I received at work, only six months ago. A mere season has passed, but it feels like a lifetime. The phone call delivering the dreadful news of Daniel's death dances across my mind, and I steel my resolve to face her without tears in my eyes.

"John, it's the school." Grace walks toward me, lowering her voice now that she has my attention. "You can take it out front. I'll give you a moment." Grace places a gentle hand on my arm, the warmth of her friendly smile wrapping me up.

"Thank you." I pull the gloves from my hands and stride toward the office. "Hello." The phone is cradled in my right hand, and I brace against Grace's sturdy desk with my left, just in case.

"Mr. Smith, this is Principal Matthews. George Matthews." He pauses, waiting for recognition. "We met, uh, we met at Daniel's service." He forces the words out in a rush, eager to be rid of them.

"Yes. Sorry, Mr. Matthews." Words fail me at the mention of Daniel. "I'm sorry. It was a difficult day. I'm afraid I don't remember meeting you."

"I understand, Mr. Smith. Please, no apology necessary."

I clear my throat, waiting for the reason for this call. "Is there something I can do for you, Mr. Matthews?"

"Well, Mr. Smith. I wish I were calling with happier news."

My head drops to my chest, a reflex I can't control, and I wait for whatever hammer is to fall. "Yes," I manage.

"Jamie is in my office, you see." Mr. Matthews clears his throat. "I understand how difficult these past several months have been for your family, for Jamie."

"Yes. Thank you." The moisture is evaporating from my lips and I lick them, trying to still my nerves.

"Unfortunately, this time Jamie has been in a fight that has injured another student, and that student's parent is asking about the course of punishment."

"I'm sorry, what?" My fingers brush through my hair, tugging at the ends as I try to clear my mind. "What do you mean by 'this time'? Has this happened before? Is the student badly hurt? What was the fight about?" My mind is reeling, my mouth barely able to keep up.

"Mr. Smith, would it be possible for you to come to my office so we can discuss the matter? I've spoken with your wife previously, but it seems the situation has escalated. I'd like to speak directly with you before we move forward."

"Yes, of course, Mr. Matthews. I am on my way now." I hang up the phone as the principal is finishing his goodbye. His words are lost in the space between my ear and the phone's cradle.

After a brisk departure from work, I arrive at the school's front entrance. The parking lot is almost empty, save for a few cars, one of which must belong to Mr. Matthews himself. I enter through the double doors, the unoiled hinges signaling my arrival in the deserted hall. I follow the signs to the office and am greeted by the stern face of the school's receptionist, who permits me access beyond the door that separates the well-behaved students from the others.

Mr. Matthews greets me as I open the door. His face is no more familiar to me than his name was. He guides me into a cramped room with a desk, two chairs, and the light of the low sun cast through a dirty window.

"Jamie." My voice conveys my surprise at seeing my son, eye swollen and lip cut, occupying the chair farthest from the door.

"Dad, you didn't have to come." Jamie's embarrassment at my presence is palpable.

"Of course I did, son." I tilt his chin with my hand. "Let's take a look at this."

"I'm fine, Dad. I'll be fine." Jamie turns his head away, but I see the sparkle of moist eyes before he can shield them from me.

"Please, Mr. Smith. Have a seat." Mr. Matthews offers me the chair beside Jamie before sitting behind his desk, crowded with files. Folding his hands atop his desk he looks from me to Jamie. "As I was just saying to young Jamie, with this being a serious altercation, the school has no choice but to suspend Jamie for three weeks." Mr. Matthews inclines his head in Jamie's direction. "Of course, Jamie here is worse for wear than the other boys."

"Other boys? As in more than one?" My head swivels between Mr. Matthews' nodding head and Jamie's downcast eyes.

"Yes, three of them to be precise." Mr. Matthews parts his lips as his breath whistles past, a look of contemplation drawn across his face. "Bigger boys, Mr. Smith." He pauses as his eyes meet mine. "Much bigger boys."

I reply with a nod, gaining an inkling of understanding. "Three weeks?" I lean forward in the chair. "Mr. Matthews, can you fill me in here? I feel as if I've walked into the middle of a conversation."

"I suppose, then . . ." Mr. Matthews pauses as Jamie shrinks into his chair. "You and your wife have not had the opportunity to discuss the previous incidents?"

I catch myself, close my mouth that has fallen open, and regain my composure. "No, Mr. Matthews, it seems Mrs. Smith did not feel it necessary to inform me of the other incidents." Embarrassment at being put in this position sneaks in. *She's always playing me as the fool.* "Please, though, do fill me in, Mr. Matthews. Jamie is as much my responsibility as he is my wife's."

I listen as Mr. Matthews outlines several of Jamie's previous incidents, with a number of boys, including the one this afternoon. I learn of Jamie's moody behavior with teachers, his lack of attention to schoolwork, and his general disrespect for the school's rules. I steal occasional glances at Jamie as the principal paints an image of a boy so deeply wounded by grief that he uses violence to cope.

By the end of the meeting, Mr. Matthews has issued the three-week suspension but has assured me that he managed to convince the parents of the other boys involved not to take their concerns any further. I shake the man's hand and thank him for bringing the situation to my attention.

Together, Jamie and I retreat from the weary school into the sunshine of a late May afternoon. Once seated within the privacy of my truck, I lean over and wrap my son in a firm embrace. He is resistant at first, fighting the urge to let his guard down. I persist, determined not to let go until his tears have stopped flowing and his body is purged of the strain he has been carrying.

"Why are you fighting, Jamie? Why do you want to hurt other boys?" The question is heavy, but I need the answer.

Jamie's head snaps up, his eyes still bright with moisture. "I don't want to hurt them, Dad." He picks at his fingernail and sniffles. "I want them to hurt me."

My words don't form as quickly as I would like, and I am left staring at my son, unable to put together a sentence.

"It's my fault. I should have been there." Jamie's words, barely above a whisper, are thick with regret. "I should have been there, with Daniel."

"No, Jamie. It is not your fault. Don't you believe that for one minute. I can't explain why Daniel did what he did, but I know he would never have blamed you." It is my turn to let my emotions run wild, and I don't hide them from Jamie, consumed by a guilt he has no claim to.

"You weren't there. Mother said . . ." Jamie's voice trails off.

"She was wrong. You hear me, Jamie. Mother was wrong to say that to you. She was wrong to think that of you. She was hurting. She had lost her youngest son." A strangled exhale escapes my lips as I search for words to right this wrong. "That doesn't excuse what she said. Mother was wrong, Jamie. Daniel was a smart boy. He did what he needed to do, and nobody, not even you, could have stopped him. Do you hear me?"

These words, I realize now, should have been spoken months ago. *Too late again.* If there is a coward in this family, it is me. I am the one who hasn't fixed the things right in front of my face, staring me down. I am the coward, not Jamie. Certainly not Jarred or Calla. Shame gathers around me, roping me in. I am tired of playing catch-up, and a new kind of storm sparks within me. "We are going to fix this, Jamie. You and I." Determination courses through my veins as I consider the options.

"What do you mean?" Jamie's face is contorted with questions, as well as sorrow.

I look out the truck's window, putting together a plan. "School is out in a matter of weeks. Let's forget about the suspension. Let's just scrap the rest of the school year and get you somewhere for a fresh start."

Jamie nods, but I can see the wheels in his mind turning with worry.

In desperate need of a solution to ease his mind, I ask, "How about Calla and Peter's place? Maybe she would take you in for a while, until you get your legs beneath you. Cook you some of her homemade suppers." I raise my eyebrows, both of us knowing Calla's cooking is much more appealing than any of Bernice's attempts. "I bet you'd be good as new in no time."

Jamie is already shaking his head no. "I don't think that'll work." Jamie's cheeks flush red. "Peter doesn't want me around these days."

"Did something happen?" *Another surprise*, I think, and I brace myself.

"I went to see Calla, to borrow some money for a picture show. A friend with a car drove me there, and while I was asking Calla for money, Peter came home and caught my friend siphoning the gas out of Calla's car."

"I see." I can only imagine the scene, and I cringe with embarrassment for both Jamie and myself.

"Peter told me not to come back. So I'm thinking it'd be too soon to ask if I can live there for a spell." Jamie shrugs, out of embarrassment or disappointment.

"Well, it's not ideal." I thrum my fingers against the steering wheel, my mind whirling. "I'd rather keep you close, but I will call Edward tonight. Perhaps there is room with his family in Minot."

"North Dakota." Jamie's eyes grow wide. "Really, Dad, isn't there another option?"

"It is a fresh start, Jamie. I think that is more important than the place." I drop my chin and meet his eyes. "You would get spend time with your cousins. That could be fun."

"Mother isn't going like this, is she?" Jamie stares me down, a pained expression beneath his furrowed forehead.

I start the truck and prepare to head for home. "Probably not." Ignited by the knowledge of Jamie's dire emotional state, I am less concerned about Bernice's reaction than I am about protecting the others. "I'll deal with Mother. Don't you worry about that."

CHAPTER 41

February 1968
Ferngrove, Washington

Calla

The doorbell startles me. I glance at the clock above the kitchen table. *Barely nine o'clock. I wasn't expecting anyone.* I catch the reflection of my handkerchief-wrapped hair in the hall mirror as I pad toward the front door in my slippers. I unlock the knob but keep the chain in place. Tucking my body behind the wood grain of the door, I peek my head through the gap. "Dad." My voice raises in surprise. "What are you doing here?"

"Hello, Calla." His jacket collar is up, braced against the winter chill. With cap in hand, he gestures to the door. "May I come in?"

"Of course. Sorry." I fumble with the chain, flustered by my appearance and the awareness of what he is sure to know the minute the door opens. "I am surprised to see you is all." I open the door wide and take a step back, allowing him to step into our small entryway. Dad's been on my mind these past few weeks, and though this is an unscheduled visit, I am eager to speak to him frankly.

The room instantly warms as he closes the door behind him, or perhaps the warmth I feel is from my flushed cheeks. I touch my fingers to my face.

"You are glowing." Dad beams at me. "The pregnancy is suiting you, then? Four more months to go?"

I nod. "How did you know?" My question is quiet. I'm not embarrassed, but I'm not full of pride either. I decided not to tell Dad in order to keep Bernice—that is what I call her now, since the title Mother never suited her anyway—as far away from my child as possible.

"Jarred told me. I'm not sure he knew it was a secret." Dad's cheeks blush as his eyes drop sheepishly and take in my round belly.

I wave my arm wide. "Please come in. Can I get you some coffee?" I walk toward the kitchen table, and the cupboard I was in the middle of cleaning, and motion for him to sit at the table.

"Coffee would be great, thank you." Dad pulls out one of four mustard-yellow, vinyl-covered chairs and places his hands on top of the white melamine surface of the table. He examines the table, pushing his palms into it as he studies its construction.

I catch his eye and smile as I add grounds to the coffee maker. "It's not as strong as the one you built, but it works." I fill the pot at the sink before dumping the water into the machine and switching it on.

Dad nods toward where the cream-colored linoleum meets the bank of dark brown kitchen cupboards. "I see you're still sewing."

I lean against the counter's edge. "Still sewing. Only now the focus is on diapers instead of dresses." I search his gray eyes.

Dad shifts in his seat. "Did Jarred tell you he was moving?"

"He did." I pour the brewed coffee into two cups and place a carton of cream in front of Dad. "Montana, this spring. He is taking a promotion. The hardware store is expanding, and they've asked him to manage the new location."

"Yes. That's what he said." A smile lifts the edges of his lips as he stirs his coffee. "The move to Cedar Springs seemed to work out for him in the end."

We are moving into dangerous territory, I think. "Jarred is smart. A move anywhere away from here would have set him on the right path." I blow on my coffee before taking a cautious sip.

"I suppose you are right." Dad stares at the table, lost in his own thoughts, I presume.

I hesitate before asking, unsure whether he will welcome the topic. "You hear much from Jamie?" I stand to busy myself, allowing Dad a small measure of time and space to collect his thoughts. Last I heard, Jamie was still causing trouble. *Poor Uncle Edward,* I think as I move homemade oatmeal raisin cookies from a Tupperware container onto a serving plate. *Trouble has a way of clinging to Jamie like stink on a skunk.*

"Edward called last week." Dad lifts a cookie from the plate and smiles appreciatively. "Thank you. I haven't had home-baked goodies since . . . well, since you left home."

I return his smile. "Edward called last week, you said."

Dad lets out a sigh. "I'm not sure how much longer Jamie will be welcome in Minot. Apparently, he took a school bus for a joyride last weekend. Caused some awful mischief. Edward had to bail him out of jail. There is a court appearance next Tuesday."

"That can't be good." I sip my coffee and rub the baby fluttering beneath my smock.

"No. Not good at all." Dad sighs again, his heart clearly heavy with worry. "I sent Edward some money, for the bail and trouble. Edward seemed to think the court might want to keep him in a home. You know the kind? For troubled youth?"

Delinquent, I think. *The phrase you are looking for is juvenile delinquent.* I keep the thought to myself and temper my words, not wishing to inflict more pain. My own perspective on Jamie shifted a little when Peter caught him and his friend stealing the gasoline out of my car, parked in my own driveway. "And Mark? How is the strong, silent one these days?"

Dad actually lets out a laugh. "Strong and silent. That about sums it up." Dad chews on another cookie, clearly appreciating the treat. "He keeps his head down, stays out of the way. You know."

"All too well," I say before I can hide the words away.

Dad's smile edges into sadness. "I know you do. I know you do, Calla."

I let out an exasperated breath. "I won't be anything like her, you know." My shoulders straighten as defiance rights my posture. "She may have lived in the house I grew up in, but she certainly didn't raise me. I will do everything in my power to be nothing like her."

"I wouldn't expect anything else. You will be a wonderful mother, Calla." Dad, I recognize, is trying to offer me a compliment. But all the same, I stiffen at the word *mother*.

"Well, since we are talking about it, I need to ask you some questions." The nerves gathering in my belly are strong enough to silence me, but knowledge of the baby growing there propels me forward. "First, though, I need to know that you will not tell Bernice about my baby." A protective hand caresses the bump at my middle. When I first learned I was expecting, I promised myself that *she* would never be alone with my child.

Dad nods in agreement. "I can't promise she won't find out some other way. You do live in the same town, after all." Certainty is written across his face. "But I can promise that she will not hear it from me."

"Thank you." I hesitate. "I realize hiding this news puts you in a difficult position, but I do appreciate you keeping it from her."

I lean forward, placing my elbows on the table to steady my hands, already shaking in anticipation of the conversation ahead. I clear my throat. "The doctors, they need to know more about how Momma died." My voice is shaky and raw with emotion, matching my hands. "Since it all happened so close to Jarred's birth, they have concerns."

"What kind of concerns?" Dad's eyes fall to the bump stretching my smock around me. "Is something not right?"

"Everything is fine, as far as they can tell." I offer him a reassuring smile. "But they've asked me for a family history all the same. They want to know what they are up against, just in case."

Dad shakes his head. "I can't. I'm sorry, Calla, but there is nothing to tell."

"That isn't possible, Dad. The doctors must have told you something. Maybe there are records." I am rambling, desperate to find access to this information. I am her daughter; I deserve to know how she died. I look across the table into Dad's moist eyes. "Can't or won't, Dad?" My words aren't intended to challenge him, but I am scared. I need to know, if not for me then for my baby.

"Calla, please. You must understand. I was devastated when she died. Times were different then. The doctors didn't tell me anything." Dad's shoulders slump. The grief he has carried all this time must have grown heavier as years passed. "Only that she had a weak heart."

I search my brain for a memory, a sliver of recollection. Nothing. "A weak heart?" This is the first time I have heard mention of a weak heart. "How?" I try to grasp a piece of understanding. "Why did she have a weak heart?"

I imagine him trudging through the memories, both the good and the bad. All too familiar with grief's power to alter a man, I watch as Dad appears to age right in front of me. "Rheumatic fever. They said it was dormant from the scarlet fever she experienced as a child. They didn't fully understand the damage it had already done."

I think about my own heart. "Healthy and strong," my doctor told me at my first checkup as he removed the stethoscope from my chest.

"She didn't believe it though." Dad's voice cracks as the words push through. "Violet said it herself. She said, 'My heart is so full it's bursting with love is all.'"

The face of a man in love sits across from me. Through blurry eyes, brimming with my own tears, I see the love they shared. The lives lost to the inconvenience of death. No wonder he refused to let it go. Refused to let her go.

CHAPTER 42

Aᴘʀɪʟ 1969
Ferngrove, Washington

John

I pour coffee into my thermos. The morning light has yet to fill the house, but still I feel the change in seasons coming, and I welcome the warmer weather. The longer daylight hours mean more work, less time at home, and financial stability that will have me breathing a little easier for the next several months.

With only Bernice, myself, and Mark remaining in the house, mornings are a mite bit quieter. I coveted silence during earlier years, when the house was filled with the sounds of children chattering and playing. Now the quiet is a stark reminder of where my life has ventured. Neither Bernice nor Mark wake early in the day unless absolutely necessary. I begin each morning alone, in the dark kitchen.

A soft meow draws my attention as one of our two cats, recent additions to the home, purrs and moves between my legs like a slinky. After Jamie left for Minot, Bernice put up a fuss about getting another cat, the former one having died the year before. I resisted, ignoring her pleas. She took care of the previous feline about as well as she took care of her children, and I couldn't fathom how a new cat would be any different.

I walk to the cupboard and scoop kibble into two dishes before rinsing and refilling the water dish. The second cat, having heard the crunchy kernels hit the plastic, scampers toward the kitchen, tail held high before he relaxes into a seated position in front of his little blue dish. I came home from work one night a few months back to discover Bernice had gotten herself two kittens. Older kittens, but kittens all the same. They were brother and sister, she told me, clearly proud of herself, as she nuzzled one of the kittens under her chin. A coworker from the hospital had brought them to Bernice, as her own family had been unable to keep any of the litter and these were the last two in need of a good home. I raised my eyebrows at the mention of a "good home," but one look at those fury little faces and I was sold, knowing full well that I now had two cats to care for.

I grab my cap from the hook by the door. Tucking my lunch box under one arm, I reach for the knob. When I turn back to grab the thermos, I notice Mark has entered the kitchen. "Hey, son. You're up early."

Mark runs his fingers through his thick, dark hair, pushing it away from his forehead. "I was hoping to talk to you."

I am on the verge of telling him I am on my way to work when the dark circles under his eyes become visible in the light shining through the open door. "Something troubling you, Mark?"

"You could say that." Mark shuffles to the counter and pours himself a cup of coffee. It's the first coffee I've seen him pour for himself, and I wonder how much I've missed about the only son still remaining under my roof.

I place my lunch box and thermos on the table beside the door and close the door quietly, not wishing to summon Bernice. Stepping back into the kitchen, I join Mark at the table. "What is it you would like to talk to me about?"

"I've been seeing this girl." Mark stares at his coffee cup.

I wait for a beat, willing him to elaborate sooner rather than later, as I am not keen to be late to the job site. "Okay, you've been seeing this girl. Does this girl have a name?" I try to keep my tone light, not wishing to frighten him off the conversation.

"Lydia. Lydia is her name." Mark's finger traces the rim of the cup distractedly.

"Lydia. Okay, tell me about Lydia, then." I sneak a glance at the clock over the sink, considering how long this painfully slow conversation might take.

"Dad, I screwed up." Mark's eyes meet mine. Tears brim at the edges, dangerously close to spilling over.

"Mark, I promise you we have all screwed up when it comes to girls. You must really like this girl?" I reach out my hand to pat his shoulder.

"No, it's not that. Well, yes I do really like her." Mark's head drops and disappears into the palms of his hands. Tears flow freely as his shoulders heave under the strain he is feeling.

I sit across from him in silence, waiting for his distress to pass. When Mark finally looks up, his eyes are red and puffy, and I realize he has likely been crying for several hours, only having gathered himself to meet me in the kitchen.

I offer a sympathetic look and a nod to encourage him to continue.

"She's pregnant, Dad." Mark's words rush past his lips with an exasperated breath of air.

The words take me by surprise. Worries I had never had

whirl around my head. "But you're only seventeen." I realize too late that the obvious statement may not be exactly what he needs to hear, and I immediately try to cover my shock. "Why don't we start at the beginning. Tell me about how you met Lydia."

Mark hides his anguish long enough to fill in the details, at least the ones that I, as his father, can handle hearing. Lydia, it seems, is the same age as Mark. They attend high school together and currently believe themselves to be in love. I take in the information and ask a few more questions. "Do Lydia's parents know?"

Mark shakes his head. "But she is planning to tell them today. That's why I had to talk to you. I have to figure this out before she tells them. Lydia thinks we should get married. I told her my after-school job won't be able to pay the bills, and she got mad at me. She asked me what she was supposed to do?"

Uncertainty circles my head like blue, fluttery birds above a Saturday-morning cartoon character who's been clubbed over the head. Mark is waiting for words of wisdom. He has come to me with his troubles, and so far all I've done is conjure a rerun of *Tom and Jerry*.

Breathe, I tell myself as I try to steady my emotions. I'm torn between yelling at Mark for not taking proper precautions and turning on myself for the lack of parenting that has created yet another distressing situation within these walls.

"I see." I nod as if I understand completely. My gut, however, is churning wildly in disagreement of this news. I temper my thoughts, knowing very little fuel is needed to send this already fragile boy running from my house. My mind races back to the day Bernice lied to me, telling me she was pregnant with my child. I didn't know it to be a lie then, of course, and the question of whether Mark can trust Lydia does indeed cross my mind. If the situation weren't so potentially life altering for Mark, it might be downright comical.

Though I didn't know then that she'd fabricated the pregnancy, I remember feeling my life tip out of balance at news of the baby. All of a sudden, my choices were ripped out from under me. My modest dreams were scattered in the wind, and life took on a new form. I try desperately to separate my own situation from Mark's, certain that his Lydia is not of Bernice's manipulating caliber. Instead of directing Mark to marry the girl, I decide to approach it from a different angle, one I neglected to consider when I found myself in the same predicament. "What do you want to do, Mark? Do you want to marry Lydia?"

Without either of us having heard her footsteps from the bedroom, Bernice is standing at the threshold between the hallway and the kitchen. Her words, filled with sleep and confusion, ring out like an arrow toward its target. "Married? Mark? Why would Mark be thinking about getting married?" As soon as the words leave Bernice's lips, swiveling both Mark's and my head in her direction, recognition dawns across her face. "Please tell me you didn't knock up some girl? You're too young to get married. You don't even know what that word means." Bernice scoffs as she turns toward the coffee pot at the edge of the counter.

I'm not sure Bernice knows what marriage means. I bite my tongue, an attempt to skirt a nasty exchange. "Nothing has been decided," I say. "Mark and I are just talking things through."

"Christ, John, the boy has gone and gotten himself into a pickle and you're talking it through?" Bernice pours herself some coffee and leans against the counter with her arms folded across her chest, mug resting in her hand at a precarious angle.

Mark's body tenses across the table, already ducking his hands and feet into his shell to shield himself from his mother's cold and callous remarks. "I was just asking Mark what he would like to do?" My voice is taut as I try to convey support for Mark.

"Why don't you ask me what I'd like him to do?" Bernice

shuffles her slippered feet toward the living room, grabbing a package of cigarettes and her trusty lighter from the table as she goes. "I'm too young to be a grandmother, in case either of you were wondering." Stepping into the living room, Bernice, clearly not finished issuing her unwelcome opinion, reiterates her thoughts in terms too simple for either of us to ignore. "Why don't you tell her to do what all good little promiscuous girls should do. Take care of it. Permanently."

The snap of Bernice's lighter is heard over the silence that has deadened the air in the kitchen. I look at Mark and see the hurt in his eyes. "Why don't you go get dressed? Come with me to work today?" I pause, forcing him to lift his eyes to mine. "Or I can drop you off at school. Wherever you need to be today, I will take you there." I lower my voice even further. "I don't think it is a good idea for you to stay here today."

With a quick nod, Mark retreats to his room to dress for school. I have little concern about whether he ends up there or not. My worry about his future and the decision before him trump every other parental instinct.

We leave the house without another word to Bernice and climb into my red pickup truck. Mark asks me to take him to Lydia's house, and I follow his directions across town, to a quiet cul-de-sac located in a newer neighborhood in Ferngrove. The single-story home with a well-manicured lawn and a white picket fence screams upper middle class, only increasing my worry about how Lydia's parents will take the news.

After ensuring that Mark prefers to face the firing squad alone, I bid him good luck and promise him we'll talk tonight after dinner. I watch Mark make his way toward the front door, a puppy with his tail between his legs, and I do something I have fallen out of the habit of doing. I pray. I pray that God will shelter him from the angry judgement of Lydia's fearful parents. I pray that Lydia will see Mark's kindness in making sure she doesn't have to tell her parents alone. With even more fervor, I pray Bernice will never again insinuate that abortion is the solution to this situation. I shake my head in disgust at her unforgivable words—words that have the potential to send yet another one of our children running from our lives, as fast as his legs can carry him.

CHAPTER 43

JANUARY 1970
Ferngrove, Washington

John

I shiver under the thick blanket. My temporary bed, the living room recliner, is less than capable of providing a comfortable sleeping experience. As I pull the blanket tighter toward my chin, a lifetime of images mingle in my mind's eye, creating a picture show of unsettling memories mixed with a few delightful ones. I watch with rapt attention as my life, in jumbled order but entirely vivid, dashes across my mind.

I see Violet on our wedding day, a vision in white, her blue eyes smiling over me, unable to restrain her happiness. Then, without warning, the image transforms to her standing on the Cedar Springs train platform, tears streaming down her face as the train carrying me to war duty rolls away from her. Flames unsettle me as I watch them spew from the burn barrel with a witch-like cackle. Instinct pulls me away from the heat, and my resting body twitches violently. A favorite fishing spot from childhood appears, the stream flowing and splashing as I navigate the rocks and riverbank.

Jarred, tiny and motherless, cries out as a baby, followed by Calla walking away from me as she leaves our home too young. The rocky sea jars me, sending my stomach lurching in response to its swells, and the dark beachhead appears in the slowly rising morning light. I see Bernice's youthful face, her lips painted a deep red. Her eyes, confident for her age, don't shy away from mine. I feel the connection we share, before it vanishes, leaving me in a pit of despair at Daniel's graveside.

Grief consumes me as Jamie's bruised and battered face flashes across my mind. I feel his shame like my own. Mark's downcast eyes brimming with tears make my heart sink to the ground as Bernice's words cut him deep. My mother appears with another warm blanket and hot soup, tending to my fever as a small child. I open my mouth to sip the soup before a sound beyond the room jars me from my slumber.

The sensation of cotton balls in my mouth confirms the consumption of a few too many rum and colas last night. Perhaps the drinks contributed to my choosing to sleep in the recliner and to my vivid walk down memory lane.

My eyes, open barely a sliver, scan the quiet room. Bernice must have stumbled to the bedroom sometime after Guy Lombardo and the Royal Canadians rang in the New Year with "Auld Lang Syne." Nineteen seventy. Where did the time go? Where did my life go?

The rumbling of an exaggerated purr draws my attention before four paws leap into my lap, snuggling into my legs atop the blanket. The cat's warmth calms my unsettled nerves. I open my eyes and see that it is Ruffles, the latest in a long string of four-legged additions. If Bernice had her way, there would be a new creature among us every other day.

Our house has been empty for just shy of a year now. Mark was the last to leave, at seventeen years old. He decided the pressure of being a father was too much. He left last June, immediately after graduation and before his baby girl arrived. I can understand his desire to flee, as it is a desire we share as father and son. The difference between us is that I stayed. Even after all these years, I fight the overwhelming and ever-present urge to flee from any given situation and from my life as a whole, and yet here I remain.

I don't know whether Mark's decision was impacted by the selfishness he inherited from his mother or from his firsthand knowledge that staying doesn't always guarantee a picture-perfect family. All I know is that Mark didn't have it in him to stay. Not for Lydia. Not for his daughter. Even the emotional warnings issued by Lydia's father couldn't convince Mark to do what most folks would consider to be the honorable thing.

Instead, he applied for a job out of town, promising to send Lydia money in exchange for his freedom. The moment his employment was confirmed, he packed his bags and said a hasty farewell at the bus station. Lydia, I heard, was devastated. A young girl left to pick up the pieces of her heart and her life, feeling the pressures of raising a child alone.

I felt his deep longing to start life anew, and I even experienced a pang of jealousy as he boarded the bus without me. Though I cannot wrap my head around his willingness to leave a child behind, I have no right to judge Mark's actions. I pray I taught him more than how to flee.

The summer of 1969 was tumultuous for me. Mark vacated our little brick home, leaving me and Bernice alone to navigate a new and stilted reality. Then, during one of my infrequent but much desired visits to Calla's house, she informed me that her, Peter, and their young daughter were moving to Montana. Jarred, having successfully relocated to Montana the year prior, had suggested Calla's family move, as he had found not only a career he loved but also a wife.

Berkley's nails tap against the kitchen linoleum as our dachshund wobbles toward me on his short, pudgy legs. Ruffles stretches in my lap, lifting her head to ensure Berkley notices the space is already occupied, regardless of the dog's inability to jump into my lap. "Morning, Berk." I reach my hand down to pat his red-brown head, his ears gliding through my fingers like silk. Light streams through the curtains, and the budgies, right on cue, begin to chatter to each other from their cage in the corner of the room.

I stretch my arms above my head and wonder how many animals will be enough to fill Bernice's void. As it stands today, we've accumulated three cats, one dog, and two budgies, and just last week she was talking about setting up a fish tank.

I've begun to notice a change in Bernice these past several months, whether due to our now-vacant home or a lifetime of poor choices. The woman seems to cling to me a little more than before. She has stopped eating for the most part, instead consuming caffeine and nicotine for fuel.

Her collection of age-reducing creams and expensive, trendy clothes is piling up, and I am unsure whether she is experiencing a midlife lack of confidence or has found another tactic to manipulate me. No matter what I am busy with, Bernice frequently needs me to take care of things for her. This, of course, is in addition to my taking care of all the animals.

Perhaps 1970 will be the start of something new. My hand runs against the soft fluff on Ruffles' back, and I try to imagine the possibilities through the fogginess of my dreams. My imagination, squashed by years of disappointment, offers little. Instead, the weight of a life not lived well settles upon my chest. Its overwhelming presence smothers me.

I recount the years I've lived, and though I see how things have gone wrong, I am unable to find an alternate path I could have taken. Is my unhappiness due to fear? Despair? Was I too kind to the wrong people? Is it the result of a brutal and costly war? Or the loss of a beloved woman? Or did the unthinkable, the loss of a child, set me off course? Perhaps, the daily act of surviving led me astray. I know better than most the suffocating isolation survival can bring. The inability to see light. The lack of emotion. The bitterness of knowing you are dying a slow death but being forced to carry on and move forward.

I can barely believe my life has led me to this moment. I still have more questions than answers. I will be forty-five years old this June, and I cannot comprehend how I allowed my life to end up this way. Even if I won a few battles throughout the years, I have a sinking feeling that, even from the beginning, I was destined to lose the war.

In hindsight and with the assistance of Calla's letter, which I've read more times than a sane man should, I am aware that the most crucial war I lost was the fight for my children. I protected them as best I could, stepping in when warranted, stepping aside when I thought it meant an easier time for them. My actions, however, were not enough. Not even close. I shut myself off from my emotions, but making myself unavailable only made certain that I was out of touch. I suppose it was a self-fulfilling prophecy of sorts.

I run my hands over my face as Ruffles stirs in my lap. Tears push at the corners of my eyes, and I wish I could go back in time. I am certain that, if I could do it all over again, I would find a way to be the man and the father I should have been.

CHAPTER 44

January 1980
Toole, Montana

Calla

The shrill of the party line pierces the air. One ring for Campbells, two rings for us. Two rings! Who could be calling at this hour? Before I can even bring myself to speak the question aloud, let alone drag myself from the warmth of our bed, Peter is in the kitchen. He lifts the receiver and gives a subdued, "Hello."

His muffled voice is all I hear. I sit up in bed, wiping sleep from eyes and tugging the covers with me. Peter flicks on the bathroom light, which shines dimly into our bedroom. "What is it?" My voice is coated in sleepiness.

"It was Jarred." Peter's voice is steady, just like he is.

"Jarred! Is everyone okay? The kids? Monica?" I push myself farther up the bed, swinging my legs toward the edge of the mattress and turning my back to the doorway where Peter stands.

"Jarred is fine. Everyone at their house is fine." It is the way Peter says "at their house" that tips me off. A shiver grips me as my feet find the floor.

"Peter. What is it?" I stand abruptly and reach for my housecoat at the end of the bed.

"It's Jamie. Calla, I'm so sorry, but Jamie is dead."

Peter steps toward me as my legs go weak. My hand finds the bed, and I rest my unsteady body back onto the mattress. "Jamie? How? Why?" Those are the only questions that come before the tears arrive. I haven't heard from my brother in several years. Last I knew, he was living with a lady in Sioux Falls and working construction. Though the news of Jamie's death shouldn't surprise me, given his volatile battle with life, it does.

A sadness creeps in when someone you love, someone you wished better things for, passes from this earth. Though he gave me a fair share of headaches over the years, he also brought laughter into a home that desperately needed it. "Jamie." His name slips from my lips. *Jamie Jesus,* I think, and a small laugh escapes through the tears.

Peter interrupts my silent thoughts. "Jarred is waiting for your call."

I nod. Peter meets me at my side of the bed and hugs me, long and tight. His embrace is like my own personal shield from the rest of the world. When no one else is able, Peter can protect me from it all.

I tiptoe down the hallway, not wanting to wake our two girls, asleep in their beds. Peter affords me the privacy I require by tucking himself back into bed, though I doubt either of us will locate an ounce of sleep tonight.

I dial Jarred's phone number. He picks up on the first ring. "Hey."

"Hey," I reply.

"You okay? I mean, well, you know?"

"What happened? How did you hear?" The questions are waiting patiently in line, one ahead of the other in my head, though I want to know both everything and nothing at all.

"Dad called. They are headed to Sioux Falls already." Jarred clears his throat, and I know he is avoiding saying her name. "Bar fight." I can almost hear Jarred shrug. "I guess he lost that one."

"Sure did." A heavy sigh leaves my lips. "Does Mark know?"

"I left him a message. Called him after I hung up with Peter. I don't know if he'll even call me back. You know how he is."

"Strong and silent." I offer the words like an echo. "It's been, what, ten years since we heard from Mark?" The crackle of the old phone line fills the air. "We aren't so different, you know. If you get out alive, you tend to just keep running. Never look back."

"That is one way to look at it." Jarred laughs nervously. "She gave up driving. Did you hear?"

"No, but I don't really expect to hear anything these days. Seriously though? How does that work?" Nothing about Bernice should surprise me, and yet here I am, baffled by something new.

"Yeah. I guess Dad is driving her everywhere now." Jarred laughs again. "I'm sure that is going over really well."

I shake my head. "You know, I thought it would end."

"What would?" Jarred asks, his voice muffled by the sound of crunching. "Found a bag of chips in the cupboard. I think Monica is hiding them from me." He laughs again. "I'd share, but you know, you are there and I am here, so . . ." He pauses, crunches again. "What would end?"

"All of it. The nightmares, the memories, the fear that she will just show up at my door unannounced and demand something of me." I pause. "I know. Crazy, right?" A nervous laugh escapes my pursed lips. "I don't know how, but she is always there, lurking in the dark, ready to condemn me for the tiniest infraction."

"I don't know, Calla," Jarred says in a serious tone. "Maybe it never goes away."

We both laugh at our inside joke. "It" is in reference to Bernice, and even as adults, with families of our own, we still laugh at a juvenile joke that only we share.

"You know, the other night I put dinner on the table, and both girls turned up their noses." A nervous giggle bursts forward, but a defeated smile settles upon my face. "I couldn't help myself. Bernice's words echoed in my head and came right out of my mouth. 'There are children starving in China. You'll eat what is put in front of you.' I was mortified. I think I may have even gasped."

"I remember that one." Jarred laughs.

"Of course, even though I wanted to, I stopped myself from offering up my standard reply to that comment, the one I only said inside the safety of my own head. I don't want my girls to think they can get away with cheek."

"What was the reply? I don't know that one." Jarred pesters me. "Come on, Calla, what did you say?"

"I used to think, 'Then they can eat this slop.'" Laughter fills the airways between us.

Jarred is laughing so hard he can barely speak. "Man, she sure was a terrible cook."

"Really, Jarred? She was a terrible everything."

"Yeah, I know. I know." The line is quiet. "So, I'll call you if I hear anything else. I don't imagine there will be a funeral or anything, but Dad said he'd call once they are back from South Dakota."

"Okay. I won't hold my breath, then."

"Hey, Calla, try and get some sleep. Jamie is at peace now. We can be grateful for that, at least."

"I will. You too. And you are right. I am grateful for that."

"Be seeing you." Jarred's words bring a fresh tear to my eye. No matter where we go, we remain connected to each other.

"Be seeing you, Jarred."

CHAPTER 45

October 2009
Ferngrove, Washington

John

The pedestal of the dining table is coming together. I run my hand along the smooth, rounded edge of the base and picture the solid maple tabletop. *A deep stain,* I think as I carefully examine the carved ridges.

The young couple came to see me just over two months ago. Referred by a mutual acquaintance, they told me of their upcoming nuptials. The bride-to-be beamed as she talked about their autumn wedding. The groom took her hand as he showed me the drawing and told me he wanted a custom table as a gift for his bride.

They wanted a table they could share meals over, both romantic and the family sort. A table that would see them through the good times and the challenging ones. A family heirloom for their children and their children's children.

A sturdy table, just as strong as their love for each other. He spoke the final words while gazing into her eyes, and that was when I saw them. Her cornflower blue eyes shone bright as gemstones as she looked at her future husband, with adoration a mile long and a heart full of love.

I quoted them a price far less than the craftsmanship and the hours involved. I toss aside the thought of remuneration. This is a project of love. I saw us in that young couple. I saw Violet and me, our hearts full and our dreams nestled in each other's arms. *This one is for us, Vi.* I run my hand down the pedestal's base one more time.

The ache centers in my chest. I'm overcome with emotion, with memories. I wipe the tears from my eyes, certain the table before me is drawing out the pain of losing her. The pain is intense. Working in the carport, protected from the light drizzle, my heart feels like it's being squeezed by a giant's fist while being pierced by a hot poker. As the sweat beads on my forehead, I picture her, Violet, dressed in white, a delicate netted veil at the back of her curled hair. The crispness of her satin gown shimmers in the sunlight and, as if in time with my memory, a beam of sun bursts through the clouds.

A slice of white-hot pain grips my left arm, and the sander I was holding drops with a thud. I lean on the table's base for support, feeling like a knife is twisting deeper into my chest. "Mother." My voice is quieter than I expect. My strained vocal cords carry sound no farther than two steps in front of me. I gather my strength and take a step toward the house, my eyes blurred by pain-induced tears.

The third step takes me down. Unable to support my own body weight, my knees buckle and I tumble, taking the pedestal and tools with me as I fall. The crash, though earsplitting, seems to occur in slow motion as I grapple through the air. Unable to steady myself, my body slams into the packed, cold ground. My vision narrows and then fades as I watch Bernice's slippered feet move close to my face, before I lose all consciousness.

I wake to the sound of a steady beep. The room is shadowy despite the stark white ceiling above me. The covers that lay over my weak and exhausted body are thin and scratchy. I turn my head to the right at a snail's pace. My groggy eyes find Bernice, slouched in a chair, her head leaning at an awkward and presumably uncomfortable angle. Her light, rhythmic breathing fills the space between us. I shift from my uncomfortable position, using my elbows to steady myself as I lift my hips and move ever so slightly.

Bernice's breathing alters beside me. "John." She sits upright with a swiftness I haven't seen in decades, rubbing her neck with one hand while reaching for my hand with the other. "How are you feeling?"

"Like I've been hit by a truck." My mouth smacks, unable to find moisture beyond my lips.

"Close." Bernice smiles but has a furrow between her eyebrows. "You've had a heart attack. Doctors say they need to run some tests."

Bernice stands and walks to the other side of my bed. My eyes follow her movements. She reaches for a cup from a tall, narrow table on wheels, and she fills the cup with ice water before lowering the straw to my lips. "Drink this."

I do as I'm told, and the cool water washes away the drought within my throat like a summer rainstorm. "How long have I been here?"

Bernice places the cup back on the table and rests her bottom on the edge of my bed. "Several hours. They said they will need to keep you a few days though."

"How did you get here?" I remember Bernice's inability to drive, having given up her license over a decade ago, due to what she called an unrelenting fear of operating an automobile. Her decision created a royal pain in my behind, since I was at her beck and call to drive her wherever she needed to go. Her refusal to drive came on the heels of her sudden inability to manage the bills, which dumped more responsibility on my shoulders. The longer we have been alone in the house, the more Bernice has relied on me for every aspect of her life. Trapped under the responsibility of two, it's a wonder I didn't have a heart attack sooner.

Bernice's voice rings through my thoughts. "I came with you. In the ambulance." Her fingers tap the designer purse in her lap, an indication that she is eager to pop outside for a cigarette. "Though, I suppose I'll have to call Miriam when the time comes for us to go home."

"You can't stay here until then." The words are sharper than I intended, but even she should have had the common sense to know that. I soften my delivery. "You'll need to go home, get some rest, feed the animals. Get a good night's sleep, and then come back in the morning." There is no workshop for me to escape to in this hospital, and I may very well die if I have to spend the next several days in this room with Bernice.

Bernice's silence tells me I've taken a misstep. I ignore the notion. If ever there was a time to take a liberty or two, it's after having a heart attack. "Why don't you head on out for that cigarette. I am sure the doctors will be in soon. They'll only shoo you out anyway while they do their checkup." I offer her a weary smile. "Go on. I'll be fine."

Bernice stands, a small sigh escaping her lips.

"Can you pass me my jacket, though, before you go?" I incline my head toward the open locker, where my clothing and personal effects are neatly folded.

She may have a desire to inquire as to why I want my jacket, but her desire for nicotine wins out over staying here to lick her wounds. "I won't be long." Bernice lays the jacket across the bed before she pats my hand. Tucking her bag under her arm, she walks out of the room with her head held high.

I test my strength by shifting positions once more, this time sitting up with the help of the motorized bed. Looking around the bleak room, I think of the last time I visited a hospital. I was summoned to Sioux Falls by an early morning phone call on a winter day. After a long and slippery drive over icy roads, I entered the hospital with dread in my heart. I insisted Bernice wait in the truck. She didn't need to see another of her boys like this. The officer had told me of the bar brawl and the freezing temperatures that likely led to his death after he presumably passed out in the bar's back alley. But, still, I've not yet managed to push the image of Jamie's body on the stainless steel table to the back of my memory.

Jamie's wild side was not easily curbed. Whether he was at home with us or in Minot with Edward and his family, Jamie's willingness to fight his way through life was at the very core of who he was. The fight within him only intensified with Daniel's passing. I wondered then, and I wonder now, how do you convince a child that he is not at fault for his brother's suicide? The truth is I couldn't say the words that mattered most because of my own fear and my own shame. I believed Daniel's death was my fault, and my words to Jamie were trapped under a bedrock of shame and guilt. Two boys died when none had to. The tears well in my eyes so easily these days. With less life ahead of me than behind, the emotions I've tried to keep at bay over a lifetime surface like oil in water.

I tug on the envelope tucked in the inside pocket of my jacket. Unfolding the letter with care, I read Calla's words once more. The paper is worn now, unfolded and refolded over the years. The truth of her words keeps me coming back for more. Seeking salvation from a letter, I know in my heart the time has come to say the things that need saying, even if only so she can hear them. At the very least, I owe her that.

A nurse interrupts my thoughts, and I hurriedly tuck the letter under the covers as she walks toward me with a wide smile. "Mr. Smith, so nice to see you awake. How are you feeling?"

Understanding my time is short, both on this earth and until Bernice's return, I seize the opportunity and ask the friendly nurse for a favor. "Will you call my children? Tell them to come?"

"Oh, Mr. Smith, I am sure your wife will take care of that for you." The blood pressure cuff wraps around my arm, squeezing the life from the limb as it inflates. I wait for her to remove the stethoscope from her ears and begin again.

"Please," I all but beg. "I cannot count on my wife to reach out to them. This is important."

Tears well up in my eyes again, and the nurse offers a comforting hand on my forearm before reaching into her pocket for a notepad and pencil. "Do you happen to know their contact details?"

I shake my head no. My embarrassed look feels too comfortable, as if it has become my permanent facial expression.

"All right then, let's go with first and last names and their last known place of residence."

Grateful to this angel in pink, I rattle off all the details I know for Calla, Jarred, and Mark.

"Thank you." The words are far from adequate, but they're all I can offer before Bernice enters the room, cloaked under the familiar cloud of cigarettes inhaled far too quickly.

"You get some sleep now, Mr. Smith." The nurse tucks the covers into my sides as she leans over and whispers, "I'll see what I can do."

CHAPTER 46

John

After two days in the hospital, I am itching to vacate the drab place. Unfortunately, the doctor's conclusions do not permit me a speedy escape. I am sullen, but I understand my remaining time is now measured in hours rather than months or years. Besides, my legs are not in any shape to bear the weight of my now-frail body. I pass the time flipping through magazines I've never been interested in, but feigned appreciation for when Bernice brought them from the gift shop three floors below.

I am about to succumb to an afternoon nap when a light knock comes at my door. Bernice looks up from her women's magazine, her lips pursing as she closes the glossy cover. Her mood is already put out at the arrival of a visitor. The friendly-faced nurse enters the room with a smile, and upon casting my eyes toward her, my hopes of seeing my children plummet a little farther.

Movement, seen out of the corner of my eye, captures my attention. I almost don't believe my eyes. There, with nervous smiles, are the older but sweet faces of Calla and Jarred. Bernice shifts uncomfortably in her chair before standing and closing the gap between my bed and the door.

Calla flinches and instinctively moves behind Jarred's much broader frame, and Jarred squares his shoulders and lifts his chin. A shiver of familiarity runs through my mind, sending a chill throughout my body. As I myself know, time doesn't heal all wounds, and my heart aches at the sight of Calla shrinking as Bernice steps within striking distance of my children. After a lifetime of protecting Jarred from everything she could, the roles are now reversed as Jarred steps in to do the protecting.

I have no desire to watch an argument unfold, and I never wish to hear Bernice's foul words spewed in the direction of my children, no matter their age. But I can't help but feel proud to bear witness to a love no one could destroy, not even Bernice. Despite the many years of heartache shared together and alone, Calla and Jarred are family. This both comforts and saddens me, knowing I could have been included in their version of family too.

"Mrs. Smith." The friendly nurse cuts in. "Do you think you could come with me to answer a few questions?"

Bernice's smug look is replaced with one of annoyed confusion. "Questions?"

"Yes, it seems the doctor neglected to ask you about your living arrangements, and you see, we can't let Mr. Smith go home until we know what type of layout you have. You know, stairs, washroom access, that sort of thing. I hate to bother you with this, especially since your guests just arrived, but I really do need that information before the doctor will even consider signing the hospital release paperwork." The nurse, obviously practiced in the art of gentle manipulation, pauses before adding, "I promise it will just take a jiffy and you'll be back here in no time to visit with your guests."

"All right." Bernice slings her latest designer purse over one shoulder before following the nurse out the door. She says nothing and keeps her head and her eyes tilted down as she moves past Jarred and Calla.

As the door whispers closed behind them, Jarred steps forward. "Hey, Dad." He reaches his hand toward me, and I shake his firm grip with my much weaker one. "The old battle-ax listens to a nurse these days? What's with that?" Jarred's smile is contagious. He keeps the conversation light, given our reunion is taking place in a hospital room. "So, how are you feeling?"

"Better, now that you two are here. Much better." I notice Calla taking a few tentative steps forward. "Calla." I reach toward her, and without hesitation and with the exuberance of a small child, Calla falls into my waiting arms. She buries her face into my shoulder, and sobs gathered from a lifetime of pain and disappointment land there. I could hold her tight forever, let her cry a river of tears, but even that would not make up for all she has had to endure. I squeeze my arms around her as tight as I can manage, wishing I could wear her turmoil as my own. I never intended for my children to live a life they longed to escape, yet that is one of the few things I passed down to them.

Jarred busies himself by repositioning two of the three chairs in the room. He places one beside my bed, where Calla can sit once she unfolds herself from my embrace, before moving the chair Bernice vacated a little closer to my side. I already anticipate the awkward situation should Bernice return, thoughts born from the survival instincts I have cultivated over the years.

Calla wipes her face with the back of her hand, gripping mine with her free one. I smile at each of my children. "I am so happy to see you both. Thank you for coming."

"Mark won't be able to make it, Dad." Jarred, burdened with

delivering bad news, examines his hands before looking up to meet my eyes. "He said he just couldn't do it. Not if *she* was still alive." Jarred shrugs. "Can't blame him, really. I guess we both knew we weren't welcome 'cause we weren't her kids and all." Jarred gestures between himself and Calla. "But Mark is her own flesh and blood, and she cuts him down like no mother ever should."

A tear sneaks past my eyes, snaking a salty path to my lips. "I understand. Please tell him, when you see him . . . tell him I understand. And that I love him and I always have." I look from Jarred to Calla, intent to say what I should have been telling them all their lives. "I love you both." I pause to steady my voice. "I should have loved you better, but that isn't to say I didn't love you, because I did, with every bone in my body."

Calla's gentle hand squeezes mine as tears flow freely down her face. Jarred's larger and more calloused hand fumbles into mine, and then he reaches across my legs and gathers Calla's free hand in his own. "We love you too, Dad." Jarred's words are shaky, but the message is sincere.

The door to my room flings open and Bernice steps through, assessing the scene. Her eyes, narrowed to slits, scan the room before resting on the only remaining chair. With little space or inclination to relocate the chair, she sits with a huff at the opposite end of the room, arms crossed over her chest, glare fixed in place.

"Oh, stop your maudlin." Bernice brushes invisible fluff from her lap. "I've just filled out the paperwork. He'll be back home in no time." Her eyes are filled with fear instead of coldness. "He has to come home. Who is going to take care of me otherwise?"

In an instant, I feel sorry for Bernice. I am aware now, a lifetime too late, that this is the only emotion I should have ever felt for her. Oddly, the discovery puts me at peace. All these years I have battled her as she threatened to reveal the secret she held over me. My shame, I realize now, comes from allowing her to manipulate me long past the day she told me of her deception. Now I understand completely. I was never meant to feel anything other than sorry for her. She is like an abandoned puppy with an abusive past, one no family could ever love enough to cure of its aggressive behavior. All she knew was to live with pain, and when there was none, she created it. There was never anything we could have done to give her what she needed. We were pawns in her game of chess, mere obstacles for her to play against. I see now the game, the strategy, and the deep-seated and cruel necessity for her to play.

I offer Bernice a sad smile, knowing her game is now over. I am not going home. This I know for certain. My shallow breathing and my body's weakening state are clear indicators of my impending end. Bernice has always been deathly afraid of being abandoned. In the end, her own lifelong actions toward others will deliver her this most feared status in life. She will live out the rest of her days as a lonely, bitter old woman, with no loved ones to mourn her passing when her time in this world comes to an end.

My greatest regret is not having understood these things a lifetime ago. If I were a smarter man, a braver man, I would have taken more of an active role in my own life. Instead, I let life happen to me. It has taken me eighty-four years to learn this lesson. I've heard it said that when you've finally learned what you came here to learn, there is no more life to live.

That is where I find myself now, with no more life ahead of me. Perhaps it isn't the choices we make that alter our life's path, but the choices we don't make. The ones we fear. The ones that paralyze us and breed inaction. The ones we allow others to make for us, believing falsely that they are stronger. These, in the end, are the choices that decide our fate.

Calla and Jarred exchange glances. "We'd better go. Let you

get some sleep, Dad." Jarred stands, his hand still clasped in mine.

"Wait!" My mind races as our time together grows short. "Calla, wait." I pull my hands away from hers and scavenge around beneath the covers across my legs. The look on Calla's face turns to concern. "I've got something for you."

Letter held tightly in my grip, I pull my hand from beneath the covers. Crushing the paper into her hand, I clasp both of my hands on top of hers, wrapping them with as much strength as I can muster, determined to convey the importance of my words. My eyes look desperately into her cornflower blue ones. Eyes just like her momma's. I smile at the memory of Violet. Her face is so easy to imagine when its truest counterpart stares back at my own.

A quick glance in Bernice's direction and I push ahead, undeterred. "Calla. I need you to know that I understand now. No one should ever come between a father and his daughter." I nod my head toward her. "Do you hear me? No one." My voice is strained with emotion, but my determination to make her understand overrides my weakened state. "I choose you, Calla. I choose you."

Tears fall from our eyes. With our heads together, it is impossible to tell where her tears end and mine begin. Connected together, as we always should have been. I can feel Violet's presence, smiling with a heart overflowing with love, as she watches her family. Bernice was right about one thing; she never could compete with a woman like Violet. I doubt anyone could.

CHAPTER 47

AUGUST 2014
Toole, Montana

Calla

The nightmares have vanished. They disappeared two weeks ago, after the phone call announcing Bernice's death. Relief is the primary emotion coursing through my veins. The relief is sometimes giddy, other times subdued, but it is complete with the knowledge that she can no longer hurt me. Fifty years have flown by since I walked away from my home, my brothers, and my father. All because of Bernice and her hateful vengeance.

Jarred's wife, Monica, telephoned Peter and me with the news, a hint of jubilation in her voice. Not one of us shed a single tear. There would be no service, no flowers, no gathering to remember the deceased. Yesterday, Monica telephoned once more to inform me they had parked at a rest stop on the way home from Ferngrove and tossed the ashes into the canyon below. I thought getting out of the truck to do so was a step further than I might have gone, as Monica's laughter filled the airways between us.

I am not the only one feeling the burden that was Bernice lifted from my shoulders and my life. After Dad passed, Jarred and Monica took on the arduous task of settling his affairs. I wanted nothing to do with Bernice, and since Jarred had remained in contact with their household, via an annual fishing trip with Dad, he was the one to inherit the chore. Less than a week after Dad's funeral, it became clear to Jarred that Bernice, then seventy-six, was in no state to care for herself. He placed her in a care facility, where a group of friendly professionals would meet her immediate needs.

The staff were, initially, eager to help her settle in, but Bernice's antics rallied against any such possibility. She acted out with inappropriate words and actions, getting herself expelled from the first facility in record time. Thus began five years of constant relocation for Bernice. Jarred transferred her from one home to another in search of a hospital that would tolerate her for longer than a few months.

Though Jarred's stories of Bernice's outbursts were lively, her behavior added a new layer of stress to his and Monica's lives. Bernice never did make it easy for anyone but herself. I remember, about two years after Dad's funeral, sharing hamburgers and beers on Jarred and Monica's back deck. They told tales of Bernice hiding in coat closets, behind bushes, and under beds to sneak a few drags from her coveted cigarettes. Nobody knows how she obtained the contraband, and if that had been the only concern, perhaps a solution would have been found.

Bernice loved attention and didn't seem to discern the difference between a positive spotlight and a negative one. When refused cigarettes, Bernice first turned to hurling insults and cussing out anyone who attempted to help her. When that didn't elicit the desired response, she raised the stakes. She adopted a habit of disrobing and placing herself in locations throughout the hospital where she was sure to be discovered by some poor individual. I laugh out loud at the thought of a seventy-eight-year-old woman running about a pristine and antiseptic environment in the nude. The hospital's solution was to place her in a jumper with no buttons, zippers, or fasteners. I snicker at the thought and can only imagine her distaste for such a generic ensemble.

I place the small rectangular shoebox on the table. My and Peter's girls are coming to visit this afternoon, as the time has come to tell them Bernice is dead. I remove the lid of the shoebox. I needed some time. Time to figure out how I feel. Time to prepare myself for the questions they are sure to ask when they hear of their grandmother's passing. Time to convince myself the power she held over me is really gone forever.

Peering into the box, at its sparse contents, I am comforted by the black-and-white image of Momma staring back at me with a wide smile, her hands placed on the handle of a baby carriage. The photograph is the only one of her alone that I have. I collected the few items in the box from aunts, Uncle Edward, and both sets of my grandparents when Peter and I traveled to Cedar Springs on our honeymoon.

The love Peter gives is unending. He encouraged me return to school as an adult, a step that boosted my belief in myself. I graduated at the top of my class and went on to earn a degree in accounting. Peter is the kind of father I desperately wanted for myself as a child. He is part navigator and part warrior, and he has guided and protected me and our two daughters all these years. Together, we have built a family that stands on trust and is filled with love, acceptance, support, and laughter.

I reach into the box for a photograph and look at Dad's handsome face. He's dressed in his army uniform, and his expression is dashing but serious. I contemplate whether the photograph was taken before or after the war that changed him forever. The picture of Momma and Dad at their wedding is by far my favorite. Their smiles are contagious, and the photo, taken without their knowledge, fuels my imagination as I ponder the love and joy they shared.

Reaching into the shoebox, my fingers grace the little red box that holds the pearl earrings Momma wore on her wedding day. The gift from Aunt Iris was accompanied by a laundry list of qualities I share with Momma. On a rare and talkative visit, Aunt Iris confirmed my love of and talent for handicrafts was passed directly from Momma. Apparently, Momma left me more than just my cornflower blue eyes. Aunt Iris helped me see Momma in my mannerisms, my smile, my desire to create beautiful and wonderous things, and most importantly, my ability to love and keep hope alive. Momma instilled these notions in me long before I could understand them myself.

Placing the box of earrings on the table, I reach for the last piece of thinning paper. Crinkled and folded more times than I can count, the letter I wrote to Dad fifty years ago is the thread that binds us together, even after he drew his last breath. Little did I know the words I wrote him as a desperate and distraught sixteen-year-old would stand on their own some forty years later. When he returned them to me on his death bed, begging forgiveness and plying me with his unending love, I knew I had never been far from his heart. I had already forgiven him by writing the letter, and on his last day on earth, he found the grace to forgive himself.

Fifty years ago, I felt the pull to sacrifice my familiar life to seek something more. Though difficult, that decision has served me well. I am happy. My life is full of joy, and I am pleased with the woman I have become. I wouldn't be the person I am today had I not experienced the challenges of my past. I struggled and I worked hard to make ends meet in the beginning, but no matter how difficult the road, I never gave up hope for a better tomorrow. Momma's final gift to me was the understanding that hope always exists, and I feel her presence each time the sun shines a little brighter on my face. I was so lucky to have a momma who could fit a lifetime of love into a few short years.

The sharp, piercing sound of the doorbell yanks me from my reverie. I scoop up the fragments of my past and place them with care into the shoebox. I hear the animated chatter of our daughters through the screen door as I pass through the living room that has witnessed many family gatherings. I reach the door with a smile as wide as my eyes are bright. As I open the door to welcome my girls with a warm embrace, I know this conversation, too, will be easier because of the love we share as a family.

Looping a hand through each of my girl's arms, I guide them toward the kitchen and the box that waits for us there. Glancing toward heaven, I whisper my gratitude for the gift of my family. It was all I ever wanted.

EPILOGUE

March 7, 1964

Dear Dad,

I have so much to say to you, and yet the words do not come easily. A lifetime of hurt and unanswered questions lies between us. I was a small child, left without a mother. You were all that I could cling to for support, for love, for guidance. I would be simplifying things if I were to say you disappointed me. But I have never felt your grief after losing the love of your life, left with two small children to care for. Only to be followed by a lifetime of regret.

You were not the father I wanted you to be. You were not my knight in shining armor who would rescue me from the evildoings of a storybook stepmother. Instead, you remained silent, stoic, immersed in your own hell. You missed out on getting to know me. The real me. You missed out while I was a child and a teenager, and even as I grow into an adult. I was forced to scrape my way out of a dark, dank pit of despair, with no tools but my sheer will to survive and the strength in my small hands.

You withheld from me things of great importance. You kept secrets that needed not be kept. You were detached when I needed you to engage. You let time slip away from us. I should never have had to beg for my father's love.

So many times, I felt as if I was a burden to you, the reason you had to go on without her. Were my eyes too blue, like hers? I never meant to hurt you, Daddy, or cause you any pain. Did you ever consider that perhaps I was the gift she left behind? I was the one who was to remind you of her love?

I need you to know that I forgive you. I want you to understand that I have not only survived but thrived, not because of you, but in spite of you. I want you to embrace my reconciliation of our life together and apart.

I saw the pain. I saw the heartache. I felt the dysfunction and I still chose you. Even when I argued. Even when I was silent. Especially as I leave. I choose you. So, you see, Daddy, no matter the circumstance, I'll go on loving you, just as I believe Momma would have done.

I choose you, and I will love you forever.

Your daughter,
  Calla

AN INTERVIEW WITH THE AUTHOR

∽

CJ Armitage is a writer and bookstagrammer on Instagram. You can find her at @one.chapteratatime.

CJ: Hi, Tanya, Thanks for talking to me today. When I first talked to you at an author signing, you mentioned that you started writing *A Man Called Smith* a couple of years ago but stopped to write two other books. Can you tell me more about that?

Tanya: Thank you for having me. Yes, *A Man Called Smith* was slated to be one story, complete within itself. I was about a third of the way through writing the first draft when two female characters from within the story began to insist that the story needed to be shared from their own perspectives.

I woke in the middle of the night with a conversation taking place inside my head. It was two women. The first was demure, polite, and soft-spoken. The second was brash, demanding, and several octaves louder. They were Violet and Bernice, John's first and second wives. These two characters, or my imagination of them, literally woke me with their dialogue for weeks on end each night around 3:00 a.m. Violet was ever so polite in requesting I allow her to tell her and John's story through her own eyes. Bernice, in contrast, was in a huff of an argument, demanding that if Violet was going to tell the story from her own perspective, then she would do the same.

This nightly routine continued for weeks, and during the day, I contemplated, between yawns, the possibility of creating a trilogy instead of a single story. It was a quote I read in a writers' magazine that pushed me toward one story told from three different characters' perspectives. The quote said, "Every character is the hero in their own story." For me, the lightbulb went on. I was having difficulty entertaining the thought of allowing Bernice a voice all her own. I already knew the type of character she was, but giving her a spotlight to peddle her misguided and oftentimes nasty demeanor was not a task I looked forward to.

Once I decided to give Violet and Bernice their own stories, I set aside *A Man Called Smith* and began work on *Becoming Mrs. Smith* and *Stealing Mr. Smith*. The original intent was to create two novella-length stories, but as you can see from the disparity in length between the two, Bernice managed to get a full-length novel out of me. And that is how the three titles that started solely as *A Man Called Smith* came to be.

CJ: I know exactly what you mean. I've been pulled off course by characters too. I appreciate that *A Man Called Smith* can be a stand-alone book too. New fans can start here and go back later. Now, in this book, Calla has chapters, and then for the first time, John also has a voice with chapters from his point of view. By the way, is there any historical significance to the name John Smith? How did you choose the name for your leading man?

Tanya: There are a multitude of John Smith's throughout history. Some are well known, as in John Smith the explorer, and others are famous only within their family tree. The name is actually considered a placeholder name, and John Smith is one of the most common, relatable names used to demonstrate the everyday man. The man who seeks the simple things in life. In *A Man Called Smith*, John's name is juxtaposed to the life he lives throughout the story, as his life is anything but simple.

CJ: John warned us at the beginning that, since the war was over, he would avoid conflict for the rest of his life. Little did we know how true that was! Is avoiding conflict more effort than just nipping something in the bud? I mean, there were plenty of times that if John had just shipped Bernice out, everything could have been easier for the family. He did speak against Bernice and take the children's side a few times, but it wasn't enough. Was it an option to leave his wife in those days? I suspect the concern would be that she would take the children with her and then they would still be in danger. What alternatives did John have in those days?

Tanya: When I wrote *A Man Called Smith*, I was trying to understand the nature of choices in a person's life. I've always leaned toward the idea that not making a choice is the same thing as making a choice. It is choosing to be inactive toward a particular decision. So I wondered what happens to a person if they allow the majority of their decisions to be made by default instead of active participation. After the war and Violet's death, John was one of those characters that let life happen to him more often than not, and though circumstances were not always in his favor, John's own inaction created much of his turmoil.

Every single day of his life, John had a choice, as do we all. I believe he tried to the best of his ability, with the weight of his past experiences tied around his waist, but I can't disagree that John didn't do enough to make things right for his children. The choices we make every day, whether they are premeditated or reactive, are what make up the experiences of our lives. We always have a choice. We may not like the choices laid before us at every turn, but we always have a choice, even if it is only to choose an alternate way of looking at a situation.

I suspect John's experiences during the war and the devastating loss of Violet were at the core of why he became a bystander in his own life. After the war, he was adamant he never wanted to fight again. He held a very ingrained belief that fighting solved nothing. However, in the beginning of his relationship with Bernice, John might have felt some relief in having Bernice take charge and make decisions, as he was already weary by the time they married. What may have begun as a relief from the pressures of daily life for John was soon a situation beyond his comprehension or control.

Though divorce was an option of the times for John, I am not sure he was capable of seeking it out. Factors that might have influenced his consideration against seeking a divorce were his faith-based upbringing, fear of what the neighbors would think, or the financial expense of a divorce, which may have been beyond his means. He was also well aware of Bernice's antics, and seeking a divorce might have been beyond what John could knowingly sign up for, given his already defeated state in life.

CJ: To be honest, I was furious with John more than once. What are your thoughts on John and why he had to mess up so much?

Tanya: [laughs] I understand. I am glad you were furious with John. I think being disappointed with John's character is a natural reaction to have. I have very mixed feelings about John myself. He is likeable and probably pleasant to be around. He is a nice guy, the helpful neighbor, the war hero, the quiet and hardworking man, but I can't say I have a lot of respect for him. I find it difficult to comprehend a parent who cannot stand up for the safety and well-being of their children.

I grew up in a loving home with parents who would protect me. Sadly, my upbringing is not the only norm in the world today or throughout history. John's story is not an uncommon one, and perhaps reading about a situation such as the Smith family's will offer us the ability to expand our hearts with compassion and understanding for others who have experienced a reality different from our own. I don't know how other authors feel about this, but I believe that all fiction begins from a nugget of truth; some truths are just easier for us to digest than others.

CJ: The word *Mother* had a lot of weight in this book. It is a term used for a birth parent and a step-parent, and even between husband and wife. Was this a purposeful choice because of the times?

Tanya: Mother was a common term for a parent during that time in history. That being said, I imagined something attracted Bernice to the title; she might have viewed it as a role of power and control. I think Bernice wanted that kind of power from both the children and John. This type of thinking speaks to Bernice's unstable nature subtly throughout the story.

On the flip side, John refers to his own mom as mother as well. However, the relationship between John and Mother Smith is loving, so the negativity that cloaks Bernice's use of Mother isn't present for Mother Smith. I also needed to differentiate, for Calla's character, between Violet (Momma) and Bernice (Mother), otherwise we all would have been confused.

CJ: Tanya, the hardest part for me was what happened to Danny. I'm trying to forgive you for that. What drove you to end his life so young? And then Jamie too!

Tanya: I am sorry. Daniel was one of my favorite characters as well, and I cried while writing those chapters and then again through every reread. In fact, I still get teary-eyed when I think of Daniel. However, it was important for me to show how a family living in as close to the same reality as possible could each interpret and act on those experiences differently.

Each individual Smith child reacted uniquely to the experience of living in the same house. This demonstrates even further how the choices we make affect our lives. I have a sister, and we grew up in the same stable home, yet when we talk about our experiences growing up, it never fails to amaze me how differently we both view a single situation. For my sister and me, it is often comical. For the Smith family, it was tragic.

CJ: Let's focus on a happier note. There were some lovely moments in this story with John and the children. What is a favorite of yours?

Tanya: There are so many that pop into my mind. John truly loved his children, and it came across in the simple yet brief exchanges between them. My favorite, though, is when John visits a pregnant Calla at her home. Calla serves him coffee and home-baked cookies and they talk things through. John is often a man of few words, but it is during this conversation that Calla fully understands the love John had for Violet and why he could not let her go. It is a sweet moment between the two of them, and though the story doesn't end there, to me it was a reconciliation of sorts.

CJ: The ending is touching with Jarred, Calla, and John together. Tell me about the significance of "I choose you."

Tanya: John was referring to the letter Calla wrote him when she left the Smith family home at sixteen years old (see epilogue). As a teenager who had lived through a significant amount of upheaval, Calla desperately wanted her father to do the right thing, not just for her but for all of her siblings. She still believed in him. Calla knew the man he could be, and she wanted that part of him to take a stand against Bernice.

Calla wanted John to choose a life with his children over a life with Bernice. It took John almost forty years to say those words back to Calla, and even though he was too late to right so many wrongs, John was determined not to leave this earth without making amends with his children. In the end, there was a reconciliation, there was love, and there was acceptance and understanding. And Calla could take that with her forevermore into her future.

CJ: Thank you again, Tanya. I'm sure this was a roller coaster of emotions for others too. I appreciate the chance to hear your thought process and "behind the scenes" glimpses of the creation of *A Man Called Smith*.

AUTHOR NOTES

~

One of the greatest privileges I experience as a historical fiction author is stepping back in time through research, interviews, film, and many other forms of media in a quest to capture a time period I have little to no personal experience with. The internet is a vast and occasionally overwhelming place for an author on the hunt for a particular bit of information so it is with a grateful heart that I am indebted to the individuals (real people in the physical form) who I spoke with while acquiring historical tidbits for this book.

Another great privilege of being a historical fiction author is that I am able to take historical accounts and tweak them for the sake of fiction. I do my best to convey a sense of time and place throughout history while still allowing the fictional side of the story to weave its own path. Doing so sometimes alters the precise details of history and so I try to note those details that have been altered for the sake of the story.

First, I should mention that both Cedar Springs, South Dakota and Ferngrove, Washington are fictional towns. Cedar Springs, in my imagination, is located in the general vicinity of Beedle county. In contrast, Ferngrove was a name my husband came up with as we drove from Tacoma towards home one cloudy afternoon. A fun bit of information is, the reason for our trip through Tacoma was so I could take a peek at the house that inspired Hilda's home in Stealing Mr. Smith. I had seen the home a few years before on a real estate listing and after being captivated by every available photograph, I jotted down the address in the hopes of one day stopping by. The home did not disappoint and though we only saw it from the street, It was just as lovely as I imagined it to be.

Though John and Bernice reminisce in 1951 over an intimate moment shared while the unattended barbecue charred their burgers, the Weber charcoal grill was not invented until 1952. Before George Stephen, Weber's inventor, dramatically changed the way families used their backyard grill, food was often charred on the outside and undercooked in the middle. Grills prior to his invention were often riddled by smoke and unsafe in nature.

In December of 1951 Bernice obtains one of her dinner recipes from the back of a soup can. After lengthy investigation and several phone conversations with Campbells, I learned the first recipe printed on the back of a Campbell's can of soup took place in 1959. I was unable to ascertain if another soup company in the 1950s printed recipes on the back of their cans, but the image of Bernice being able to manage a simple dinner such as one from the back of a can had already resonated in the story so I chose to keep mention of it.

The Motel 6 Calla has her sights set on as she packs her things to move out of the family home did not exist in Washington State in 1964. The first Motel 6 was opened in California in 1962 but did not expand into Washington state until years later. The hotel chain did feature a $6.00 per night price point while offering simple furnishings and pay per use black and white TV.

Sears and Roebuck began issuing a Christmas Book catalog in 1933 and though it was commonly referred to by Sears' customers as the "Wish Book" Sears did not officially change the name of the catalogue to the Wish Book until the Christmas of 1968. It is often assumed that the Wish Book was a catalog solely made up of toys, however since the first Christmas edition was produced in 1933, the catalog offered a variety of gift ideas suitable for the whole family. The iconic holiday inspired covers came to be in 1934 and continued for the life of the Wish Book.

In a memory, John recalls his brother Edward getting into Mother Smith's stash of chocolate that was set aside to send to John overseas. Though I did not make note of it within the story itself, one of the reasons for Mother Smith's strong reaction to the chocolate Edward devoured would have been due to the number of ration tickets she would have needed in order to purchase the chocolate in the first place. I imagined Mother Smith, saving her rations like a miser and gathering up a collection of items before packaging them and sending them off to John. I was fortunate to hold and peruse a ration booklet during my research (thank you Aunt Irene) but it was difficult for me to imagine what the tickets represented and how the ration booklets were used and given that rationing was a constantly evolving situation, I am certain there would have been a steep learning curve for those that had to use them as well.

When Hilda and Bernice's father visit the Smith family's new home site in Ferngrove, an argument between Bernice and Hilda erupts. Bernice makes mention of Hilda's Gucci shoes. Though the argument takes place in 1958, the Gucci brand did not become well known in the USA until its products were endorsed by the likes of Grace Kelly, Audrey Hepburn, and Jackie Kennedy in the 1960s.

John's memories of war were inspired by real events, real dates, and the very real accounts of soldier's experiences. This particular research took me into the depths of the horrors of what man is capable of during wartime. It humbled me, horrified me, and made me weep crocodile sized tears as I read, watched, and listened to personal accounts of the second world war. I specifically do not mention post-traumatic stress disorder by name in this work of fiction as it is not my place to say whether a label or lack of one, makes any significant difference to those who continue to suffer long after a war has ended. All I know in my heart is that war changes everything and not a single soul comes away from it unscathed.

Calla too, is a survivor of war, as are all the Smith children. Though she never experiences the raging of guns herself, she lives with someone who did and thus John's unsettledness was inadvertently passed down to her. In all honesty, I did not intend to set out to portray Calla as having a similar experience to John's and it wasn't until my editor made mention of it that all the pieces fell into place and I understood fully the circle of sharing, only a family can know. As a WWII veteran said in the documentary D-day 360, "You have to learn to live with chaos, to operate in a chaotic environment."

Thank you for reading A Man Called Smith. If you enjoyed the story, please visit your favorite book retailer, BookBub, or

Goodreads and help book lovers like you discover A Man Called Smith.

For a glimpse into the special box Mother Smith keeps tucked beneath her bed, please visit my website and sign up for my twice monthly newsletter to unlock some of Mother Smith's treasures.

www.tanyaewilliams.com/landing-page/

ACKNOWLEDGMENTS

~

My family is the cornerstone of my world. It is where I come from, where I can be completely myself (warts and all), and most importantly, where I am loved. Thank you for allowing me the time and the resources to take the idea of A Man Called Smith and turn it into the three stories that it is today. I am forever grateful for the support, the research assistance, the words of encouragement, and the comedic relief that was provided along the way. In particular, a huge thanks goes out to my parents for more than I could ever express here.

I am exceptionally grateful to have friends who are well versed in reading, listening, advising, walking, celebrating, commiserating, believing, loving, and occasionally kicking my butt when I need it. Hugs and thanks to each and every one of you. Donna, Kari, Ginny, Caroline, Carla, Kelsey, Tammy, Kelly, Tanya, Stefanie, Irene, Janice, and Glen.

As always, I am deeply indebted to my editor Victoria Griffin, for her outstanding insight into what is lurking in the corners of my brain but is missing from the page. Her patience with this project is what made the story what it is today. Thank you for always knowing what I had in me, even when I didn't see it myself. You are truly valued, both as an editor and as a friend.

Ana Grigoriu, your simple yet powerful artwork captures the essence of the story beautifully. The magic is in how you are able to achieve this without a complete story to draw on. I am, as always, amazed by your talents and very honored to have you as my cover designer.

Rose O'Toole, I am over the moon that our paths crossed (thank you Lillian) as you are the voice the story needed. Your ability to scoff where only I had imagined there to be one, along with your accents, inflections, and passion for the story are what take the audio books to the next level. Thank you for your enthusiasm in all things.

Though the writing life might often be viewed as a solitary endeavor, I am fortunate to never have felt like I was going at it all alone. Many of my friends are authors and they are a constant guiding force that encourages me to locate my true north and follow it with reckless abandon. Some, I have known for years, others have graced my life only recently, yet all of them make me a better writer as well as a better person. Thank you for towing the line alongside me.

To my early readers, you are an author's dream. You are patient, thoughtful, intelligent, and oh so generous with your time. I am thrilled to share my stories with you and even more delighted that you eagerly await them. I hope I have done you proud and you have enjoyed A Man Called Smith as much as I enjoyed writing it for you.

Dave and Justin, you are at the center of a world in which I orbit around. You are full of love, joy, inspiration, laughter, stories, insight, advice, and more. I am thankful every day for both of you. Everything that I do is greater because I get to share it with you. XOXO

ABOUT THE AUTHOR

A writer from a young age, Tanya E Williams loves to help a reader get lost in another time, another place through the magic of books. History continues to inspire her stories and her insightfulness into the human condition deepens her character's experiences and propels them on their journey. Ms. Williams' favourite tales, speak to the reader's heart, making them smile, laugh, cry, and think.

facebook.com/authortanyawilliams

twitter.com/tanya_breathes

instagram.com/tanyaewilliams_author